THE ALBION CHRONICLES
Book 2

Seven Druids

Also by Nelly Harper:

The Albion Chronicles:
Queen of Betrayal
(short story prequel)

The Girl of Two Worlds
The Battle of Brigantia

******

The Jet Necklace

The Albion Chronicles
Book 2

Seven Druids

By

Nelly Harper

The Albion Chronicles – Book 2
Seven Druids
Published by Goblin House
www.goblinhouse.co.uk
Paperback
ISBN: 978-0-9932748-4-8

www.nellyharper.co.uk

For Becky and Ciaran.
Thank you for getting me through my darkest
days.

Acknowledgements

As ever, I wish to thank my editor, Katharine Smith, of Heddon Publishing for all her work and for being such a lovely friend. Thanks also to Katherine Willis, for finding the time during the busiest schedule ever to beta read for me and offer such wonderful suggestions and to Ciaran Copland, for all his hard work on the series covers.

Pronunciation guide

Anniel	-	An-yeal
Beithe	-	Beh-he
Belatucadros	-	Bella-too-kad-ross
Bodach	-	Bo-tach
Cailleach	-	Kai-lee-ach
Dair	-	Dar
Dei	-	Day
Dimmi	-	Di-mee
Dun da Lamh	-	Dun da Larve
Eburos	-	E-boo-ross
Faela	-	Fay-el-a
Martaani	-	Mar-tar-nee
Nantosuelta	-	Nan-toe-soo-elta
Naraic	-	Na-rake
Nighean	-	Nyee-uhn
Raien	-	Ray-en
Rurann	-	Ruar-ran
Samhain	-	Sa-wain

SEVEN DRUIDS

1

Cobalam woke and stretched out his aching body. It was stiff and cold and more than a little damp from the morning dew. The early sun promised another glorious day. It seemed wrong that the weather should be so fine lately when they were going through such torment. He rose to his feet, nodded his thanks to Cailleach and stepped out of her stone circle. Inclining his head to acknowledge the other two circles, Cobalam headed towards the village. He took the longer route to avoid passing his own home and that of his old friends. It was lonely in the nemetons now they were gone. He knew Raien would be returning once he had recovered sufficiently but the loss of his mentor, Dei, was still more than he could bear. Instead of facing it, he had thrown himself into helping Drost rebuild the village. Many of the homes had suffered from Martaani's attack; some, such as Drost's own crannog, had been entirely destroyed. A hastily thrown-up house was now his base and here he intended to stay until all his villagers had their homes rebuilt.

Already a number of roundhouses had new thatch on. The scouts sent by Lord Alpin had taken word around all the nearby villages before they had left to return to their own lands, and support had been quick in arriving. From all around people had brought supplies of wood for building, fleece for lining walls and thatch for the roofs, along with food and essentials to help them undertake all the work. The first task had been to see to the dead. Cobalam had never dealt with so many funerals in such a short space of time. His heart lay heavy in his chest at the toll these good people had been forced to pay.

In the grand scheme of things, they had been lucky. The losses could have been so much greater, but even so the ten new graves at the edge of the village were testament to the bravery of those who had tried, unsuccessfully, to stand up to the Roman forces. When it was time to lay Dei to rest, Cobalam had struggled with what to do. It had taken a night of meditation inside Cailleach's circle before he could proceed.

The small pyre had been built over the very spot where the druid had been killed. Cobalam would have preferred something grander, indicative of the arch-druid's standing, but wood was much in demand and the living were more in need of it than the dead. Every piece of broken and charred wood that could not be re-used in the repair work had been carried over to the pyre; the people were honoured to contribute whatever they could. One small girl even brought over her wooden dolly that Dei had made for her, dutifully handing it over with big, solemn eyes. Cobalam had lifted her up so she could place it at the head of the pyre where it could keep Dei company on his long journey in the afterlife.

Despite the lack of wood, the pyre had burned hot and long, fully consuming the body.

Afterwards, people had scattered ashes all around the village, to help them feel that he was still close. A small amount was taken by Cobalam to the ceremonial circle at Moraig. Here they had held a midnight ceremony of farewell, releasing Dei fully into the care of the gods.

Cobalam sighed as he remembered the great man. He did not feel worthy of filling his shoes but there were no other feet to take on the roll. In time, the druids would gather from far and wide to acknowledge his new position. He hoped he would feel ready by then.

The sound of laughter broke through his reverie. He came out of the trees and into the village to see Carina with one of the villagers, picking wool clean, ready for carding. He watched with a smile as he made his way over to the edge of the loch. Her laughter, reflected in the shine of her eyes, warmed his heart. Her long red hair was tied at the nape of her neck and the sun, shining onto the strands, made it glow. In the short time since she had returned, she had brought a new zest to the village. Always happy and free with a smile, she chased away the blackness and made every task she turned her hand to fun.

'It is amazing, isn't it?'

Cobalam turned and saw Drost approaching. 'After all Martaani did to her, you would think she would be broken.'

The druid agreed. 'She is a survivor, that is for sure.' He looked at Drost, whose hair was starting to grey around the temples, and there were more lines around his eyes than there ever used to be. The last year had taken its toll on him. It was a heavy burden to endure and Cobalam had the utmost respect for him. Many others would have caved under the pressure.

Carina looked up and saw them watching. She waved at them and said something quietly to her friend. They both collapsed in laughter again. One of the older women wandered past. 'I have never seen anyone take so much joy in such a boring job,' she told Drost, shaking her head in disbelief. 'At this rate they will get through the rest of the year's fleeces in one sitting.'

'Shall I ask her to slow down?'

'Ye Gods, dinnae be doing such a foul thing.' The woman's hands flew up in mock horror. 'That used to be my job. I'm more than happy to keep spinning. And if we get through the wool sooner then we can all enjoy a wee break afore the next shearing. Just make sure she leaves enough wool for lining your new walls.'

Drost chuckled as the woman went on her way. 'Talking of lengthy jobs...' He raised his eyebrows and looked at the pile of logs on the shoreline. Sighing, he looked at Cobalam. 'Shall we get it started then?'

The Druid moved to the water's edge and raised his hands. In front of him, peeking out of the water like old charred men, were the remains of the crannog's supporting posts. The sun shone down on the rippling water, which sparkled and danced gently with the stilts, licking the wood and teasing memories from all who watched. The day the crannog had burned was a day scorched into all their minds. Cobalam pushed his own memories

4

firmly away.

'Tatha!' he cried out.

Behind him, the men who would be working on the crannog gathered around Drost. A number of the other villagers stood and watched. Carina skipped over and eased her small hand into her father's. He squeezed it, smiling, but kept his eyes forward.

Cobalam waited, arms still raised. Everyone held their breath. Would she come? They searched the surface of the water for any sign. Only Cobalam saw the figure rise from the water. Her hair was the colour of the algae-covered piles; brown with the merest hint of green. It fell in ringlets over her shoulders, covering her bare breasts. How long it grew, he never knew. She only ever rose up to her waist. Her eyes were a deep berry-red, they spoke of richness and vitality. Everything about her should have been alarming but instead she exuded passion and calm.

'Blessed Tatha,' Cobalam held his arms out towards her. The villagers stared blindly to where his hands led.

'Aide us, we beseech you, as we build this home anew. Allow us our presence in your waters and we will respect your benevolence with gratitude and offerings.'

At her nod he stepped forward into the shallows and produced a small flint blade from within his sleeve. He brought it sharply across his palm and let the blood run down into the water. He squeezed the last free-flowing drops out before bending and rinsing his hand. The goddess smiled, her deep eyes reflecting her gratitude. She did not speak but slowly lowered herself back into the water. As she did so, Cobalam called out to her. 'Blessed Tatha, we thank you.'

His words were echoed by everyone on the shore and the waters broke once more as the goddess brought her face out of the water to look at them again. Then she turned and was gone, the resulting ripples the only indication that she had ever been there. The villagers cheered at the sight of them; it was a sure sign the goddess had blessed their build.

Carina skipped back to her pile of wool and the men made ready with the first of the new piles. Oak and elm would be driven into the loch bed as stilts to support the alder frame that would form the base of the crannog. The old piles would remain in place. Some of the least damaged ones would be re-used; the others would stand as a reminder of the day they nearly lost everything.

Cobalam returned to Drost's side. 'The crooked glen of stones beckons,' he told him. 'I may be gone longer than usual. I need…' the druid's voice broke.

Drost held up his hand. 'Take all the time you need,' he said, 'I am sure the gods will forgive us a late Beltaine this year.'

2

Sirens screamed. Those who weren't already aware of the burning building were soon jolted from their homes. Acrid black smoke hung like a veil, blocking out the late evening sky. There was a sharp crack, followed almost immediately by the sound of falling glass as one of the windows blew out. A bolt of fire roared out through the empty frame.

'Pull back,' came the cry as the fire crews, bundled up in safety suits and breathing apparatus, were called out of the stairwell. One of them pulled off his helmet and shook out his sweat-soaked hair.

'No one could have survived that, Sir,' he told his chief. 'Best we can do here is contain the damage.'

The chief nodded his agreement and shouted new orders to his crew. To the policeman nearby he called, 'Can you get these people further back? We need room... and get the fancy dress crew out of here. This isn't a party.'

The policeman glanced over to where the chief indicated. Two men were standing in the shadows, quietly watching. They were dressed in dark woollen cloaks, fastened at the right shoulder with a buckle. Under these the policeman could make out some kind of tunic that ended just below the knee. They wore nothing else apart from lace-up leather sandals. He chuckled to himself as he made his way over to them. They moved off as he approached, without a word, and the policeman watched for a minute. Whatever party they had been to didn't seem to have made them very happy.

Morning broke to more sirens, this time in the park; the blue flashing lights and wailing police cars at odds with the usually calm surroundings. A man sat at one of the café's tables with a blanket around his shoulders, barely holding on to the paper cup full of coffee a kind officer had brought him. His two dogs fussed around his feet whilst police tape was rolled out, sealing off the whole area, including the bandstand café. The owner came and sat down with her own drink. Her face was streaked with tears and the remains of her hastily applied make-up. They both looked up as a black transit van drove slowly past.

At the rocks, the scene the dog walker had found an hour earlier was also cordoned off. Blood covered the area. It was splattered up the stones and pooled beneath the crumpled body that lay there. Drying to a dark brown colour, it looked as if the rocks were rusting in the early morning light. Despite the blood, it had only taken a second for the café owner to identify the body as that of her waitress, Kariss. The very same person whose flat had gone up in flames the evening before.

A policeman lifted the blue-and-white striped tape to let the two men from the black van pass through. They lifted the woman's bloodied body and placed it into a thick black body bag and slid up the zip. The two men in Roman costume watched silently from the trees. One of them ground his teeth in anger.

'We are too late.' He cursed under his breath. The other man smiled.

'Maybe not. Maybe we are just in time.'

'What do you mean?'

His friend turned to him. 'She has saved us a job, now we can go home. If we hadn't seen this, we would still be searching for her.'

They turned from the scene and walked across the park to a deserted, overgrown area where the public rarely ventured. Here a stream ran through the undergrowth. They followed it a short way, carefully avoiding the thin, prickly ropes of brambles that grew everywhere. Most people avoided this area until the berries were in fruit, even then they did not notice the two yew trees on the far bank. They were growing so close together that two of their branches had fused together to form an archway. Checking no one was following them, the two men stepped over the stream, through the gateway, and disappeared.

3

Lord Hightern accepted the cup in a shaky hand and though he wanted to drink deeply, he sipped the ale slowly to avoid pouring most of it down his chin. Despite the warmth of the day, he wore his woollen cloak pulled tightly around him. He was aging fast, everyone around him knew it. He closed his eyes for a moment and willed himself to be strong. He could not afford to die just yet. Brigantia needed him to keep his throne until all the pieces were in place and Kariss could take over. He felt his aching heart give a lurch; how he hoped the girl turned out to be everything they needed. It was not just the lives of his subjects that Hightern was worried about. He did not want to be known as the last king of Brigantia under the old gods. The person whose reign had failed to set in place the defence of everything they had held dear for centuries.

The despicable Martaani had been hovering around Stanwick like a scavenger. He knew she could smell victory. For all her false smiles and incessant attendance, she would not hesitate to step in and finish him off if Kariss were to fail. For a long while he had stayed away at Ingleborough, not ready to face the coming months; but when he had finally returned to his main fort, it was to be met with the news that Martaani had kept herself in her lodgings for weeks. The word her guards had put out was that she was ill, but the Brigante leader was not fooled. Old he may be but he was not that gullible. Martaani was up to something, but so far his spies had been unable to find out what.

The cup trembled in his hand and he felt someone lift it from him. He opened his eyes to see Volisios. Hightern offered him a weak smile. He had no need to pretend to his personal guards.

'Has there been any word yet about the viper?'

Volisios glanced over his shoulder to check that the room was clear.

'One of the night guards was found unconscious at the western gate early this morning, Sire. The walking guard returned from his check on the palisade and found him in a pool of his own vomit.'

The King gave the guard a shrewd look, his mind not yet as slow as his body. 'I take it you suspect foul play?'

Volisios nodded. 'The guard says he ate the same as the other men, but the old crone who lives by the guest quarters was found in a similar condition this morning. Viroco has gone to speak with her.'

A servant came in with a platter of bread and cheese. Volisios took it from her with a polite nod and waited while she re-filled the king's cup. As soon as she had left the room he continued. 'It is well known that the crone was a gossip. She does not sleep well and has caught out a number of folk who like to wander between beds during the night.'

Hightern chuckled. The deep, earthy sound had endeared him to so many people over the years, yet now it rattled with age. 'Ahh, Breta, what a rascal she is.' His eyes shone as a memory prodded at him and his voice resonated with a brightness that was so often lacking of late. 'She nearly brought my house down once, you know. Many years ago,

11

when you were just a bairn on your mother's teat.'
He waved his hand to another chair, indicating his
guard should sit.

Volisios placed the platter on a nearby table and
eagerly pulled the chair closer. At 27, he had heard
most of the stories of Hightern's long reign but this
one was new to him.

'I was not long wedded, and in those days I had
more than my fair share of virility.' A smile hovered
around the old king's mouth as he remembered. 'I
had always had a tendency to play around with
whoever took my fancy, and being married had not
curbed that desire.'

Volisios was unsurprised at this revelation;
Hightern's reputation for his wandering hands was
still legendary. He nodded his head in recognition
of such an understandable pastime, though in truth
he had always been faithful to his own woman.
Ever since the day he had first laid eyes on Callimai
he had never so much as even looked at another
woman. Though forbidden to marry, guards were
encouraged to have a woman for their pleasure. It
was considered poisonous for them to keep their
manly urges unspent, but legal commitment to
anyone other than the king was expressly
forbidden.

'One evening,' Hightern continued, 'I had just
finished enjoying the delights of a lovely servant
girl named... err...' He waved his hand absently.
'The town was in darkness and no one stirred as we
crept between the houses. Suddenly a voice carried
across the night air. "Who is that sneaking about in
the shadows?" Breta demanded. She chased the girl
away and grabbed at my arm. "Shame on you," she

hollered, raising her stick as if to beat me. Just then, the moon came out from behind a cloud and she saw who she was accosting. She dropped to her knees, but the damage was already done and a number of people had come out of their huts to see what the fuss was about.'

Hightern reached a trembling hand out for his cup. Volisios passed it to him and waited patiently as he took a careful sip.

'You know how quickly news travels in a town,' the king continued.

Volisios nodded and took the cup from him.

'Well, needless to say, the news reached Temitria the next day and the result was...' He grimaced. 'Not pleasant.' Hightern pointed to the platter and Volisios broke some bread and cheese off and handed them to him.

'I cannot imagine our Queen was happy at the news,' the guard said, ever a tactful man. He was not going to openly refer to the late Queen's insistence on loyalty above all else.

His Lord chuckled again as he took a bite of the bread. 'Oh, she was in a rage fit to challenge the gods themselves,' he admitted. 'I was forced to relinquish all other women and the girl was whipped in the slaughter yard with the whole town as witness.' He shook his head. 'No woman would come near me after that.' He chewed on the hard cheese with his few remaining teeth, whilst he sank deep in his memories.

Footsteps at the door roused Volisios and he turned to see Viroco enter. As usual, Hightern's other personal guard was unsmiling. At 23, he was young for such a responsible position but his serious nature and commitment to duty had pushed him quickly through the ranks. His skills were respected by the general guards, but unlike Volisios he had few real friends. Too many men thought him dour and depressing company. Volisios, however, liked him, even if he did find his manner frustrating at times. Viroco walked up to the king and dropped to one knee.

'Creala!' The king suddenly cried, spraying cheese crumbs over the guard. 'The servant's name was Creala, I knew I would remember in time. Lovely thing, she was. I wonder what happened to her?'

Viroco frowned at Volisios, who shook his head, smiling. 'Shall I try to find out for you, my Lord?'

A wicked grin appeared on the king's face. 'Do you think I could still service her?'

'I think you would be happy to try, Sire.'

Hightern turned his attention at last to Viroco and waved him to stand.

'Well, what did the old crone have to say for herself?'

'I went straight to her hut after the news came in,' Viroco told them. 'I passed no one on the way and saw no one close by, but when she didn't answer my summons I entered her dwelling and found her dead on the floor with a broken neck.'

Hightern's breath hissed between clenched teeth. 'Your suspicions were right.' He stopped when another guard appeared at the door.

'Martaani has requested an audience with you, my Lord.'

'Has she, now?'

'She says her health is at last restored and she wishes to speak with you.'

Hightern looked pointedly at his two personal guards. 'This should be interesting,' he muttered before looking back towards the guard at the door. 'Show her in.'

Martaani marched into the room with a look of disdain carved on her beautiful Mediterranean face. Her long black hair hung in coils, still damp from her morning bath, and her coal-black eyes were smudged with tiredness. She would have strode right up to the king had Viroco not barred her way a respectable distance from his chair. The Roman glared, expecting him to back down, but Viroco kept his arm across her path and met her stare with a firm determination.

'It is good we meet at last.' Hightern spoke. He could not do much to hide the frailty in his voice, but he fully intended to keep the sharpness of his mind hidden for now. 'I am sorry you have been ill. I expect our climate is not to your liking.' His watery brown eyes took in every detail of her, noting the strength of her stance and the healthy colour in her cheeks that belied her story of being ill. He suppressed the shiver that ran down his spine as she turned her cold eyes in his direction.

'This land does have an overabundance of damp and dreary weather.' She tilted her head back slightly as she spoke. 'It is nothing that I will not get used to, given time.' Looking pointedly at the chair that Volisios had just vacated, she waited for an invitation to sit. When none was forthcoming she carried on. 'It is indeed good that we meet at last, though I would have liked this meeting to have occurred when I first arrived in Albion some months ago.'

Hightern held up his hands. 'Alas, my commitments took me to the far reaches of my kingdom. The workload of ruling an area as large as Brigantia is not easily put to one side.'

Martaani's features softened but the coldness behind her eyes did not entirely disappear; a fact that was not lost on the king and his personal guards. 'A workload that is surely too great for you to continue with on your own. I would be happy to help ease your burden. I can also put my men at your disposal. You only have to say the word.' She smiled, and Hightern once again felt a shiver run the length of his spine.

He inclined his head and met her with a smile of his own. 'I am not alone my dear, I assure you, but I may be able to find some work for your men if that is what you wish. After all, it does not do men good to remain idle.'

A brief flash of anger crossed Martaani's chiselled mask of calm, so quickly that most people would have missed it. 'Anything to help, my Lord.'

'I will see what can be done. Now I am afraid I am expecting council with one of my advisers. Is there anything else I can do for you just now? I will of course look forward to your presence in the evenings now you have recovered your health, and you can bring any further requests to me then.'

'There is one thing,' Martaani said, refusing to be dismissed so readily. 'There was quite a disturbance outside my rooms last night, I do hope your guards do not allow this sort of thing to happen often?' she ran a condescending look over Volisios and Viroco.

'What sort of disturbance would that be?' Volisios asked.

'I was woken to the sound of men moving through the town. I am used to silence throughout the night; I will need to move my quarters to somewhere quieter if this is likely to happen again.'

'Did your guards not go out and investigate?'

Martaani bristled at the question and levelled an icy stare at Volisios. 'I see no reason to mount a formal guard at my doors inside the town. To do so would be to assume I was not safe here.' Her eyebrows rose as she spoke, inferring her acknowledgement of the disdain her hosts had for her. 'But as it happens, one of my men did go out to see what was happening and saw a number of men walking towards the eastern gate.'

'I will ensure the matter is investigated fully, my dear,' Hightern promised, just as voices could be heard coming from outside the room. 'It sounds as if my adviser is here already.'

Dismissed, Martaani turned and strode to the door. She was almost there when a tall, slight man with long brown hair and warm honey-brown eyes entered and almost bumped into her. Martaani took a quick step back and almost hissed at him as she quickly skirted around him and out of the room.

The Brigante arch-druid watched her go. He could feel the power of her venomous nature, and almost taste the taint of the Roman gods oozing from her. His lip curled in distaste and he turned towards his king. 'I take it that is the Roman contingent?'

Hightern sighed and nodded his head; he took another sip of wine as the druid took the empty seat.

Corio had assumed the role of arch-druid five years earlier when his predecessor, Bodvoc, had grown too old and senile to carry on. He had, in fact, been picking up the pieces of his predecessor's failings for a number of years prior to that, so he had almost ten years of experience in the role. He was going to need every one of them for the coming months. 'She reeks of her gods.' He commented, reaching for a piece of bread.

'She is certainly a viper,' Hightern told him. He looked to his guards, 'Leave us if you will, I will be safe enough for now with the door guard. Try to find out as much as you can about last night. But do not raise any hint of our suspicions.'

The guards nodded, inclined their heads respectfully to Corio, and left, doubling the guard on the room as they went.

The druid raised his eyebrows and helped himself to a piece of cheese.

'I have a feeling Martaani has been away from Stanwick, and only arrived back in her rooms late last night,' Hightern confessed. 'It will have been a shock to find we had returned to the town in her absence.'

Corio nodded thoughtfully. 'It would explain why she failed to show herself at yesterday's Beltaine celebrations. She probably timed her return knowing that most people will have been the worse for wear after the drink and revelry; she will have hoped to enter the town unnoticed.'

'She did not counter for good old Breta.'

Hightern shook his head. 'Who knew the nosy old crone would have her uses at last?'

4

The rain coursed down the thatch, finding the only weak spot in the otherwise perfect roof. It had taken a full day and half the night for the unrelenting deluge to finally edge its way through to the inside of the house. The resulting drip, drip, drip had been driving Martaani mad since she woke. Not for the first time, she strode over to the doorway and peered out at the sky. A solid mass of grey replaced the azure blue she so loved from her homeland.

'This dismal land is driving me crazy.' She turned to her serving girl. 'Have the scouts returned yet?'

The girl shook her head and looked down at her feet. She knew to her cost not to make eye contact with her mistress when she was in a temper.

The Pontiff had assured her that they were his best scouts, yet it was over a week since they had been dispatched to kill Kariss wherever the gods had sent her, and still there was no word. She was beginning to wish she had gone herself. If truth be told, the thought of travelling through time filled her with dread, but she would not be cowed by something her enemy could clearly do with ease.

She had thought that she had been so clever, attacking from both sides at once. Almost as clever as Kariss and her putrid Albion gods had been. She spat on the rush-covered floor. The thought that those imbeciles could have conjured up such an ingenious plan made her blood boil, but they had beaten them at their own game. Kariss could no longer travel between worlds, she was as vulnerable as she would ever be, but still they had failed to find her. Martaani's fists clenched, her nails cutting into her palms as she re-lived her failure. Even the death of Lord Alpin and the scourging of his stupid wife had only sated her fury for a little while.

Finding that Hightern and his entourage had returned to Stanwick in her absence had done nothing to improve Martaani's mood. Whilst the deception about her 'illness' seemed to have worked, she now had to be much more careful. The king himself was too old and decrepit to be a cause of concern, but his two guards were another matter. Shrewd and far too conceited for their own good, they would have to be watched carefully.

'How long does it take to kill someone?' She glared at one of the men sitting by the hearth. 'Has there been no sign?'

The Augur rose to his feet and inclined his head in respect before speaking, choosing his words tactfully. 'I have seen nothing to indicate anything definite, but this rain tells me that the land is being washed clean. I would like to think it means our worries are being washed away.'

Martaani's face creased into a sarcastic smile, 'You would like to think.' She humphed a disgusted noise and strode back to the centre of the room, leaving the door open. The serving girl rushed to close it before the rain started to pool on the floor.

It wasn't unknown for scouts to disappear. Many years before, numerous augurs had reported feeling the tell-tale ripples in time that indicated someone had passed from this world. The Pontiff had sent men to follow, and although they almost caught them numerous times, Kariss and her family always managed to evade them. One set of scouts had mysteriously failed to return. Now it seemed the same might have happened again. Martaani turned to the second man. 'Are you sure you sent them right?'

This man did not rise. He did not defer to Martaani. His role here was clear, defined by the Roman Emperor Caracalla himself. Guilty of fratricide and the mass murder of his brother's supporters, Caracalla was not one to cross. The Pontiff was lucky to be in his favour. He also knew what an excellent position he would be in when Albion fell; and if he was secretly relieved to be out of Rome, he was not letting on. He lifted his eyes, and held her gaze.

Martaani blinked and turned away. The man was infuriating, but he was needed. She allowed him this small victory. When the time came, she would remind him just who her allies were in Rome; key of whom was none other than Julia Domna, mother of the sibling emperors, Caracalla and Geta. Julia, overlooked by the Pontiff, knew all about the clandestine meetings the priest had enjoyed with Geta before he was murdered. The younger of the two ruling brothers was the picture of his father, Emperor Septimus, and a favourite of the senators. It was no wonder Caracalla had felt threatened enough to resort to such violence. The Pontiff had been one of the few astute enough to keep his liaisons with Geta private, and as such had kept his head, when most were losing theirs. It would take only a careful word in the right ears, and his position would become treacherous once more.

Martaani's gaze fell on the serving girl. 'Do something about that bloody dripping.'

The girl raced for another pot, this time filling it with a scrap of cloth. The sound of the drips was instantly quelled.

'You are quite sure she did not get the blessing before she was banished?' Martaani turned back to the Pontiff.

'My spies would have informed me straight away.'

'And how would they know?'

The Pontiff's eyebrows lifted in amusement. 'I fail to see how the raising of an army would get past anyone. Kariss would not have wasted any time. The call would have gone out immediately and no messengers left the fort before we banished her. Besides which, the man we left there will inform me of any news.'

A holler from outside marked the arrival of visitors.

'Enter,' Martaani barked.

The door covering was pulled aside. Two scouts ducked their heads and stepped under the lintel, bringing a gust of wind and a smattering of rain to soak the nearby rushes. They bowed to Martaani and nodded in the direction of her companions.

'Is it done?' she demanded.

The men's faces were unreadable but their rounded shoulders betrayed their discomfort. The air thickened. 'We arrived too late,' the larger of them admitted.

'What do you mean, too late? Explain.' Martaani almost spat the words out.

'Her house was ablaze when we arrived, and nearby we watched as they took her body away.' The man's voice reduced to thread. He straightened his shoulders and stared ahead. It was one thing to fail, quite another to look like a failure.

Martaani swung to look at the thin, pale Augur who still stood by the hearth. Disdain oozed from every pore. 'And what do you think now?'

He ignored the look and turned to the scouts. 'How did she die?'

'What does it matter how she died?' Martaani snapped at him. She was starting to wonder why she had ever thought he was one of the best at his job. 'Either way, she will be back here now.'

The Augur remained calm, 'If she died at the hand of another, that is one thing.' He inclined his head. 'If, however, she died at her own hand, that would suggest she has far greater knowledge than we gave her credit for.' He glanced at the Pontiff. 'We are both agreed, are we not, that she was cut off from her gods once you had Janus seal the gateway?'

The Pontiff nodded his agreement. He was still annoyed at Martaani's slight.

'It would therefore mean that either she was no longer able to cope with her life, and will have returned here by surprise, not understanding the consequences of her actions... Or,' he hurried on when Martaani made to interrupt, '... she was able to reason out exactly what would happen should she take her own life. And, have the courage to see

24

it through. If that is the case then surely we are looking at far greater an opponent.'

All eyes rounded on the scouts. Again, it was the larger one who spoke, 'It appeared that she had slit her own throat.'

Everyone waited for the explosion, but the silence that followed was broken by Martaani laughing. The air in the room suddenly seemed easier to breathe, if still charged with tension.

'I hope she enjoys her surprise,' she told the stunned men. 'When she finds Alpin dead, she will realise she cannot defeat me. The prophecy was very clear. His blessing was all-important, and he cannot give that from beyond the grave.'

5

The late spring storms finally blew themselves out. For six days rain had lashed the north of Albion, whilst the wind tore at thatch and uprooted trees. There was barely a pot left in Stanwick that had not been commandeered to catch the drips falling from leaking roofs.

Corio peered out of the window. Children laughed as they gathered great armfuls of scattered thatch, relieved to be finally outdoors again. They took them to the worst-hit houses, where they swapped their bundles for fresh-baked bread or pieces of fruit. Everywhere, people were busy repairing the damage. A woman struggled to round up a number of geese that had scattered in the bad weather. She waved a long stick to try and keep them together as they made their way between the houses. Above it all the sky was clear blue, with not a trace of cloud, but in Corio's mind he could still see grey.

'Come, sit and do not fret.'

The druid turned and looked at the three men in the room. Along with Lord Hightern sat Cartivel, the ruler's closest friend, and the aged druid, Bodvoc.

Cartivel continued. 'Help us arrange the midsummer gathering, it will keep your mind busy.'

Corio snorted. 'You do not need me to tell you what needs to be done. It is the same every year, the only difference this year is the vote for the heir. No one needs to be informed. The whole region, and far beyond, will be in attendance. No one is going to want to miss this.'

Hightern pointed a gnarled finger at the druid. 'You forget yourself. There is much to be planned, as you know full well. We need to be ready should the meeting descend into chaos. If Martaani does not accept the vote then there is no doubt that there will be war. The prophecy hints at as much, or why else did Kariss have to chase right up to the Vacumagi lands in order to attain the support of the northern regions?'

The druid looked suitably mollified. 'Forgive me,' he said. 'But I must leave and speak with the gods, something is very wrong.' He turned back to the window; one of the geese had managed to get inside an open doorway and was honking as it was chased back outside by a disgruntled woman with a broom. An argument was brewing between the two women.

'You cannot change events by staring out of a window.' Cartivel spoke again. 'We need to wait.'

Corio remained at the window. Cartivel may have been used to commanding men before his accident, but druids were not warriors. 'I have waited long enough,' he snapped. 'I will not be deterred any longer, you must find a way to keep the viper's men busy.'

Hightern raised his right hand. 'Enough,' he said. 'I have listened to this argument for days. It ends now. We achieve nothing if we begin to fight amongst ourselves.'

Corio inclined his head to the king. 'Apologies, my lord. I do not mean to let my frustrations spill out so.' He shook his head and pulled at his long beard. 'I cannot shake the feeling that something is gravely amiss; it grows in me day on day.' He hung his head, looking down at his bare feet. The mud was slowly drying on them now he was indoors. When he looked back at the men they were surprised to see his eyes were bright with unshed tears. 'It has been half a moon now and still there has been no news as to what caused the great shift in the air. Something dreadful has happened.'

He would have continued to speak but he was interrupted by low mutterings coming from the old druid. Bodvoc sat with his eyes closed, rocking backwards and forwards. His lips moved as he spoke but the words were incoherent. After a few moments he stopped making noise and was still. For a while it appeared he was asleep but then he inhaled deeply, shuddered and spoke.

'I have lost a friend,' he said. 'I feel the loss like a great stone weighing me down. Fianntan, the great red-and-white tree, is reaching for me.' He fixed his bright blue eyes on Corio. 'You must go to the Eburos and seek answers.'

Cartivel made a noise at the back of this throat and shuffled on his seat. A thoughtful man by nature, he did not like to rush at things. His years leading the warriors of the Brigante tribe had taught him that haste rarely brought rewards, but he knew these arguments could never stand up against Bodvoc's message.

'The time for waiting is past,' Corio announced, even more irritated now that Bodvoc had appeared to pick up a message he himself had not heard. 'I must leave today. How soon can you be ready?'

With an exasperated sigh Cartivel threw hands up in defeat. 'Give me enough time to set a distraction and have an escort ready for you.'

'I will take no escort.'

Cartivel rolled his eyes. 'The escort will only be with you until they are sure you were not followed. Once you are clear of the town they will wait for a day and then return.'

Corio nodded; if they followed him too far, he would soon lose them.

As the druid slipped through the trees and into the quiet calm of the forest, he let out a breath of relief. Behind him, two guards were following, making sure Martaani did not send anyone to trail him.

There had been no real effort to disguise the fact that her men were keeping a close eye on his movements. They wanted to stop him leaving the town where he could speak with the gods in peace, and find out news from the north. So far he had grudgingly agreed to stay within the palisade but as the days wore on with no news, his usual patience had been reduced to snapping point. His thoughts turned to the two men she kept closest to her. The Pontiff and the Augur. Both were clearly priests, but he could not work out their specific roles. As soon as he returned, he would make it his business to find out as much as he could about the pair.

A nightjar flew past him, its long wings cutting through the air. He watched as it landed on a low branch and turned so its body was in line with the limb. It huddled down, perfectly camouflaged to wait for dusk, and its usual time to be awake. The signal was clear. Enough was enough. Corio stepped behind a holly bush and disappeared himself. He would get nowhere travelling through the forest with the noisy warriors crashing behind him. Even sticking to the paths, they had alerted most of the wildlife to their presence after only a few steps. Cartivel had meant well, but even a seasoned warrior was no match for a druid in the forest. Corio continued his journey using invisible druid paths. The two men could take their time searching for him but they would never find him.

Now that he no longer had the guards in tow, he turned from his westerly direction and headed south. His bare feet made no sound on the damp forest floor. Here and there he came across uprooted trees that had been unable to hold on in the saturated ground any longer; their root stocks were still dripping with soil. In one place, a tree had not fallen right to the ground, but was caught up in the branches of its neighbour. The creaking of the trunks rubbing together carried like an eerie warning and Corio's deep-rooted feeling of dread deepened.

Eburos stood in a clearing surrounded by ash trees. It was the oldest yew tree in the forest and revered by the druids. Three hours' walk from Stanwick, Corio reached it early in the afternoon. The bole of the tree was huge and in places the inside had wasted away, forming hollow spaces perfect for nesting owls. A number of branches had grown down into the ground around the base and rooted to form a natural support system, helping the old girl stay upright.

Corio placed both palms on the trunk and rested his forehead against the rough red bark. With his eyes closed he offered his silent greetings to the tree. After a few moments he heard a voice in his head. *You are not the one I called.*

Forgive me, he answered. *Bodvoc is old and infirm, unable to make the journey quickly enough.* He brought an image of the old druid onto his mind and replayed the morning's conversation.

Old and infirm he may be but he knows how to listen.

Corio was given no time to realise what her words meant; his mind filled with a feeling of utter peace. His body no longer hindered his thoughts, and he felt himself floating higher and higher. The space his mind filled grew until his awareness was infinite. A sound echoed through the ether, tugging at him. He resisted, the sense of belonging was too strong to interrupt, but the sound kept on repeating itself until he was forced to listen.

Dei. It called. *Dei.*

Suddenly, Corio understood. The connection with Eburos was broken as he staggered to the ground. He lay amid the dried needles that coated the earth for a long time. The tranquillity his mind had been filled with was now replaced by questions needing answers. A charm of goldfinches flocking into the yew disturbed his grief. Their liquid chatter filled the air, reminding the druid that life still went on. Like the bright yellow flashes on the finches' wings, the future offered glimmers of hope - if only they were strong enough. He pulled himself from the floor and took out the small flask that was hanging on a leather thong around his neck. He poured the wine on the ground in front of Eburos.

The news was indeed dire, he told the tree as he left the offering. *But I thank you none the less. May his spirit ever soar with the gods.*

His journey back through the forest took a different path; Hightern would have to wait for his news. He had missed hearing Eburos when she called, so what else had he missed? The presence of the Romans in Stanwick had made him reluctant to call on Brigantia. The foreign gods were mighty and vengeful; he had not wanted to risk his beloved goddess when patience would bring him all the answers he required. Patience, however, had been the last thing he should have used, that much was evident now. He had got it wrong, and it did not sit well on his shoulders. Martaani was far more of a risk than they had ever envisioned before her arrival. The prophecy had lulled them into a false sense of advantage but now the rival heir was here, any thoughts that she may be a weak, malleable individual had been ground to dust under her warrior boots. She had more than earned her viper reputation.

They had not needed to be resident in Stanwick when she had arrived with her substantial entourage for news of the disruption they had caused to reach them. All across the Brigante kingdom, unusual occurrences were disturbing the peaceful way of life the people had enjoyed during Hightern's long reign. Fires broke out with alarming frequency. Accidents, arguments and thefts had turned the peaceful citizens into wary neighbours. The druid network had their work cut out calming the people, and keeping them focused on the true nature of the disturbances. Evidently one of Martaani's tactics was to attempt to divide and conquer. He should not be so surprised, therefore, to discover she had other, more deadly, strategies at hand.

The land began to head downwards slightly as he neared his second destination. The trees to his right still rose steadily to the summit of the hill known locally as How Tallon, but in front of him they began to thin out as he dropped down to his destination. The early evening light spread shadows from the circle of stones onto the surrounding grass. The stones were not tall; only about half the height of a man. The shadows were already longer than that. At the far side of the ring a gill carved its way between How Tallon and the adjacent hill, the Eel. Beyond the gap, Corio could see right out over the moor. The north stretched out as far as the eye could see. Somewhere there, he hoped, Kariss would be making her way to them.

Keeping the boulders on his right-hand side, Corio walked sunwise round the ring of stones three times before entering it from the north. Once in the centre he turned, sunwise again, and sat facing the gill. He bowed his head, stilled his thoughts, and focused on his breathing. Once it was slow and steady, he imagined fine roots growing out of his buttocks, fixing him firmly to the ground. Up his spine, he worked a long thread all the way to the top of his head, extending it right up into the sky. It held his back elongated and connected his consciousness to the ether. The knot that had been tightening in his gut all day fought to control him. He blew the tightness out of his mouth with every exhalation, replacing it with calm inward breaths. It took a long time before he reached the state he required. Once there he brought his beloved Brigantia into his thoughts.

She was the Mother goddess and guardian of the Brigante nation, and she was the one Corio had always had the closest connection to. Every druid had a stronger connection to one god above all others. It was with this god that they worked the closest, though they interacted with all the gods as necessary. Unusually for an arch-druid of Brigantia, his predecessor Bodvoc had always favoured the Maiden goddess, Verbia, but then he was from Illecliue, beside the river Weorfe, where Verbia was most revered. Together, Brigantia and Verbia along with Cailleach - Maiden, Mother and Crone - formed the Great Goddess. There were a number of these triple unions amongst the gods, though it was very rare to see all three gods together. Many druids were never blessed by such a sight.

Nine years ago there had been a meeting at Barmr Craggs, further to the south, where just such a sight had occurred. It was possibly the only time in Albion's long history that such a meeting had been called. The craggs covered a huge area and acted as a natural temple. Rock formations had been carved out by the might of the gods, and stood far taller than the rowan trees that grew amongst them. In places, enormous rocks balanced on smaller ones, acting as a warning to any who would stray into the sacred area. Only the druids dared to walk there without fear of being crushed to death.

The meeting had consisted of six druids. Each

arriving separately, guided there by their respective gods. It was only when they were all together that the years of planning, and the depth of detail to save Albion, were revealed. Each druid was linked with a different god or goddess, and each had been called for a specific reason. Other gods would of course have a part to play before all was done, but they would appear only if and when needed, and so formed no part of this main, elaborate plan.

Inside the protection of Barmr Craggs, the gods and goddesses had appeared to the assembled druids. Even this had been deliberately arranged. Six was the number of balance and harmony, the most stable of numbers. It was also known for its sacrificing and protecting qualities. Nothing was being left to chance. No one present, god or druid, was in any doubt just how much danger they would be in. The Romans and their gods had tried to break Albion once before, but they had never mastered her intricacies. They could not understand the druid's power, and so they had targeted them mercilessly. Martaani was expected to be no different. Yet the use of this number also held a dire warning. At its most negative, the number six could cause destruction.

The druids had come from all over the north. Corio and Bodvoc from Brigantia; Nectan from the Vacumagi lands in the far north; Darnus from the Carvetii lands to the west. Lastly, from the Parsii nation in the east, came Umar and Torwain, although Torwain had long since abandoned his homelands to wander reclusively around the Isle of Albion. His life was as close to that of Cernunous

35

as he could possible get it. All he was missing was the god's horns. To those who were not used to him, he was quite alarming. He had long since abandoned 'normality'. He was animalistic, fecund and wild, in looks and mannerisms.

The other druids also reflected the gods they most closely associated with. Bodvoc was impetuous and full of anticipation. He delighted in new projects and saw possibilities in places most people only saw gloom, just as the maiden goddess Verbia did. Corio, like Brigantia, fussed and mothered over the people of the Brigantian nation. He angered quickly when they were unjustly treated, and would no doubt stand in front of the whole Roman army if it meant protecting them. Patient and quiet, Nectan was a deep thinker, often spending hours pondering over the tiniest details. Like the goddess Cailleach, he could be relied on for his wisdom and his ability to see the bigger picture. Whereas Umar would anger quickly, strike first and ask questions later. Just like Belatucadros, the god of war and battles, Umar was the strongest ally you could wish for. Darnus, on the other hand, studied all his options before acting. He was calmer, seeking the best way forward. He was a druid of Maponus, the warrior god of the north, worshipped by hunters and warriors alike.

Corio tried to drag his thoughts back to the present but the memories had flooded his mind, refusing to leave. That meeting so long ago was the time he had met Dei. The unexpected druid had walked late into the natural temple at Barmr Craggs and was immediately welcomed by Cailleach. The symbolism was not lost on anyone; a seventh druid meant a measure of luck was being introduced to the plan. Corio resisted the urge to pull on his beard. Now that Dei was gone, had that luck gone with him? A hand caressed the side of his head and Corio opened his eyes to see Brigantia sitting in front of him. Like a typical mother, she had not waited to be called but had turned up exactly when needed. Her dark blonde hair hung in waves, flowing down to mingle with the moss-laden grass beneath them.

'Cailleach took Dei back,' she told him bluntly; the truth would be no easier to hear if she tiptoed. Her fingers slid along the lines of worry etched in the druid's face, as if touch alone could remove them.

'He was the seventh…' he found he could not ask. He hung his head, ashamed of his weakness.

'Cailleach is the wisest of all,' Brigantia told him. 'She had foreseen his passing and tried to avoid including him in her plans, but it was not to be. Some things even we cannot change.' She sighed. 'He was essential.' She raised his face to look at her. 'He saved Kariss on her journey north. Had he not been in the right place at the right time she would have walked straight into Martaani's trap. Is that not the luck you are searching for? He paid for that service with his life, but not before he had saved a village from Martaani's cruelty. He is at peace, Corio, you must find your peace with this news as well.'

The goddess's touch warmed Corio's face but his shame still bit deep. Ever since Eburos had scolded his failure to hear, it had gnawed at his insides. Brigantia leaned forward and ran her hands over his head, down over his shoulders and arms and flat onto the moss beside him.

'Release it,' she instructed, as she grounded the tension surrounding him. 'Let it go, it is not your dishonour.'

There was no hiding anything from gods.

'I could not call you, my lady. There is much danger in Stanwick for you now, but I did listen. I held the stones, I drank the herbs, and I tossed the bones, but I saw and heard nothing.'

Brigantia closed her eyes for a moment. It hurt to see her druid so pained. What she had to tell him would only pain him more. It would be the biggest challenge he could undertake, but he must see his way through or he would be no use to them. 'You could not see or hear us because you are being blocked. Powerful work has gone into keeping you from us; even here in this place of safety, threads of Roman magic still cling to your essence.'

Alarm flared in Corio. Involuntarily, he shuddered. He felt tainted, unclean and nauseous. 'What can I do?'

'For now, you must do nothing. The Romans must feel their plans are working.'

'But I will be cut off, unable to be of any use...'

Brigantia stayed silent, waiting.

Corio's mind raced but just as panic threatened to overwhelm him, his common sense kicked in. The gods would never give more than a person could handle. He quietened his thoughts, sifting through them methodically; the answer was in him somewhere. He kept coming back to the same question. 'Why was Bodvoc able to hear when I could not?'

Brigantia smiled, her eyebrows raising. 'It would appear the Romans do not see him as a threat. Did you never wonder why, at Barmr Craggs, when our chosen druids met, two were from the same town? Or why one of our nation's arch-druids would be a man of Verbia, and not myself?'

Bodvoc was already an old man when he became arch-druid. Now Corio thought about it, he realised that it had, in fact, been the year following Kariss's birth. It certainly made sense to have a druid of Verbia in place right at the beginning of the plan. It would give him the time to put in place all manner of things. It led Corio to yet another uncomfortable thought.

'Then what good am I?' he asked. 'If you can only talk through Bodvoc, am I to be just a decoy? A ruse to keep the Pontiff's eyes looking the wrong way? How can I be of less use to you than a senile old man?' Sadness welled inside him.

Brigantia stood and turned towards the gill and Corio knew he had disappointed her.

'Do you know how Martaani managed to kill Dei, then go on to attack Dun de Lamh and kill Lord Alpin when she was safe in her quarters at Stanwick?' the goddess asked without turning back to him.

'Lord Alpin? Dead?'

Brigantia turned. 'Lord Alpin, his youngest son, and now his wife.'

'But not...'

'I cannot give you all the details. You know this, Corio. Already I have said more than I should have. Now is not the time to need such cosseting. Think!'

He felt the reprimand like a slap across the face.

His pride had reduced him to a petulant child. He cast it from him with a shake of his shoulders. If the answer lay in how Martaani had fooled them all, what was he missing? She had almost been too clever in her deceit. Had it not been for Breta, they might have believed the guard had truly fallen ill. The decoy she had used had been illness. But Bodvoc was not ill, he was senile. Corio gasped, surely not!

'Bodvoc is not senile, is he?'

Brigantia smiled, 'Keep going.'

'If Martaani thinks I am much less of a danger now they are blocking me, and Bodvoc is not worth watching, they will not see the damage we can cause until it is too late.'

The goddess resumed her place before him, her eyes lit with pride. 'Do not leave the safety of Stanwick again until called, and do not speak to anyone, not even Bodvoc, of this. If there is anything we need him to tell you, he will find a way to let you know. You cannot do much with the Pontiff and Augur so close, but you can prepare. The Pontiff is a pernicious man and he is powerful. He has the ear of his gods, a little like yourself, but he needs an augur to guide his actions and read the signals of the land. Between them they are a dangerous combination, do not underestimate them.'

An involuntary shiver ran down Corio's spine at the thought of them using their magic on him. Brigantia reached for his hand and raised him to stand in front of her. 'Take back the news of Dei, but keep it quiet amongst yourselves. Let the Romans feel their plans are working, that you are without your power near them. But do nothing to give them cause to harm you. We will need you. I will need you and the people of Brigantia will need you. There is so much more to you, Corio, than your ability to talk to us. You are vital to the people of Stanwick. Do not forget also that if it were not for your healing skills, Lord Hightern would have no chance of lasting until midsummer. If he dies before Kariss can be confirmed as his heir, war will surely break out. If that happens, most of our planning will have been for nothing. Never again doubt how important you are.'

She leaned forward and placed a kiss on his forehead, and then she was gone. Corio wasted no time in leaving too. As he hurried back to Stanwick he digested the news. The gods truly had foresight to have hatched such a long-term plan. Long enough to train Corio in the things he would need to know for this moment. It was just the kind of plan Verbia would love: daring, exciting and full of possibilities. For now, they had two powerful druids in Stanwick, and two could do so much more than one. Once back in his rooms he would meditate on those lessons he had thought were obscure. Those he had put down to the tired, failing mind of his predecessor. For he could be sure now that there was a reason for everything. He sent up a silent thanks that the Pontiff could not block his memories.

6

Cailleach's wavy hair hung loose and wet down her back. Salt-and-pepper colour, Kariss thought absently as she waited for her to speak. The old crone goddess held both her hands. Her skin was loose and so thin that it felt almost papery. When Kariss moved her thumbs across the backs of the goddess's hands, the skin followed in waves of wrinkles. Old age had a beauty all of its own, if only people took the time to notice it. Wisdom showed in the eyes, and Cailleach's eyes were a depth of knowledge and understanding. They sat, piercing green, deep within her shrivelled face, the lines of which reminded Kariss of contour lines on the maps of the highlands she had spent so many hours poring over on her long journey up here to the Vacumagi lands with Naraic. As she studied her, Kariss realised her aura was a little sharper, the calmness she usually associated with her presence was less pronounced. There was a tension she had never felt from her before and it was nothing to do with the rain. It unnerved her.

'As you rightly noticed, I am worried, my child.' Cailleach said finally. 'The dangers increase day by day as more of Martaani's Roman allies arrive from over the waters. I feel them invoking their gods and desecrating our sacred places. Worst of all, it has come to our attention that their god Mercury and goddess Muta have been invoked together.'

Even goddesses can shudder, as Kariss found out just then. She raked her memory for what she knew about the Roman gods. 'Mercury is an important god, isn't he the messenger god?'

'He is the one they turn to for messages, yes; communication is one of his stronger aspects. He also watches over trade and travellers, even guiding souls to the afterworld.'

'Surely it is understandable that they should be speaking with him?' Kariss could feel a knot of concern building in her chest. There was something coming that she did not want to hear, yet she knew there was no way around it if Cailleach had come with the news.

'True enough,' Cailleach acknowledged. 'But he is also known for his guile and trickery. Muta, you may not have heard of. She is a lesser goddess; a nymph who came to the attention of Jupiter when she revealed his affair with another god's wife.' Cailleach's lip curled in disgust, sending the wrinkles in her face running into yet more contours. She released Kariss's hands and tightened her own into fists. 'Jupiter, who is their god above all others, was so angry that he cut out Muta's tongue and sent her to Mercury in the underworld. Mercury, however, fell in love with her, forced himself upon her, and made her with child. Then he hid her away where Jupiter could not find her. She is revered now as the Roman goddess of secrets.'

Kariss had heard some of the stories that surrounded both the Roman and Greek gods. She knew they could be shocking but she had never heard of one raping another. No wonder Cailleach was so disgusted with them. She pushed her thoughts past the shock and on to the other word that had stood out to her. 'So Martaani is trying to reveal our secrets?'

'We believe there could be a plot to try and intercept your journey and make sure you do not reach Stanwick. That Muta was invoked would imply that Martaani's priests feel there is information they need, which they have so far been unable to find out.' Cailleach sighed, a look of frustration clouded her face. 'All this is very dark to us; we have not been able to read the signs clearly yet. We need more time, but there is none. For now I must ask that you do not take the direct route back to Lord Hightern at Stanwick but that you go by hidden ways, keeping to just a small group.'

'But what about the warriors? They are amassing to travel south with us. Surely we would be safer amongst so many?'

'Would that that were true.' Cailleach opened up her hand to reveal a mass of ants. 'In large numbers there is more chance to hide spies, more chance for someone strange to get close to you, because you will feel safer. You must trust no one but the select few already known to be faithful. It will be hard, but you have faced a hard journey before and thrived.'

Kariss laughed. How much of that statement was truth and how much was flawed thinking, she was not sure. That journey had, after all, ended, almost along with her life, trapped in the Insh mire. On the way she had been drenched in ice-cold water and almost died of hypothermia, and had it not been for the druid, Dei, they would have walked right into one of Martaani's traps. Then again, the journey had led her to Anniel; by far the greatest ending any journey could have.

44

'You will be watching us?' she asked. 'We will not have to travel without your aid?'

Cailleach squeezed her fingers again, tightly. 'It pains me to send you with so much still unknown, but have no doubt, we will always be with you. Though you will not always see us, messages will be sent to you when guidance is needed. Keep your eyes, ears and heart open. The Roman gods will be watching us, just as we are watching them; our messages may not be as direct as you have been used to.'

Kariss wondered if the Roman gods were watching them now; could they hear what was being said?

Cailleach shook her head. 'My old friend Belatucadros is keeping them occupied.' She chuckled, her eyes shining with mirth. 'He can be quite persuasive when he wants to be. One more thing,' she added, her face turning serious again. 'Do not repeat any messages you get, even to Anniel.'

Kariss frowned.

'Knowledge is strength, but it can also bind. Our plans may have to be cut to the finest of lines. Any deviation may result in danger for you all. If others need to be warned, they will be, and they too will be asked to keep such warnings to themselves.'

'But why?' Kariss did not want to return to the burden of carrying secrets. She had thought all that was gone now she was fully in one world.

The goddess felt her heart lift; Kariss had stopped following blindly. She was starting to need more answers, to understand why she needed to do the things she was being asked to do. It could be important in the future. Cailleach answered her as honestly as possible. 'Because telling someone else could change the way the future happens. We are not the only gods at play here, so we do not know all. If we are warning you, then we have an idea of what is set to happen. Remember, we are bound by our own laws, there are ways of doing things. Already we are pushing hard at the boundaries of what can be done. If you are told something, it is because you and you alone need to know. There will be learning in it for you, an opportunity to grow in knowledge and experience. You must use such messages wisely, and have faith that we are watching over you. All of you.' The goddess's essence was starting to fade. More questions would only cloud things and she could hear Belatucadros calling her. 'Trust us, Kariss.'

Her parting words echoed. Kariss felt the air drop a little as the goddess left. She stayed where she was for a long time, until the rain drove her to seek the shelter of the fort once more.

The path up the hill had become slippery and she tried to make her way through the trees to the side but bushes of holly and vicious brambles had been encouraged to grow there, to stop unwelcome visitors from hiding their approach. She was soon forced to return to the path. How on earth did the druids manage to make their way to the fort's entrances without being seen?

She paused at the top of the hill, and looked over to where Inan was buried. Already, the earth was settling over the little hero's grave. Kariss felt the lump of sorrow return to her throat. It was never far away these days. Everywhere she turned there were reminders of what Martaani had done. She imagined how much worse it would be if Martaani were to win. Thunder rumbled overhead and the rain answered by increasing its intensity. Still Kariss did not hurry. Maybe the heavier rain would be more successful at washing away the pain, and cleansing her soul.

The new wooden gates looked incongruous in their mountings. The wood was yet to weather, though this rain would certainly hasten the process somewhat. She thought they looked like great wounds on the otherwise impressive fort. Inside the new thatch was just as obvious, though she was glad the men had been able to get all the roofs fixed before the rains had started. They had worked night and day, making use of the light nights the northern summers enjoyed. She made her way towards the great hall. There would be a fire burning in one of the hearths and she would be able to dry off. Then she needed to find a way to tell everyone that they were not going to leave with the warriors.

In the end, it was far easier than she had hoped. Both Mailcon and Anniel had been inside. They understood the sense of Cailleach's plan straight away and immediately began discussing the best way forward. The only problem had been with Fayern. Walking in as they were planning who should be included in their small party, she had been horrified to hear that they were even considering travelling without a full warband to ensure their safety. Nothing they said had calmed her. It was the first real reaction she had given to anything since the funerals. Eventually, Mailcon led her outside, his hand at her elbow, guiding her gently. He was able to get closer to her than anyone else now. She had put up barriers to everyone she loved, as if her heart would shatter to let any of them near.

Anniel and Kariss carried on with their plans, but Fayern's distress had drained them. The mood in the hall was sombre as the servants came in and began setting up the tables and benches. Fayern did not appear for the communal meal that evening. Mailcon had managed to get her to accept that the goddess knew best when it came to Kariss's safety but still, she had pleaded a headache and retired to her private quarters to eat alone. Later, when Kariss took her a sprig of lavender and a tincture of meadowsweet, specially prepared by Brean, she found her calm, but withdrawn. Fayern looked at Kariss with wary eyes, as if she expected her to announce something else to cause her anxiety to rise again.

'I am sorry I made such a fuss,' she said once she had drunk the tincture. 'I...' Her hands fluttered at her throat as she struggled for her words.

Kariss took hold of them and kissed her friend on the forehead. 'You have nothing to apologise for. It is such an unexpected plan, but that is why it is the safest thing for us to do.'

Fayern blinked back tears and forced herself to try again. 'I...I agree,' she stammered. 'When M... Martaani came, all the warriors were here, but even they could not stop what happened.' Her voice was tight with emotion, it wavered threateningly, but she managed to keep hold of her composure. 'But in taking you away and hiding you, Anniel kept you safe. I see now that you will be safe this time, too. You must follow Cailleach's advice.'

Kariss could see the immense amount of strength it was taking Fayern to say this, and she took heart. Her friend's core was pure Vacumagi royalty. She might be broken with grief, but time would heal that.

7

'There is one thing I don't understand,' Kariss said to the old druid before her, the next day. Nectan stopped rubbing his gnarled fingers together and waited. His joints were protesting greatly. Four days of endless rain had made everything feel damp. Even here, next to the fire in the great hall, the ache deep within his bones did not ease much. 'If I was born at Wendell, how was it that you were the one to make the prophecy? And why was it made here, instead of down there?'

'Do you know, my dear, I don't believe anyone has ever asked me that before. Everyone just seemed to accept it at the time.' His eyes shone as he remembered the day, so long ago, that Cailleach had come to him and told him Kariss had arrived. He had known she was expected, but Cailleach had bade him to wait for her news before he could make his announcement. It had taken ten days; ten long days waiting at the pre-arranged meeting place, to prove he was worthy of his part in all this. For he had no doubt that Cailleach had already known the exact time the babe would be born. Indeed she had told him as much when he hinted at her lateness.

Some felt the gods played with them for their own amusement but the druids - most of them at least - knew the truth. The world they lived in was really one of chaos. The gods, being as powerful as they were, had the ability to bring some kind of order to that chaos, but no one could ever truly control it. The challenges the gods made were their way of testing that a person would be strong enough for the path ahead and not buckle when the forces of chaos descended, as invariably they would. Chaos was the ultimate power. No matter how ordered or calm something may seem, it would never, could never, last. All anyone could do was put their trust in the gods, and keep the faith that everything would be alright in the end. That if chaos managed to scatter their well thought-out plans, the gods would find a way to bring the pieces back together again, somehow.

Nectan jumped as the touch of a hand on his arm brought him back to the present. He looked up to see Kariss looking at him with concern. 'Are you feeling unwell?'

'I am sorry, my dear, my mind seems to wander off into the past so often these days.' A flash of worry clouded his eyes for a moment but it was gone before Kariss could be certain she had even seen it. She glanced at Anniel and saw the almost imperceptible shake of his head, so she held her tongue as Nectan continued. 'Whilst Bodvoc's predecessor...' he shook his head irritably, 'I forget his name now... was presenting you to the world, my dear, I was up here announcing to Lord Alpin and Anyetta that the blessing of their life was destined with the chance to save not only the Brigante nation but also the whole of Albion. The news was then carried to Brigantia by Torwain, the wandering druid. You will meet him, no doubt, before all is done.'

'I hadn't realised druids travelled so much,' Kariss said, surprised.

'Most of us do not,' Nectan explained. 'The only

travelling we do is within our homelands. Some who live in the furthest reaches of a nation's land would not see a druid for years if we did not. But there are a few, mainly those who serve the god Cernunous, that choose a solitary, nomadic life. Often they seem quite mad to the rest of us and I should warn you that Torwain is no exception there.'

A noise outside the doorway made them turn. Mailcon entered with Fayern just behind him.

'Did I hear Torwain's name mentioned?' the new leader of the Vacumagi asked as they made their way over to the fire.

'Nectan was just explaining to me how some druids choose to travel the land,' Kariss said.

'I remember Torwain visiting us a number of years ago,' Mailcon told them. 'My sister's children were having nightmares for weeks afterwards.'

'I had heard he was in the area,' Nectan said. 'I missed him, though Brean had a chance to speak with him. It would appear he has become even more primitive than when I saw him last, and he was feral then.'

Kariss felt a shudder hurry through her. She was not looking forward to meeting Torwain. Mailcon noticed and laughed. 'I would not worry. He is a harmless soul, just a strange one.' He moved further away from the fire, the smell of wet wool was heavy in the air now their cloaks had begun to warm.

Nectan's face grew serious. 'Oh, Torwain can be very menacing when roused, Mailcon. He is not one to underestimate. Think of him more like a great stag. Most of its life is spent calmly grazing in the forest and hills, but those antlers are not just pretty ornaments on its head. They can attack just as well as they can defend. The stag only has to turn his head and you are impaled.'

'He sounds dangerous.' Fayern's complexion had lost the healthy colour of only a moment ago.

Nectan appeared not to have noticed; he was looking at Kariss. 'He may live in the forest and shun the luxuries of normal life but there is no one who will protect you more, should he decide you are one of his flock.'

'Then he is just the kind of person you need to have around you,' Fayern told her, not quite managing to keep her voice even. To Nectan she added, 'Brean asked me to tell you that Raien has arrived home safely. His escort has just arrived back.' She nodded to them and quickly left the hall, pulling the hood of her cloak over her head as she ducked under the lintel.

They watched her go in silence. Mailcon could not hide the downcast look on his face.

'She is getting so much better,' Anniel tried to reassure him once his sister was out of earshot. 'It is going to take time.'

Mailcon nodded. 'I hate to say this but I think the sooner you leave, the better it will be for her... I know, I know it is an awful thing to say,' he added as Kariss made to disagree. 'But every time she closes her eyes, she sees her family struck down in turn by Martaani.'

'That is understandable, surely?' Anniel argued. 'Naraic tells us Tharain is just the same, though his work with the animals is keeping his mind off it, through the day at least.'

Mailcon closed his eyes and inhaled deeply. He threw out the breath. 'Yes, but does your brother see the same thing happen to you and Kariss, every time he looks at you both?'

'No.' Anniel shook his head, confused. 'Because we were not there.'

'Even so, that is what Fayern sees.' Mailcon dragged his hand through his damp hair. He had stepped up to leading the Vacumagi with the efficiency of someone who had been training for the role his entire life. However, the situation with Fayern was something he had no experience with, and his inability to take away her fears tore at him like a rust-blunted blade. 'Every time she turns her head, she sees blood covering the flagstones; every time she hears a child cry, she sees your brother Inan murdered; loud noises become your mother's screams.'

There was silence as they each thought about what he had said. They all knew Fayern was struggling to come to terms with what had happened to her family at the hands of Martaani, but most of them had not realised how deep the torment ran. After a few moments Mailcon threw his hands up in resignation.

'I was hoping that Tharain would be able to accompany you when you leave. It would do him good to be away from the fort for a while, and give him something else to focus on, but when I tried suggesting it to Fayern she would not hear of it.'

'She needs time, plenty of time,' Nectan said thoughtfully. 'And plenty of love. She may never recover fully, but she will hopefully heal enough to live a decent life. Brean was out collecting more

Rock Rose for her last night. He has already told me how deeply she is suffering. He too feels she will not begin to heal until the fort returns to normal.'

Kariss looked at her husband. 'How soon can we leave?'

'The men have been preparing for days; as soon as the rain ceases we can be gone almost immediately.'

'I will deal with any concerns from the northern tribes,' Mailcon assured her. 'I have Anniel's statement to reinforce the call already sent out. Though by now I would expect many are already gathered and waiting to ride south.'

Kariss looked around the hall, 'I have grown to love this place. Just as I love you all, but I cannot cause Fayern any more pain than I already have. Whether the rain has passed by the new moon or not, we are leaving then.'

8

The sky was a freshly washed blue, with only the faintest hint of cloud. Already the air felt pleasantly warm, though the sun was barely visible over the hill tops. Where the road followed the edge of long water, the ground was boggy and the horses and dog were plastered with mud. Once the path turned away from the loch and up the hill they fared better. The slope and the increasing amounts of gravel had kept the route well-drained, giving Brean had a much easier job of hiding their tracks.

Martaani would be expecting Kariss to head south on the swiftest route. Instead they had decided to avoid the recognised pathways and travel across the country. For this they needed Carrick to guide them. His loyalty was to Lord Alpin and although he had agreed to help Anniel once before, there was no guarantee he would continue to do so now that his father was dead. Anniel's personal guard, Garth, had spoken to him that last time, whilst the rest of them hid on Long Water island. Carrick had agreed to lay a false trail to lead Martaani's men away from the area. Once done he had told Garth that he would make his way to Dun da Lamh in case he was needed again, but so far no one had seen him.

As they approached the clearing where Carrick's homestead sat, they dismounted. They did not want to alarm the hermit. Seven armed riders approaching in a group would be sure to set his teeth on edge - he didn't like visitors at the best of times. It was a surprise therefore when they noticed five saddled horses already hobbled close to the hut but no sign of the two horses Garth had left with him. Alarm flared. Without a word spoken, Garth and Anniel moved in front of Kariss, drawing their swords. Behind her, Naraic and their two guards did the same. Kariss glanced at Brean. The druid pulled a long dagger from his belt and moved to her side. She itched to draw her own sword, but her instructions were clear. If there was trouble here she was to run and let the others do the fighting. It went against everything she had been training for, and she had argued long and hard against the plan. It was Naraic who eventually convinced her. 'The whole of Brigantia is counting on you,' he had said. 'Without you, all is lost. We did not come all this way for you to die in a pointless skirmish.'

His words echoed again in her mind. With her heart thumping in her chest, she nodded at Brean and pulled her own dagger from her belt. She might not be able to fight, but she could still protect herself. Her eyes scanned their surroundings for her best route of escape as they crept forward cautiously.

'Hail.' A voice called from the waterside, shattering the tension. They turned to see Carrick hunched over the stream. 'Yer can put those away,' he told them. 'There is only me here.'

Anniel looked pointedly at the horses; fresh mud still clung to their legs.

'Had me a spot of bother,' Carrick said, holding up his arm. Blood gushed from a long wound running from shoulder to elbow, 'but the Roman woman now has five fewer men to help her. I ran into them on my way back from the western isles.

Nasty lot they was too.' He nodded respectfully at Kariss as she stepped into view. 'I lost your two horses in the fight, though. They ran off as I was laying my ambush' He shrugged. 'S'pect someone will find them eventually.'

Anniel waved away the apology. 'There is much we need to tell you,' he said. 'Will you hear us?'

'Aye lad, I will that.'

They settled around the fire. Anniel lost no time with the introductions.

'I am honoured to meet you,' Carrick told Kariss. 'Your story has fascinated the people here for a long time. I know my Lord was very anxious as to who would be taking his son away. I expect he is not disappointed.'

'He was not,' Anniel said. 'Though I have grave news to impart.' Quickly, he told him what had occurred at Dun da Lamh. His hands shook as he spoke about the deaths of his family, though he managed to keep his voice reasonably calm.

Carrick took the news quietly enough, asking only a couple of questions. There was nothing on his face to indicate how he was feeling, but after a few moments he rose. He pointed to the carcass of a small hind on the ground near the hut. 'Help yerselves,' he said, his voice gruff with emotion, before striding away into the woods.

They let him go.

Anniel frowned. He realised he had done his father's old friend a disservice. He should have broken the news in private. Anniel rubbed his face; lost as he was in his own grief, he had rushed to get the news told. He needed to remember that this intolerable pain was not his family's alone to bear.

Kariss squeezed his hand and he smiled in return. He would make a point of apologising later.

The hind was skinned, roasted over the fire and half eaten by the time Carrick returned. He took a small knife from his belt and cut of a chunk of the meat. Cloud shuffled over and beat his tail on the floor. He was rewarded with a rib bone and ran back to Naraic to lie crunching it at his feet. Carrick brought the talk swiftly back to Dun da Lamh.

'So, how is Mailcon faring?'

'He is coping well,' Anniel answered. 'The fort was in complete disarray when he first arrived. He jumped straight in and began organising the clear up. The people needed someone to look to, and he gave them just that. I think he will settle well.' He thought briefly of his sister's parting look, and how she had reached for Mailcon's hand when she thought Anniel had turned away. 'Those who answered my father's call for aid have mostly left now, gone to take word back to the nations. It is our hope that they will unite and help us defend Albion.'

'Alpin had time to send out the messengers, then?' Carrick shook his head, 'That bitch must have a mighty force with her, if she can bring down such a man.' He had control of himself now the shock had passed, and it was reassuring to know that his friend had gone down fighting.

'I am surprised you did not come across Tholarg on your journey,' Anniel said. 'My father sent out messengers as soon as he knew Martaani was coming. The Caledone king sent Tholarg with a band of warriors.'

Carrick shook his head ruefully, 'I did not follow the main route west for very long. Soon as I realised I was being followed, I led them a merry dance over the hills. Bringing them all the way back so I could corner them in a gully close by, where I would have the best chance at taking them all out. I never saw hide nor hair of any war band. That reminds me, one of the horses took a stumble. I should go and take a look.'

'Will you go?' Anniel asked the two guards, 'And can you unsaddle them and clean them all up?'

Carrick waited until the men were out of earshot. It was obvious Anniel had sent them away on purpose. Even more obvious was the fact that this visit was not just to inform him of Lord Alpin's demise. 'So,' he said firmly, looking at Kariss. 'What is the plan, and where do I fit into it?'

'I would like you to take us south,' she told him. She was not sure yet whether she could like this man. There was something about him that unsettled her. It was almost as if ghosts lived inside his eyes. The thought was ridiculous and she pushed it away. She didn't even understand what it meant.

'I want to go the hidden ways, so Martaani will not see us coming. You are the best man for the job, I am told.' She pointed over at the two guards. 'The Vacumagi have lost a number of good men and the nation is not a large one. This is all I felt Dun da Lamh could spare at this time. Men from further afield are joining up to make their way down to meet us. They are hoping to provide a distraction, should Martaani attempt an ambush.'

'After my father's funeral, word was taken far and wide,' Anniel said. 'I hope many more will choose to join them. This is no longer just the Brigantes' fight. In decimating my family and that of Drost's, Martaani has brought the wrath of the north down onto her shoulders.'

Carrick cut another chunk of meat and thrust his knife into the earth in front of him to clean it. 'I had always planned to disappear once yer father was no longer here,' he admitted. His manner was as calm and assured as ever. He may have shed his grief in the woods, but his next words showed he had not shed his allegiance to the old leader.

'But I never expected he would meet such an end. I cannot go until justice is brought.' He turned to Kariss. 'You have my word that I will do all I can to help you defeat the bitch. If you fail, I will keep going until she is dead, or I am.' His arm prickled. 'Damn it!' he cursed, seeing the wound was bleeding freely again.

'It is lucky we have our healer with us,' Anniel told Carrick as Brean began preparing a thick paste of yarrow and plantain. He cleaned the wound and coated it with the mixture.

'I will redo it again in the morning before I leave, but after that you will need to keep applying plantain for a good many days. You should have no trouble finding fresh leaves at this time of year.'

'Are you not travelling south?' Carrick asked, surprised.

'I am only here for my abilities to eradicate the horses' tracks,' Brean said, wiping his hands on his robe. 'Now Kariss is far enough away, my skills are better served at the fort.'

They left early the following morning, travelling only a short distance together before parting. Brean headed east back to Dun da Lamh, taking the remaining horses with him to be added to the fort's stables. They plodded, heads hung low, roped behind him. Weary after their long trek over the hills. The rest of the group dismounted and followed Carrick south into the woods. For a short way it was hard going. Branches hung low to the ground and vicious blackberry vines coated the floor. Before long they glimpsed water through the trees. The woodland opened up and a shallow loch pointed the way forward. Mounting up again, they clung to its sandy shoreline until around midday, when the loch end came in sight. They rested for a while and one of the guards removed his footwear. Inching forward slowly, he carefully stepped into the water. When he came to a good sized rock on the bottom, he eased himself lower and reached in with his hand.

'What on earth is he doing?' Kariss asked, her fingers idly playing with her hare amulet.

'He is guddling.' Garth told her. 'Catching a fish,' he added when she looked even more puzzled.

Suddenly the guard gave a flick of his hand and a trout was thrown clear of the water to land flapping on the shore. The other guard soon rapped its head on a stone and held the prize up for all to see.

'That would be fish for supper tonight, then,' Anniel said with a laugh.

Naraic watched with interest. 'How is it done? My uncle used to do it but he called it tickling, not guddling; he was going to show me how but…' his voice trailed off. Cloud's nose pushed against his leg and he reached down and scratched behind the dog's ears.

Garth came to his rescue. 'You rub your fingers slowly along the fish's belly and it goes to sleep. Then you scoop it out of the water before it wakes up and swims away.'

Two more fish followed the first and after a good while the guard left the water to dry his feet. 'That is all I can find,' he told them. 'Still, three is better than none.'

'There is another loch further on,' Carrick said. 'We can stop for another break there.' It was one of the first things he had said all day. They had tried drawing him into their conversations but, getting nowhere, had soon given up. Clearly, the spy was not one for small talk.

'I will give you a lesson, then,' Garth told Naraic. He still had a soft spot for the lad. When they were hiding out in the soutterain, he had taken him under his wing, impressed with the fact he had managed to get Kariss all the way from Brigantia to the Vacumagi lands without getting caught. He had heard all about his uncle's death and, like Kariss, did not believe Naraic was really to blame.

The loch was soon far beneath them as Carrick led them up into the hills. The animal track they were following had been turned into a rivulet during the storms. It was not so bad for the first couple of horses but their hooves quickly churned the sodden ground into a quagmire, making the going much harder for those following. They would have spread out but the land around the path was covered in spiky gorse bushes. Warblers in the bushes fussed and chirped as they passed, threatening them not to come any closer and raid their nests.

'They say if you can smell the flowers, yer loved by Cailleach,' Carrick called back, surprising them. He pointed to the bright yellow flowers covering the bushes. 'The stronger you can smell it, the stronger her protection.'

To Kariss, the smell was almost overpowering. She inhaled deeply, loving the distinct smell. She imagined it wrapping them all in the goddess's safe-keeping. Garth, however, looked abashed. 'I cannot smell a thing,' he admitted. For the first time since she had known him, Kariss could see worry in his face.

'Aha!' Carrick cried, as if he had found a prize. 'That means you must be in the hands of another; Bodach, maybe?'

Garth thought for a moment. 'I do love the thunder.'

'You love the rain as well, you daft man,' Anniel added.

Garth nodded his agreement. The signs of worry slipped from his face as quickly as they had arrived.

'I thought Gorse grew in sandy soil?' Naraic asked, grabbing his horse's mane quickly as one of its back legs slipped from under her. Cloud just managed to jump out of the way of the errant hooves.

'Aye, yer right there, lad,' Carrick answered. 'They have their feet in sandy soil, but the ground changes higher up, it becomes a vast boggy moorland that stretches farther than the eye can see. This is all the run-off water bringing the bog down with it.' He resumed his silence, as if he had run out of words as suddenly as he had found them.

They stopped again by the loch near the top of the hill. Garth upheld his promise and took Naraic to guddle fish. The two of them came back wet but happy. Naraic was full of the account of how his one had got away, but Garth had caught two more to add to the previous three.

'Well, we won't be feasting like kings, but at least we won't starve,' Carrick said as he finished redressing the cut on his arm. 'I hope yer not too used to the good life, my Lady.'

Kariss laughed. She had begun to warm to the man since he had made the comment about Cailleach, but there was still a feeling of ghosts around him. 'Oh, Naraic managed to feed us both just fine on our journey up here, but I would hardly call it feasting. And please, call me Kariss.'

'Do you remember the woodcock I shot on the first night?' Naraic said, his face alight.

Carrick's interest piqued, he looked at the bows tied to the boy's saddle and back to him. 'You have a fine pair of bows there, lad, and you must be a damn fine shot to bag a woodcock.'

Naraic flushed with pride. 'It was flying too,' he said. He took his bows and showed them to their guide. 'I made this one myself.' He handed over his ash bow. Carrick ran his hands up and down the shaft, wincing a little as he moved his arm.

'Can I string it?'

At Naraic's nod he fastened the string to the bow and made a few gentle pulls on the cord. 'Not bad,' he told him. 'But a little light now for a lad your age. Can I see the yew?'

Naraic took back his bow and handed over the heavier, slightly longer one, made of yew. 'Tharain gave me this one when we were leaving. I have not had chance to get used to it yet.'

The yew bow was a handsome-looking weapon, comprising pale wood on the outside and darker wood on the inside. The light wood was the sapwood and worked the best under tension, the darker wood on the belly of the bow was almost red in colour. As the bow string was pulled back, this red heartwood compressed. Once the string was released, the tense sapwood would instantly spring back to its rightful shape, shooting the arrow forward with incredible force. Carrick strung the bow and gently tried the string, pleased with the tension. He unstrung it and handed it back.

'That is a mighty fine bow, yer a lucky lad. Tharain must think a lot of yer.'

'We were good friends,' Naraic told him. 'I am going to miss him.'

Carrick clapped him on the back. 'I think we should get you to catch our dinner each night, what do you think?'

Naraic nodded eagerly, he would relish the chance to impress him with his shooting skills.

'I might even join you,' Carrick went on. 'Between us we should be able to catch ourselves some tasty meals with those two sticks. That's if you don't mind me using one.'

Naraic's nod turned to a shake. There weren't

many people he would be happy to let use his bows but he had heard enough about Carrick to be fascinated by him, despite the gruff demeanour. Tharain and Inan had spoken of him in almost reverent tones. Of course, his mysterious work for their father would fascinate any boy. He felt a sharp stab of regret when he remembered the boys. Leaving Tharain behind had been hard, especially so soon after losing Inan, but they were almost men now and they had responsibilities. He hoped his friend was enjoying the parting gift he had left him, as much as Naraic would enjoy the yew bow. The scrawny pup would take a fair bit of nurture if it was to survive but if anyone could do it, Tharain could. Naraic had come across one of the guards carrying the hairy bundle down to the river to drown it.

'T'waint survive,' the guard had told him but he gave in when Naraic persisted. 'Anything for a quiet life,' he told him. 'But it better not come back to bite me.'

Black as night in colour, the trembling pup had melted Tharain's shell of grief the moment he laid eyes on it. He had stayed up for next three nights, nursing it. The morning they were gathering to depart, Tharain had rushed over to Naraic. Bleary-eyed from exhaustion, he had thrust his yew bow into Naraic's hand. Then he had pulled at the sleeve of his tunic to reveal the tiny pup curled up, fast asleep in the crook of his arm.

Grinning from ear to ear, he told him, 'She is feeding well, she is going to live. Take my bow and make sure that you do too.'

9

The stream babbled away as it chased over the water-rounded pebbles. Not far away, a hopeful dipper bobbed on a stone by the shore, its little white bib, a sharp contrast to the rest of its brown and black feathers. The dawn had broken with an ominous sky. The heavy clouds appeared to drop lower and lower and very soon they found themselves surrounded by mist. Carrick's earlier warning about the boggy ground rang in their ears and they carefully picked their way nose-to-tail behind him. Cloud, heeding Naraic's commands, stayed close. Now was not the time to chase birds or bound away looking for food. They made a solemn group trudging across the moor. The only noise was the fall of the horses' hooves and the running water. Occasionally, other sounds cut their way through the blanket of fog but by the time they reached them they were muffled and strange. Only the dipper seemed unperturbed by the weather.

Kariss jumped as a deer barked nearby. She couldn't remember a fog so thick. The eerie stillness was unnerving.

'This is actually a beautiful moor,' Carrick called back to her. 'In summer the reeds cover the bog with yellow flowers. It is bleak, I grant you, but...'

'The last time I was in a bog it didn't end well,' Kariss interrupted him. She hadn't thought about that day much since it had happened but now she did, she realised how frightened it made her feel. 'It was deep with snow and we couldn't find our way. If it hadn't been for Cloud, Naraic and I would have both died.'

'Aye, they are dangerous places,' Carrick said. 'But yer've got nothing to fear this day, my Lady. We are only skirting the moor and I know this route well. We should be across before we stop for the night.'

The ground started to slope downwards as they neared the far edge of the moor. Stream after stream ran the excess water away. When they stopped for a drink they found the water had a strong, peaty taste. As they descended, the air finally started to clear and they found themselves heading into the end of a valley. Down at the bottom was a long, narrow loch but Kariss could see the valley ran into a far larger one, leading much further east into the distance. She was so busy enjoying the view after a day of such limited vision that she failed to see the change in Cloud. The scruffy dog had lifted his head and was busy smelling the air. His tail began to wag, slowly at first then faster as the scent he had picked up grew stronger. When he could contain himself no longer, he raced, barking, towards the small shieling where Carrick had suggested they spend the night. The noise brought a tall, thin man from the hut and he scooped down to embrace the dog like an old friend. As the horses neared, he straightened. Kariss realised that it was Cobalam, the druid who had saved her life on her journey north.

He waved a hand in greeting. 'I did not think to see you here,' he called.

'Nor I you,' she answered. 'Why are you here all alone? Has something more happened at the Tai?'

The druid held his hands up in a sign of calm. 'Everyone is as can be expected. I was needed here to put out the stones at Beltaine. It has been my job for many years now. I usually stay a day or two and repair the shieling. Come rest by the fire and tell me your news.'

'What do you mean about the stones?' Kariss asked after everyone was introduced. Cloud had settled down with his head on Cobalam's knee; the druid patted the dog absently as he spoke. 'A short distance away lies a small shieling called Tigh Na Cailleach. It is the home of a family of stones; two large and a number of smaller ones. Cailleach gave us the stones hundreds of years ago and a druid of old built the shieling to protect them. Every Beltaine we get the stones out of their little home and face them down the valley to guard the people and their cattle. Come Samhain the family is tucked safely away inside the shieling for the winter. I will show you later.'

'I would like that.' She paused for a moment, trying to find the right words. 'We heard about Dei. I am so very sorry.'

Cobalam blinked a couple of times but when he answered his voice was calm. 'It has been hard,' he admitted. 'He had been my mentor for so many years. I must admit I have been hiding away up here, afraid to return and face my new role.'

'Raien has returned,' Naraic told him. 'He was eager to get back to help you but Nectan would not let him leave until he was fully recovered.'

'The news reached us just before I left to come

here. I am sorry, Anniel, here I am wallowing in my own grief I forgot you have your own to bear.'

Anniel was not the man to take offence easily and he waved away the apology. 'Martaani has a lot to answer for my friend.' He threw another log onto the fire. It hissed as the moisture was forced from it by the sudden heat. 'I am fortunate that I have Kariss to keep me strong but I admit I see their faces every night in my dreams. I see my mother tortured, and my father killed instead of me.' He paused, 'My little brother...' He picked up another log and threw it onto the fire, sending sparks chasing each other into the air. No amount of sparks, though, could chase the visions his words had given him. 'Naraic, will you help me hunt something for our meal?' he asked, changing the subject abruptly.

Naraic jumped up and gathered his bows.

'I heard noises in the woods over there a short while before you arrived.' Cobalam pointed to the woods clinging to the side of the valley. 'I have a trap or two in there you might check for me, if you would?'

Garth made to get up and go with them but Kariss shook her head. 'Let him escape for a while.' She watched her husband disappear into the woods behind Naraic.

'It is a hard line he has to walk,' Garth said.

'The line between grief and happiness is always thus,' Cobalam agreed. 'He has found a wife, yet lost most of his family. His emotions must be pulling in all sorts of directions.' He seemed to dig deep within himself for something positive to add. 'Of course for us it has been wonderful to have

Lord Drost's daughter, Carina, returned. She has been instrumental in putting the heart back into the village.'

Later, when they had eaten, the druid took Kariss to see the shrine. 'This small valley is known as Glen Cailleach, the larger one is the Crooked Glen of Stones.'

'I remember you telling us that name when we last saw you,' Kariss said. 'So that must mean that Tai water is somewhere down there?'

'At the end of the valley and south slightly, yes, though it is a very long way.' Cobalam looked along the valley. 'I need to head back tomorrow; I have been away too long.' He looked at Kariss. 'Though now I know why I was guided to stay when the rains ended.'

'Cailleach has a knack of getting us in the right place at the right time,' Kariss told him.

They were approaching the small shieling. It stood only an armspan high with stone walls and a neat turfed roof. At the front of the hut, basking in the evening sunshine, stood the miniature family. The weather-worn stones had discernible bodies, with narrower necks and flattened heads.

'Here is Cailleach.' Cobalam pointed to the largest stone. 'Next to her is Bodach and these are the Nighean.' He pointed to the smaller figures.

Kariss crouched down to look at the figures. 'Why are there so many of Nighean and where is Brigantia?'

'There so many goddesses,' Cobalam told her. 'All over the land they are called many different names; here we know Cailleach's daughter as

72

Nighean but she has many daughters. It is easier for us to call them by the name we understand.'

The next morning, they said their farewells to Cobalam. 'Tell Drost I am very grateful for all his support,' Kariss told him. 'I am glad he has his daughter back.'

Cobalam nodded, 'Take care. Remember, the gods are always with you. Even you, boy,' he added to Cloud as he pulled on his ears one last time.

As they were moving off, he reached up and tucked something small into Naraic's hand. 'Shhh. Keep it safe but not in your pouch,' he told him in a low voice so none of the others could hear. 'When you run out of options, this will be your last hope.' He slapped the rump of the horse, and it hurried away, giving Naraic no chance to question him. The boy looked down and saw a smooth, oval black stone that fitted perfectly into his palm. It was so shiny he could almost make out his own face on its surface. He twisted around in his saddle to look at Cobalam, but the druid was already hurrying on his way.

Puzzled, Naraic turned the stone over and over but he could not fathom what on earth it was. Or how it could possibly be his last hope. He had nowhere to keep it, apart from his pouch, but Cobalam had been very clear about that. He racked his brains until an idea came to him. He carefully placed the stone into the bottom of the bag of essentials he had carried all the way from Brigantia and pulled out a bone needle and some thread. This was another gift from Cobalam, given to him when they had arrived at the nemetons on their journey north and he had seen Naraic's tunic sleeve was torn and tied with a leather thong.

On the bottom of his tunic he made a small hole in the hem, recovered the stone and slipped it inside. He gave silent thanks to the fact he was wearing his uncle's cast-off tunic, with an extra deep hem to make the length right. He slid the stone around until it rested against the side seam and sewed it in place. Then he stitched up the hole. There was nothing he could do to hide the bump it made but he hoped no one would notice. Its weight was reassuring and he found himself touching the bump often, hoping some insight as to its meaning would materialise, but nothing did.

10

The Pontiff called Martaani to him at Stanwick. The weather had finally cleared and the smell of damp being driven from the thatch filled the air. The Augur sat quietly in the corner, letting his counterpart do the talking.

'I received this today.' The Pontiff showed her a stone, the size of a man's head.

She snorted, 'Brigantia is full of stones, what is so special about this one?'

'It comes from Rome herself. It is time we performed a rite to the god, Terminus.'

'The festival of Terminalia is in February. Why did we not do it then?'

The Pontiff tapped his foot as he answered. It was the only outward sign that he found her attitude annoying. 'On Capitoline Hill in Rome, the shrine of Terminus lies in the centre of the Temple of Jupiter. We need to sanctify this stone here to verify your claim on this land, so that the gods know exactly what it is you are claiming in their name. Or you can continue to sneer at the gods and risk their wrath.'

Martaani's sneer evaporated. 'When and where?'

The Pontiff allowed himself a secret smile. 'Naturally it needs to be here in Stanwick, and as soon as possible. Obviously we cannot perform the ceremony out in the open as Terminus demands, so I propose we do it here in my room and open a hole in the roof, as was done at the Temple in Rome.'

His answer was rewarded with a nod. 'How long

will the preparations take?'

'I need a sacrifice.'

'That would be my area.' The Augur stood. 'I will leave immediately.' He ducked out of the room, eager to be out in the fresh air.

The rites were performed that night. The rain dripped down on them through the new opening in the roof. Martaani watched as the bones, ashes and blood of the Augur's victim were placed into a hole along with a handful of grain and honeycombs, dripping in sweet golden honey. Fragrant red wine, the colour of rubies, was poured from a stone flagon over the offerings whilst the Pontiff spoke the words which Terminus, the god of boundaries, required. Finally, the stone sealed the hole and the Pontiff brought the ceremony to an end.

He moved back to the table. As he sat down, he knocked over a bowl of salt, spilling its contents across the wooden surface.

Martaani made to speak but she was stopped by the Augur, who jumped to his feet and held up his hands. Eagerly, he studied the spread of the salt

Finally, he smiled and turned to his companions. 'We need to go north.'

He pointed to the salt, most of which had fallen in one thick stream across the table. Some of the salt, however, had separated and taken a different line, only to join up with the rest where it culminated.

'I believe Kariss is coming,' his finger followed the thin line. 'But I do not think she is coming with the rest.' He looked to the Pontiff, 'You have men watching them. I trust they will stay with her?'

'Of course.'

'Then we need to be close enough to get their messages. By the time they reach us here it will be too late to use them.'

Leaving only a handful of men behind, they departed Stanwick the next day and rode north. At Martaani's side rode Proculus. He was the Praefectus, or leader, of the cohort that formed her personal guard, and the man she trusted the most. Many in Rome had doubted Martaani's claim to the Brigantian throne, and she was the object of some ridicule amongst the elite of the city. Only her friendship with Julia Domna kept her from being publicly shunned. Proculus, however, had been her friend for many years and her lover for the last three. His cohort had served in Rome, protecting Julia Domna who had insisted they accompany her on her quest to Albion.

The cohort were mainly Syrian in origin and as such had only been recruitable as legionaries since Caracalla had issued his Antonine Constitution. The edict declared that all men in the Empire above slave level were now recognised as Roman citizens and so eligible to be enrolled into the main army. Before this they had served as auxiliaries. Citizenship gave them better rights, but did not change their ingrained convictions. Whilst they believed wholeheartedly in the mighty Roman Empire, they had great respect for what Martaani was trying to achieve. Unlike the proud Roman-born Centurions and their ranks of legionaries, they had immense faith in the abilities of those not born to the privilege of full Roman citizenship. Martaani kept them close at all times, using them as a buffer between herself and the condescending ranks making up the bulk of her Roman support.

Their destination was The Eildons, a triple hill right at the edge of the Votadini and neighbouring Selgovae lands. The three hills together formed the third point in a triangular connection with the two major Votadini forts of Ad Gefrin and Dumpender Law. It had been a very important area in Cartimandua's time. The Selgovae had not recognised the full strategic importance of the hills. They held them sacred, due to their triple peak and supposed hollowness, and had built a small fort on the summit of the northern-most hill. When the Romans had first arrived, though, they abandoned the fort and left the hills to the gods. The Romans had defiled what they had left and built a tower right in the heart of the fort, staying until they were driven from Albion. In the intervening years, the Selgovae had reclaimed their sacred hills and built a complex fort surrounding the top of the north hill.

The tower was not the only thing the Romans had built there. Close to the bottom of Eildons, by the banks of the river, they had built their own large fort, which they called Trimontium, the ruins of which were now crawling with men. Officially, they were there to make it habitable again, but this also served as a useful cover for Martaani's troops.

Not all of the legionaries now in Albion wore the standard army clothing of red tunics and light body armour. Most of the men at Eildons wore a standard white tunic, making it harder for the residents of Albion to get any firm idea on the true number of soldiers Martaani had at her disposal. Each man looked just like any other man, and shift working ensured that only a third of the men were ever working at any one time. The other two thirds were tucked away inside, overcrowded and eager for action. Every fortnight, two waggons went to the coast to pick up supplies of fish and other goods from the ships that traded with the Empire. More men hid within each cargo, and so the Roman population grew. Not all stayed at the Eildons fort. Some of the units hid out in the forests in leather tents. Each small unit of soldiers was called a contubernium and consisted of six to eight men. Like those hidden at the fort, these men wore plain clothes and were growing restless. They hated the damp weather, and the need for all of the secrecy. It was not how the Roman army usually operated.

Martaani had been glad to get out of the claustrophobia of Stanwick. She could not abide the constrictions placed on her movements there. The presence of druids so close by made her flesh crawl. She longed for the time when she could purge the land of their presence. She watched with envy as the messenger galloped away from them, his quest to inform the Pontiff's network of spies as to their new whereabouts. Martaani resisted the urge to put her heels to her horse's flanks. They had a long ride ahead, it would not do to tire the animals at the very start.

Four days later they arrived at Trimontium. Martaani looked at the complex with dismay. This really was a backwards country. She could not understand why the people had not made the most of the luxury buildings that the Romans had left behind. Without adequate maintenance they had soon fallen into disrepair. The intervening 145 years had not been kind. The woodland had encroached into some of the smaller buildings, roots had torn through walls, and many of the outer buildings had given way completely to the trees now growing inside them.

Her men had worked hard in the months they had been here. Along with a number of men from the Votadini lands, now serving them as auxiliaries, they had managed to make good the great hall and rebuild two of the smaller buildings and roof them. These were now being used as the private rooms for the Centurion and his key officials. The rest of the men slept in the hall, hidden from any prying eyes.

Martaani immediately took over the best of the finished buildings. The Centurion stiffened his spine. He was not used to being ordered around by a woman. They were not allowed into the army and were never in a position of authority over a Centurion in the Empire; but this was not the Empire, he reminded himself. His orders had been to do whatever it took to help Martaani secure the throne of this region. Once done, his advancement in the army was almost a certainty. Provided he kept his head.

He had been promoted to the leader of the Centuria only the year before. It was not a well-positioned group. The Legate had not wanted to risk his best men here. The battle for Albion was not expected to be successful. The leading

80

members of the army were amused at the thought of a woman in command. He bristled at the humiliation he had suffered from his counterparts, but he would show them. He would ensure victory if it came to battle. Then his lowly hundred men would become the First Centuria of the many that would arrive from the Empire. He would be catapulted to First Centurion, and as a result would lead the First Cohort.

For the last few months he had drilled the prospects of advancement into his men. No longer were they to think of themselves as the laughing stock of the Roman army, despite the fact that Martaani held the inferior Syrian ex-auxiliaries in higher regard. He dangled the opportunities that would be available to the most experienced fighters in this foreign land, appealing to the soldier's pride. His work at turning the men already defeated by their placement on this forsaken isle into a truly inspired fighting force was further aided by the reports of Martaani's love of aggression. Her brutality towards the family at Dun da Lamh was discussed endlessly amongst the soldiers. As was her treatment of the legionaries who had displeased her. Against all the odds, this woman was one that instilled both fear and admiration in the men. Whether they had developed a newfound respect for her or just a desperation not to find themselves on her wrong side, the Centurion was not sure. Either way, they had stopped complaining quite as loudly, and there was an eagerness to their military practices that had not been there before.

The Centurion retired to the lesser of the two buildings and waited for an audience with Martaani.

He tried to ignore the indignation of appearing to concede ground to a praefectus. In the old days, before the Antonine Constitution, it was not that uncommon for the auxiliary forces to form personal guards, leaving the official army free to fight. In his eyes, and those of many of the Roman-born men, the edict and the intervening two years had changed nothing. The auxiliaries may have been raised to legionaries with their new found status, but they would always be considered as lesser soldiers. He swallowed his ire and thought again of the possibilities in store when they took this land back.

11

Shortly before noon, they entered a small glen.

'Cobalam recommended we come through here instead of taking the straighter route,' Carrick told them. 'He wanted us to stay as close to Cailleach as possible and this is another of her glens.'

Kariss soon became aware of a strange feeling. It was almost as if someone was watching her. She looked around but could see nothing to cause alarm. The valley was banked on each side by hills, the one on their right was slightly higher. She could see a herd of red deer grazing on its slopes. She watched them as they followed the stream along the glen floor. The deer lifted their heads and eyed the travellers warily but they did not run; Cailleach loved her deer, it was no surprise they felt safe here.

The hinds were still there as they stopped for their midday rest, and Kariss's feeling of being watched had only intensified. By now there was a real sense of urgency to it. She looked again at the deer, their russet coats blending perfectly with the coarse grass and heather on the hill. As she scanned the herd, one lifted its head to look straight towards her. Slowly and deliberately, it detached itself from the herd and walked alone into a small stand of trees.

Kariss needed no further signals. Making her excuses, she left the group and walked a short distance into a shaded copse full of late spring beauty. Finding herself drawn to an old rowan tree, she sat down with her back against its trunk and stilled her mind. Whilst she waited, she watched a large mistle thrush probing amongst the undergrowth for food. It hopped closer and closer before finally lifting its head. Kariss expected to see a snail in its beak but instead she was shocked to see the hare amulet that Naraic had given her at the start of their journey. The thrush looked straight at her, walked forward, and dropped the hare onto her lap. Job done, it flew a short distance away and calmly went back to hunting for snails.

Kariss rested her head back against the smooth bark of the tree and closed her eyes. A vision flashed across her mind but it was gone before she could determine exactly what it was. She could still hear voices from the group, distracting her. She breathed deeply and willed her mind to focus. In her hands she could feel the cool bronze of the amulet. She stroked the body with her thumbs, remembering how honoured she had been when Naraic had given it to her. The vision came again, much clearer this time, staying for longer. She saw a hand reach out and draw an arrow on the ground then it covered the mark with leaves and stood a cockerel feather in the ground to mark the spot. The vision faded, only to be replaced by another.

This time she saw two birds; a male blackbird, with its bright orange beak, and a thrush. She noticed something hanging around the neck of the thrush, on a cord. It was her hare amulet. Around the neck of the blackbird appeared a string tied to two small stones and the bird fell struggling to the ground. Once there, its belly opened to allow its entrails to spread on the earth. The unhurt thrush flew away to the safety of the trees and the vision faded.

Kariss felt sick. Fear coated her skin in a sheen of sweat. The innards of the bird spread out like that reminded her of the sight that had met them when they returned to Dun da Lamh after Martaani had attacked. She looked down to her hands and found the bronze amulet was now just a smooth stone. She put her hand to her throat, relieved to find the hare still there. She untied the thong and checked it. The leather was now so worn it snapped as soon as she applied some force. Throwing it away, she threaded the amulet onto a new piece of leather lace before tying it back around her neck. She tucked it safely underneath her tunic where it sat, reassuringly, against her chest.

She 'felt' the rowan tree behind her smile and silently she thanked it. She was rewarded with a small stick, which fell to the ground beside her. She tucked it safely into her pouch, along with the hare stone the thrush had given her. Behind her, a noise made her turn and she saw the men coming looking for her Their approach disturbed the thrush and it flew up from the ground to be joined by a blackbird as together they flew out of sight, shouting their alarm calls.

'You have been so long we were starting to worry,' Anniel called out to her.

'Everything is fine,' she answered, taking a deep breath. 'I was just taking a few moments to myself.'

Anniel gave her a long look. He noted the rowan; he knew that it guarded the path that Beithe, the birch, began. Nectan himself had given him a short stave of it before they had left, for perseverance, protection and insight; along with the warning that Kariss may start getting visions. Whatever Kariss had seen, it had caused her pallor to change and her eyes to take on a panicked look.

'We will give you a moment, then, whilst we get the horses ready. We have a long way still to go before we camp tonight.' He led the men back to where Naraic watched the horses, relieved no one else appeared to have noticed anything amiss.

Riding away, Kariss puzzled over the visions. She longed for a druid to help her decipher them. Clearly the thrush with its amulet represented her. The bronze hare nestled against her skin as if it were part of her. She kept touching it, reassuring herself that it was still there and that she, like the thrush, was safe. The blackbird, though, was not safe. It was hunted and used for divination. Kariss shivered at the memory of the innards spilling out from the sleek black feathers.

She thought of the previously unseen blackbird that had flown away as the men approached. Did that mean it represented one of them? She willed it not to be Anniel; surely she could not come this far to lose him now. Immediately she was rocked with shame. How could she wish such a fate on any of them? Even Carrick? Her only relief was the realisation that Naraic was safe. Of all those in their small group, he was the only one not to have come into the copse looking for her. Again she felt for the hare. At least one part of the vision was clear – the hare would protect her. She wondered if a thrush would be able to warn her the next time the amulet was at risk of being lost.

It was only later that she remembered the first

part of her vision. Clearly signs were being written in the ground and then hidden but who on earth could be writing them? Would this be the way the gods would hide their signs when they could not approach her? She found herself scanning the ground for feathers as they rode.

She had no doubt that Anniel knew something had upset her and she appreciated his silence, but she would have to tell him something soon. She toyed with telling him the truth, but what if that meant she lost the ability to change what she had seen? The image of Anniel with his innards tipped onto the floor flashed into her mind. Try as she might, she could not rid herself of it. Nausea was her constant companion all day.

They stopped to camp at the head of a narrow loch. The smell of pigeon roasting over the fire made her retch until she had nothing left inside her but mouth-burning bile.

'I wish you could tell me what you saw,' Anniel said as he wiped a damp cloth over her forehead. 'Nectan warned me this would happen. So I know that you have good reason if you are not telling me'

Kariss could have cried with relief. At least that was one of her problems eased. 'I am sorry,' she said. 'I need to understand it first.'

'If it helps, Nectan told me to tell you that visions are often cryptic. The literal meaning you first see may not be what is intended.'

Kariss nodded to let him know she understood. The nausea was receding now her stomach was empty but the retching had caused her muscles to cramp painfully. She doubled over, blowing out her breath as if to send the pain away with it.

He had noticed her worried glances in his direction all day, and took a gamble with his next words. 'He also told me to tell you that the future is not set in stone. So whatever you have seen does not have to be what happens. You have been given the chance to change it. And I am telling you, I have no intention of dying anytime soon. I have my own vision that I fully intend to make come true.'

Kariss closed her eyes and willed his words to be true but no matter what he said, the vision was clear. There was immense danger heading towards one of the men and Kariss had no idea how to stop it.

The loch turned out to be enormous. For a full day they followed it, enjoying the sounds of the tiny waves lapping on the shingle shore. They made camp at the southern end. It had widened out here and across the water they could make out heavily wooded islands. They were much bigger than the island on Long Water, where they had hidden Kariss's body when Martaani had blocked her from Albion.

There was little grazing near the water, so the guards took the horses further away, to a patch of rough ground by the edge of a wood, staying to rub them down. The rest of them sat on the beach watching Naraic, who still had not mastered the technique of guddling. After a long while without success, he gave it up in frustration. Flinging himself onto the ground next to Carrick, he grumbled to himself so much that the older man couldn't help laughing. He had tried to keep his distance from the group, but for some reason his usual barriers would not stay in place. Almost without realising it, he was mellowing. He knew it was the boy doing it. His mind flashed back to another loch and another boy; the sound of his laughter, the glint in his eye as he held up a fish. There was only pain in memories, far better not to remember what had been taken away from him, so he shook the thought away and concentrated on the present.

'Face it, lad,' he said. 'You an' water ain't ever gonna be the best o' pals. How's about, after the meal, I teach you somat about tracking instead?'

Naraic's mood improved instantly and he nodded eagerly.

The fire was crackling, the fish Garth had caught were roasting, and Cloud was gorging himself on fish guts. It was such a lovely evening, even Kariss was beginning to relax. She had been tense and withdrawn most of the day, still fretting about the visions. She had covered her mood by claiming an upset stomach. No one thought to disbelieve her since they had all heard her retching the day before. She had tried breaking the visions down into smaller details. The two birds, she believed, represented her and the men. The thrush showed her how to protect herself, the blackbird showed her vulnerability. She asked the men all the ways you could catch a bird, but they never mentioned anything like the weapon she had seen wrap around the bird's neck. Maybe it was a Roman weapon?

As for the bird's innards, if she took Anniel's advice and did not look at this literally, then it could represent a number of things. They were not something you would usually see, so perhaps they represented something hidden? She quickly discounted that thought; everyone knew the innards were there. It could mean digestion, but how on earth that could be important she had no idea. It could also mean turning something inside out, looking too deep and only finding what was expected. Finally, not long before they had stopped, she had focused on the bird's plumage. In the vision it did not seem to have any significance.

She had jolted upright, making her horse jump at the unexpected movement. That was it, she thought. The only difference between a blackbird and a thrush was their feathers. Swap their feathers and the insides would be just the same. There was only one way she could think of that this information could be of use to her. When they got closer to Brigantia, she would not hide herself in the middle of her men. That was what Martaani would be expecting. Instead, she would disguise herself as one of the guards. She felt as if a weight had been lifted from her shoulders. Anniel had been right, she had been looking at it too literally. Now they had stopped, she was able to relax better, maybe she would even sleep tonight. She accepted her fish with thanks, realising just how hungry she was. Worry had driven the appetite from her all day. Overhead, thunder rumbled.

Meal over, Carrick and Naraic set off into the woods. Cloud made no attempt to follow them; he had found his spot by the fire and was not moving until morning. Once they were in amongst the trees, Carrick told Naraic to show him how he would walk through the wood if he did not want to be followed. Naraic had lived in the woods all his life, he had played in them as a boy and hunted in them regularly. He set off, grinning to himself. If there was one thing he knew, it was how to walk in woodland.

Carrick watched quietly, making no attempt to follow. After a while he whistled and Naraic made his way back, confident he had done well. His was astounded when he saw Carrick shaking his head.

'Ahh, don't be looking so disheartened, boy. Some things you did really well. Here, let me show yer.'

Carrick took him back along his route and pointed out the damage to the ground cover, broken stalks and trampled flowers. He lifted the damaged leaf of a hart's tongue fern and showed him the print his boot had left beneath it in the mud.

'What yer did do right was to not snap a twig underfoot, or break any of the smaller branches as yer passed. But yer only focused on not making any noise. Yer gotto remember that yer not the hunter now, yer the prey and that makes things different. The ones hunting yer will know how to find the damage yer don't even realise yer making.'

Naraic's disappointment was replaced by excitement. 'So really damage is far more important than noise? Any animal could snap a branch, but only a person could leave a footprint.'

'Though of course yer still have to be careful not to scare the wildlife. It is far quicker to head to where the animals are running from than to search the undergrowth for broken leaves.'

Naraic was thinking fast, 'What if you came across a muddy patch and there was no way round it? Would you throw a log onto it and step on that? That way all that is left is a log in the mud.'

'Yer got it, lad.'

Carrick was impressed. He was really starting to see why the gods had put such faith in the boy. Already, Naraic was looking at the ground around him and trying to work out how best to move. He seemed determined to master this new skill.

12

The small fort sat atop a low-lying hill, surrounded by a thick forest of pines. They had entered via the north-west entrance to find the place ransacked. The smoke had long since gone from the charred embers, but the acrid smell still clung in the air. A dog growled as they neared. He was fiercely guarding something. They assumed it was food but as they got closer they could see it was the chewed remains of a small hand. Cloud growled back, his hackles raised, his lips curled high to reveal sharp canines and neat front teeth. The dog gave up its stance. Grabbing the hand, it ran off with its tail between its legs.

'How many bodies?' Kariss asked when they had finished their checks.

'Twenty-eight,' Garth answered. 'Mainly guards, but also two men, two women, and six children. Two of the children have missing hands.' He glanced across to where Anniel was inspecting one of the buildings and lowered his voice. 'Both women have been scourged.'

Kariss closed her eyes and forced her voice to remain calm.

'Build pyres,' she told him. 'And Garth... try not to let him see.'

She watched as the bodies were piled onto the pyres. Anniel had insisted on helping. So much for hiding the women's backs. He made no comment as he tenderly lifted their bodies, only the steel set of his jaw and the flushed look to his face betrayed his emotions.

They were just getting ready to set a torch to the wood when the sound of a lone horse made them pause. Too late they realised that amidst the horror of their discovery they had forgotten to mount a guard.

'Quick,' Anniel told Kariss, 'hide.'

She rushed to one of the houses and pulled the remains of the leather door covering in place. There was a tear in the hide and she peered through, one hand pressing her amulet to her chest as if to stop her heart hammering.

The rider hailed them from outside the fort and held his shield high so they could see the Caledone insignia. Anniel lifted his own hand in greeting, and went forward to speak with him. After a few minutes the rider turned his horse around and galloped away. Anniel returned and called Kariss over.

'We are to have visitors. A Warband of Caledones and Epidii.'

Kariss felt a stab of apprehension. She had not spoken with war leaders before.

Anniel laughed when she said as much. 'Of course you have. My father, for one, and Mailcon. Besides, have you forgotten? Tholarg is the leader of the Caledone warriors. You got on well enough when he came to Dun dal Lamh.'

She had liked Tholarg. He was a calm, happy man, about ten years older than herself. He was not the Caledone King. That was his father, who was no longer fit enough to lead his warriors. It struck her that many of the nation's leaders were old. Albion had been at relative peace for many years; though the nations were still very distinct and a long way from being united.

She did not have long to ponder as the air was soon filled with the growing sounds of an approaching war band. Harnesses rattled, shields clanked, and horses snorted. The ground, still heavy from the previous week's storms, muffled the sound of the hoofs but it was still clear there were many. Finally, they began to emerge from the trees. In the front were around twenty mounted warriors, riding two abreast. These men rode tall and proud, in full fighting gear. Helmets and spear tips glinted in the sunlight, as did the elaborate polished pony caps on the horses' heads.

As if this wasn't impressive enough, behind followed at least twenty chariots. The simple-looking carts were each pulled by a pair of horses. Built from wood and wicker with a single iron tyred wheel on each side, they were highly adorned with bronze and enamel. Hammered bronze designs were incorporated where the shafts met the cart and many of the yoke mounts, rein guides and lynch pins bore animal forms. Owls and bulls were common, as were leaf designs and heads. Some chariots even carried blood-red enamel fittings.

Following on behind the chariots were twenty more riders and behind these were slower, larger carts carrying supplies and food. At the head of the war band rode two men. They held up a hand each to signal the convoy to halt, then proceeded into the fort. The first group of mounted warriors spaced themselves out around the fort, their eyes on the surrounding countryside. There would be no more surprise attacks today.

Beside Thorlag rode a slightly shorter, much

older man. His bronze helmet was covered in tiny horse motifs, which were further reflected on the boss of his shield, marking him out as being from the Epidii tribe from the western isles. The heavy electrum torc around his neck left them in no doubt that this was the Epidii king himself.

'One day we will meet in a great hall with a roaring fire, fine food and plenty of ale, instead of by the side of the road,' Thorlag said with a grin. He leapt from his horse and bowed his head respectfully to Kariss. 'My father sends his apologies, his health is failing fast, though his spirit is still as strong as an ox. It is a matter of shame for him that he cannot give you his presence.'

'He should not feel any shame, he has sent you and the warriors. I am grateful,' Kariss said. 'And I take you up on the next meeting. When all this is over we will have a celebration.' She embraced him and turned to the second man, who had also dismounted and had come to stand with them. She nodded her head and held her arm out in the way Lord Alpin had taught her to do when meeting important people for the first time. He clasped her arm and nodded in return.

'I am Uurad, King of the Epidii. It is an honour to meet you.' His voice was rich and deep. She tried not to stare at his strange eyes. One was green, the other blue. The eyelashes and eyebrow of the blue eye were pure white. 'It takes a lot to drag me from the islands, but already my people have been touched by the devastation of the Roman dung.'

'Lord Drost's sister lives on the islands,' Anniel explained as he clasped arms with Uurad. 'We welcome you, I am only sorry you have arrived at such an unpleasant time.' He indicated the pyre. 'It appears that the Roman dung has been spreading further than we had realised.' He was still flushed, but if the two leaders noticed anything they were too polite to mention it.

Uurad and Tholarg took a closer look at the bodies, commenting on the missing hands with shock, before Garth touched his torch to the dry kindling built into the pyre. Flames tore through the wooden pile and soon the air was filled with the stomach-churning smell of burning hair and flesh.

They rode away whilst the flames were still high, leaving by the south-eastern entrance that led down a long natural causeway.

The land south of the fort showed numerous signs of devastation. They found three more homesteads burning but the inhabitants must have seen the attackers coming and fled, for there was no sign of any bodies. Not much further on they came to a ridge, atop which was a row of standing stones. They were forewarned by a number of rooks and jackdaws rising into the air, cawing their annoyance at being disturbed. Sprawled over the stones they found the remains of a druid. He lay face-down with three arrows in his back. His robe had been torn from his body, which reeked of rot and urine. Uurad howled in horror, almost falling from his horse in his rush to reach him.

'The cowards shot him in the back whilst he was performing a ritual,' he shouted at no one in particular. 'Look, the signs are all here.' He pointed to the bowls that had once held incense and water, but which now lay uptipped on the mossy ground.

'They pissed on him, too,' Tholarg said, sniffing the air. His lip curled in utter disgust. 'Only the Romans would defile a druid in this way.'

The birds had retreated to a nearby stand of oaks but they continued to call. The sound put all on edge. Someone used a slingshot to scare them away but they only flew to the higher branches, out of reach.

'Why would they target this area?' Kariss asked. 'It does not appear significant. Is it part of the Gask ridge?'

The men looked at her blankly.

'The row of towers they built across the country?'

'Like the one we slept in?' Naraic asked. He kept his eyes averted as two warriors carefully pulled the arrows from the druid. He had pulled many from the bodies of animals he had hunted, but never from a person. The very thought made him blanch.

Kariss nodded, 'I cannot remember where they all were.'

They had not seen any sign of old Roman presence in the area; maybe they were too far up still. Anniel was getting used to Kariss coming out with snippets of information no other person could know. He understood she had been living in a world far into the future but even so, it still amazed and impressed him.

'The only person we could ask is now dead,' he said, looking down at the druid now laying face-up, his empty eye sockets glaring balefully towards the sky. 'We should build another pyre.'

Tholarg snapped his fingers and a number of his men rushed to gather the wood. Uurad pulled himself together long enough to say a few words over the unknown man before committing his body to the flames. Then once again they set off, leaving a plume of smoke reaching for the clouds.

'I am afraid we will be unable to travel any further with you,' Kariss explained that evening as they made camp. 'We are trying to get back down to Brigantia without attracting Martaani's attention.' She waved her arm in the direction of the warriors. 'Discretion is not really a war band's forte.'

'There are plenty more aiming to join up with us on the way down.' Tholarg told her. 'We are just the beginning and about as discreet as we are going to get. The northern nations might not always be the closest of friends, but none will stand idly by whilst this blight on our shores targets our people and druids.'

Uurad nodded his agreement. 'You will be safe enough with us.'

'I have no doubt.' She smiled, 'But I have received guidance telling me to take a different way. I have learnt not to question the gods' advice.'

Uurad held up his hand. 'Say no more, my dear. The will of the gods is not something to be ignored.'

Carrick had not said much since the warband had joined them, but now he spoke up. 'There could be something you could do for us, though.' He was thinking fast, trying to formulate how his plan could work. 'How many women do you have in your number?'

'I have ten,' Uurad answered.

'I have thirty-seven.' Tholarg said. The

Caledones were renowned for hosting more female warriors than any other nation. He was quick to catch on to Carrick's thinking. 'Kariss, has Martaani ever seen you?'

She shook her head.

'No doubt she will have been given a description, but so long as the hair colour is right...' Tholarg thought for a minute, then he shook his head. 'I do not think I have anyone who will do.'

Kariss had no idea what he meant.

'Oh Ho!' Uurad exclaimed as he suddenly caught on. 'I think I have just the one.' He screwed up his mismatched eyes and squinted at Kariss.

'A decoy,' Carrick explained to her. 'If it looks like you are travelling with the war band, Martaani will have no need to look for you elsewhere.'

'No!' Kariss was horrified. Already too many people had died in her place. She would not set another up to be the focus of Martaani's wrath. 'It is too dangerous.'

'Nonsense!' Uurad boomed. 'You would offend a warrior with such a suggestion.' He clicked his fingers for one of his men, giving him his instructions before Kariss could resist any more.

Before long a tall, red-headed warrior named Enda was kneeling before him.

'I have a special job for you,' Uurad said and explained the proposition.

The woman's face lit up. 'I should be honoured.' She was taller than Kariss, and the hair plaited into a long rope down her back was a shade darker, but the same basic description fitted them both.

'You would need to cut your hair,' Carrick told

the warrior.

Hair was precious to a warrior woman. It was her identity and her strength. Some did choose to cut their hair shorter but most kept theirs natural. Enda's face flushed but she nodded her agreement. Carrick took a knife from his belt and severed the plait before she could change her mind. Enda took it from him, she ran her hand down its length and closed her eyes. With her short hair falling around her face, she looked completely different. She muttered a few words and then threw the plait into the fire. Standing straight, she looked at them. 'What do you need me to do?'

When the war band left the next day, Enda rode with Tholarg and Uurad. She carried her familiar weapons, but now she was decked in one of Tholarg's spare tunics, more fitting to her presumed status. She would no longer be mixing with the rest of the warriors, who had been told that she had been recruited to go on a special mission with Anniel's smaller group. Those who knew her well would still recognise her, of course, but the majority would never know the truth.

They headed south-east on a direct route to the Brigante lands, where they would find a suitable place to gather along with all the other warriors coming from the north. Martaani's eyes would hopefully be centred on them, leaving Kariss's group free to sneak downcountry.

As a warrior, Enda was no stranger to the risks involved in warfare. She carried her scars with pride. Even the probability that she would have to sacrifice herself in order to keep Kariss alive did not crush her spirit. She had the war band at her back to help protect her, and the knowledge that she was a key person in the fight to drive the Romans from Albion. She smiled as she rode, every inward breath filling her with the courage of the gods.

13

Branches caught in her hair and snagged on her clothing, but she kept running; searching. The forest was dark and foreboding. No light reached through the leafless canopy, so the ground beneath was mainly bare. Here and there, life had started to blossom; the green shoot of a flower, a tall wispy sapling. But all had been smothered by an insipid creeping vine.

Its black tendrils were following her, sliding along behind her like a snake. She fell and tasted earth in her mouth, its gritty texture mixed with the iron tang of blood. For a moment she paused and everything went still, then the fear burst inside her again, pushing her to her feet. Her eyes scanned ahead but the raven was nowhere to be seen.

'Cailleach,' she screamed. 'I need you.'

A glimmer of light flared through the trees and she raced towards it. A small hearth was set amongst a patch of green grass. The flames danced high and bright, driving away the gloom of the forest, but there was no one there. She ran on.

'Cailleach,' she screamed again.

Each time she screamed her name, a new hearth appeared with its dancing flames. Whenever she was near the flames she felt warm and calm but she needed the raven, so she kept on running. The black vines were always just behind her, closer each time she left a fire's glow. She heard someone call her name. She turned and immediately the vines caught her. They wound their way round her legs and up her body until she could feel herself being smothered.

'Kariss!' Anniel called, shaking her.

She woke with a gasp and sat up. Her breath was ragged and she was covered in sweat. It took her a few moments to untangle herself from her cloak where it had wrapped around her.

'These dreams are getting worse.' Anniel's face was pale and concerned. 'You were thrashing around like you were fighting for your life.'

Kariss shook her head, still in the grip of the dream. 'I was running, looking for Cailleach, but all I kept finding were fires with no one around them. A vine was chasing me and when I heard you calling it caught me and…'

Her last words were muffled into his shoulder as he gathered her into his arms.

'We must find a druid,' Anniel told her. 'He will know what it means.'

Kariss held on to him tightly. She knew only too well what the fear was, but she would not tell him, or anyone for that matter. She needed Cailleach but despite calling her for days now, she had not come.

There was a small stream close by. Kariss cupped her hands and took a drink. The water was pure and clear and tasted wonderful. She rubbed some over her face, hoping to clear away the remnants of the nightmare. The fear that was choking her in the dream had been growing inside her ever since her vision with the birds. Although she felt that she had figured out that message, the thought process had brought a terrifying possibility to her. She felt for the amulet and sighed at its reassuring touch. If only she had one for her husband.

Later that day they entered a dark wood where the trees grew so close together they had to dismount to continue. The going was slow and many times the trail they were following looped back on itself until they had no sense of what direction they were travelling in.

'At this rate we will be coming out of the wood right next to where we entered,' one of the guards grumbled.

Kariss was walking at the rear with Anniel. 'There is something about this wood.' She murmured to him.

'Is it your dream?'

'No, that wood was bare, a winter wood. This path is more like walking a labyrinth. It feels… mystical.'

Anniel shook his head, 'I have no idea what you mean.' He laughed. 'You are using words from your old world again.'

Kariss opened her mouth to explain, but was stopped by the sight of a fire burning a short distance from the path, unnoticed by anyone else.

'I need to go,' she gasped. 'Tell Garth to keep the others walking on.' She gave him her reins. 'Can you wait for me here?'

The sweet smell of burning oak filled the air as she got nearer. She glanced behind her, and saw the others were already out of sight. Only Anniel could still be seen, waiting with their two horses. There was a log by the fire and she sat down. The heat felt pleasant on her skin, even though the day was not cold. She watched as the flames caressed the wood, waving up into the air. Suddenly they thickened and the wood seemed to rise up, growing and morphing until a woman stood in the flames.

'It was not Cailleach you needed, my dear. It was me.' Brigantia stepped from the flames and Kariss jumped to her feet.

The goddess wasted no time with pleasantries. 'My dear, what you are feeling is the pain of love. It is the hardest pain we ever have to deal with. There is no easy way through it. Even childbirth is easy compared to the loss of a loved one.'

'Daea Brigantia, I am so frightened I am going to lose him. I don't know what to do. I...'

The cloying fear of her dreams returned with a vengeance and Kariss could not continue. Brigantia, the great mother, High One of the Brigante nation, looked at her chosen queen and sighed.

'Oh how easily we forget what it is to be human,' she said, guiding Kariss back to the seat. Gracefully, she lowered herself to the ground in front of her.

'Your fears are understandable my child, but you cannot let them overwhelm you like this. Remember. Each one of you has been chosen for your worth and strength. Each has a significant role to play. This plan has been many years in the making and I can tell you now, Anniel's role in this is far more than just your husband. Whilst I cannot promise anyone's safety, I will tell you that he is a key part in the saviour of the Isle of Albion. Why else would we have had to put you through so much to get to him? Though it may seem like it at times, this is not a game we are playing with you.' She paused for a moment, to let her words sink in.

Kariss was glad she was sitting. If not, she would have collapsed as the overwhelming relief caused her body to tremble uncontrollably. Brigantia spoke again.

'We are bound by our own rules, just as people are bound by theirs. It would be very wrong of us to expect you to do something that you were not capable of doing. This is why we must test you. Albion is in such very great danger. If you are not strong enough for the tasks ahead then we must find ways to help.'

Kariss looked at the goddess, seeing the concern in her eyes and knowing without question that it was genuine. There was something else there, too. Fear. Even the gods were afraid. Kariss was not the only one facing losing everything. The task ahead fell back into perspective. It was not all about her love for Anniel. She had let that one fear grow out of all proportion, until it threatened everything. She glanced over to where he was standing, and saw him bend and pick something up from the ground, studying it. Giving up was not the answer, she needed to move forward with renewed vigour. To fight harder to force the danger from Albion, because nothing would be safe until the Romans were gone.

'I understand the threat to you from the Romans. I read all about it when I was in London,' she told the goddess, 'If they get their way, they will bring in their own gods and you will be all but forgotten.'

The aura of light around Brigantia dimmed a

little as she winced. 'We will not be gone, but we will be lost to the people of Albion for such a very long time.'

Kariss understood that kind of loss. She thought of her parents; she had no idea when she would see them again. They had been lost to her since long before returning to Albion.

Brigantia smiled. 'I have a gift for you. I think it may help.' She seemed to hesitate for a good few moments. Her eyes clouded over, as if she were looking inward instead of out. Then she nodded, leaned forward, and placed one hand on the top of Kariss's head and the other over her heart. 'Close your eyes, child.'

Immediately, Kariss was filled with the feeling of overwhelming love. It was joyous, soothing and oh so precious, even before her mother's face swam into her mind. There were a great many more lines around her eyes than Kariss remembered, but those lines were creased into happiness by the smile on her face.

'Kariss my darling, you must be strong now. We are still here, your father and I, but we cannot get back to you just yet, though it pains us to not be able to help you now. Have faith. Trust the gods and trust your husband. Remember, nothing worth having is ever easy. Know also that we are very, very proud of you.' Her face faded away and at once the feelings shifted to that of a strong pair of arms around her and she heard her father's voice.

'Those you love never truly leave you. They will always be in your heart, just as you have always been in ours. We will see each other again, of that I have no doubt. Stay strong, my dearest Kariss.

Always remember that you have rare blood in your veins.'

Kariss mouthed the words with him. She was laughing and crying as Brigantia removed her hands.

'They are still alive,' she exclaimed. 'But why can they not come back here?'

Brigantia rose to her feet. 'I can tell you no more, child. You must go now, and catch up with your friends. Keep your faith in us, Kariss. We will not leave you to face the chaos of eternity alone.'

With that, she stepped backwards into the fire. The flames soared upwards in a silent roar before dying to a smouldering pile of glowing embers. Kariss watched the embers until they cooled to ashes. She could still feel the sensation of her father's arms around her, and see her mother's face. A whistle broke through her reverie and she turned to see Cloud racing along the path towards Anniel. Naraic would not be far behind.

In the ether, Brigantia smiled. Even dogs could be asked to do their bidding. Reluctantly, Kariss shook off the memories and hurried to take hold of her horse just as Naraic rounded the corner.

'That dog has a mind of his own when he wants,' he grumbled, but he still bent to ruffle Cloud's head when he finally came back, wagging his tail.

'We are waiting at the end of the wood,' Naraic told them, a little embarrassed at disturbing them. He turned away, calling back over his shoulder. 'It is not too far away. Do not be too long, he will only come running back for you again.'

'I found this while you were talking,' Anniel showed Kariss a small bronze amulet. It was the profile of a stag with an impressive set of antlers and a determined look on its face. He had already threaded some leather onto it so he could hang it around his neck. Kariss grinned at him.

'I have been silly,' she admitted. 'I let my fears grow out of control, but I am alright now.' She stood on her tiptoes and pressed her lips against his forehead. 'Just promise me you won't do anything to get hurt.'

Anniel tied the leather thong around his neck and patted the stag. 'I promise.' He caressed her face. 'Was all this because you were worrying about me?'

She nodded, not trusting her voice.

'I love you.' He kissed her firmly. 'We do not know what will happen, but we will always be together. I spent all this time waiting for you in this life, do you really think I will not wait for you in the next one? I have to have faith in that, or my worries about you would consume me.' He looked over to where the hearth had been. The earth was now bare with no sign of any fire. 'I could not see who you were talking to at first, only a shimmer of light in front of you. Part of it floated over to me. Where it disappeared into the ground, the stag was there. I picked it up and remembered your hare at once. When I looked back over to you, I saw the goddess. It was not Cailleach.'

Kariss was surprised. 'That was Brigantia, the High One and goddess of the Brigantes. Did you not see her at our wedding?'

Anniel shook his head. 'I only saw Cailleach

when she gave us our stones. Was anyone else there?'

Kariss laughed, 'There were many gods there. They are watching over us whether we see them or not.'

For a short distance they walked hand-in-hand until the trees closed in tight again and they were forced back into single file. Kariss watched the back of her husband as he led the way. Worrying about someone was all part of loving them. Yet she had never been aware of him worrying about her too; part of her wished he had not kept it so hidden. Maybe it would have helped her to cope better? With a deep breath, she focused again on the fears deep within her. She imagined them now pushed tightly into a box. Instead of letting them control her, she was going to use them as fuel to power her on. In her mind she took a key and locked the box. Then she threw the imaginary key as far away into the woods as she could. Her horse shied his head away, startled by the sudden movement. She rubbed her hand gently up and down his cheek, his dark hair ruffled under her fingers. Overhead, the canopy was thinning. More and more light reached down until they found themselves at the edge of the wood, looking out onto a vast moorland.

The rest of the day followed without incident. They were just thinking about looking for a place to camp when Carrick suddenly held up his hand. He dismounted and threw his reigns to Naraic, eyes searching the ground. 'Can you see it?' he asked him. Naraic nodded his head. Hoofprints, lots of them, had joined their path and were heading in the same direction as they were. Ahead of them the ground rose slightly, blocking their view. Carrick crept forward, keeping low to the ground. He was soon back. The riders were not in sight, they had time to plan what they were going to do.

'Could it be more warriors?' Kariss asked Anniel

'Possibly, but I would rather we stick to our plan and stay out of sight until we get to Stanwick. Enda is you now as far as anyone knows; we must keep it that way. We want Martaani's eyes on Tholarg's and Uurad's war band until we decide to make our move. Remember Cailleach's warning.'

Kariss looked to Carrick. 'What is your advice?'

He considered for a moment. 'Our options are few,' he admitted. He pointed to the road that joined theirs. 'The riders have come from the lower eastern isles; they must be more of Uurad's people. We could just ride past them and trust they will keep quiet.' His face told her exactly what he thought of that idea.

Kariss shook her head. 'Martaani will probably have men watching them.'

'We could double back There is another way we could try, but it would add a day to our journey and the route is tricky.' Carrick pulled a face, 'I would rather not do that, either.' He nodded to the road ahead. 'I think our best plan would be for me to go ahead and track where they are. I will take Naraic with me and send him back for you when I know the way is clear. We should be able to follow at a safe distance until we can find a way around them.

They travelled in fits and starts, Carrick tracking a mile or so ahead before sending Naraic back for them. Five times, Naraic came back before Carrick finally relaxed.

'They have set up camp just to the side of that hill.' He pointed to a heavily wooded hill just south of their position. 'They are only a small group so have only set a basic guard, but I have found a way around. Providing we are quiet, we should be fine.' He glanced to the sky, 'But it is going to be a late night for us.'

The evening was already advancing as they followed Carrick. For a short while the sky darkened and they had to slow their horses but then the moon came out from behind the clouds and lit the land in bright night light. Kariss looked up at it; as ever, the sight of the full white orb made her smile. She took a few deep breaths as she watched. The full moon meant promise, it was the strongest it could ever be, and so held the most potent power. A cloud scurried across the sky, briefly hazing the glow. Kariss waited for it to reappear; there was something magnetic about the moon when it shone so large and bright. It was almost as if she could feel it pulling at her, urging her to be strong, filling her head with positivity. Her horse stumbled on a stone and she reluctantly lowered her gaze, but she kept glancing upwards whenever she got the chance.

'She will not disappear if you stop looking,' Anniel said, keeping his voice low. They were still very close to the camp.

Kariss prodded a finger into his side and grinned as he squirmed away.

They made camp a good way past the hill and

well off the track. Anniel took the first watch. Kariss lay looking up at the moon. It was as if the Great Goddess was shining down on her, talking to her. She noted the darker patches, which looked like seas, and wondered at the parts that shone so brightly they reminded her of the high-powered torches she had known in London. She drank in all the love the moon had to give her, until her eyelids closed of their own accord and she drifted into sleep. For the first time in days her dreams were peaceful. By the time she was woken for her own watch, the moon had hidden her face behind the clouds.

They broke camp early, still tired from the long day before. The horses were tired too, and they stamped as they were loaded up. Naraic slapped the neck of his horse as it turned to bite him when he pulled the girth strap tight. It turned its head back, ears flat, and bit at the horse next to him instead. The horse squealed and shied away, almost stamping on the guard's foot in the process. Everyone froze. Carrick glared at Naraic, who hung his head sheepishly. No sound could be heard in the distance, but they mounted up quickly and rushed down the road before the larger group of warriors could appear.

They saw no sign of anyone else that day. Rather than risk it, Carrick had led them off the main route and down yet another goat path. They made camp early that night, too exhausted to continue any further. At least the going was getting much easier now the mountains were behind them. There was only one range of high hills left to cross and then they would be almost at Stanwick.

14

For the source of such a great river, it was a pitiful sight. Just a trickle of water oozing out of the moss, hidden by clumps of tough reeds in the middle of the heathland. Yet Carrick had been quite insistent that the Tweed was a most impressive waterway, leading all the way to the Votadini coast. Naraic shrugged, maybe it was the wrong place. Carrick had been quite vague when he described its whereabouts.

A peewit called defiantly nearby. It was the time of year when they moved their freshly-hatched young from the nest to nearby feeding grounds. He moved away, so as not to disturb the little one.

The two guards and Naraic were hunting boar. It was just after midday but they were already camped. Forced to stall their journey for the day. The previous evening had been a bad one. Whilst Naraic had been away hunting, Cloud, usually so obedient, suddenly bolted from the camp, ignoring all calls to return. Carrick raced after him. He saw the dog dart into a thicket and heard him yelp. When he got close enough, he saw that he had found a young lynx cub, left alone while its mother was out hunting. The cub, not being as defenceless as Cloud had thought, had sunk its needle-sharp teeth into his nose. Carrick groaned. Lynx could be dangerous if provoked.

He grabbed at Cloud to pull him away, just as the mother lynx appeared. She launched herself at them. Carrick had just enough time to turn his body away before he was knocked to the ground.

Lynx liked to kill with a quick bite to the neck. On smaller animals this would usually suffice but on larger prey they would hold on, restricting breathing until the victim suffocated. Luckily, turning his body had deflected the attack and her mouth closed around his right arm. With Cloud worrying her back end, he frantically scrambled for a nearby branch. He was not as good with his left hand but his swing was enough to knock the lynx off him. He dropped the branch and dived into the bushes away from the cub, Cloud hard on his heels. The mother lynx followed a single pace then stopped. Her cub was safe now, and men were not her prey. She watched as man and dog crept away.

Carrick and Cloud made a sorry pair when they arrived back at camp. Not sure whether pride or flesh was the more injured, Kariss and Naraic set about tending their wounds. Cloud was not too badly hurt. The cub's teeth had just missed his eye, but one of his ears was torn and he growled when Naraic tried to clean it. Garth pinned the dog down, while Naraic inspected the wound and washed the blood away. The tear had ripped his ear almost in half from the centre down. Cloud kept up his noise the whole time but made no attempt to bite. He leapt away as soon as Garth released him, going to sulk at the other side of the fire.

Carrick had not fared so well. It was a warm evening and he was lightly dressed, his skin no match for a lynx's teeth and unsheathed claws. The mother lynx had sunk her teeth deep into his right forearm. From her back feet, he had deep cuts to his inner left and outer right thighs whilst one of her front feet had raked down his back and the other had caught his left hand, cutting into the pad beneath his thumb and across his palm.

One of the guards rushed over with a handful of yarrow leaves, which Kariss began to stuff into the deepest cuts. She was about to do the same for the cut on his hand but Carrick stopped her.

'Yer need plantain for that one just now,' he said. 'Even with all this blood, there is too much dirt in it to use the yarrow. Plantain will draw out the dirt as it heals.'

Anniel found some growing next to the path they had travelled down, where the ground was hard and compact.

'Bite the leaves a bit first to release the juices,' Carrick said, gritting his teeth against the pain.

Kariss followed Carrick's instructions, she still had a lot to learn about plant medicine. He was a good patient, well used to taking care of himself. Naraic showed her how to pound the lacy yarrow and stringy plantain leaves into a paste, which they could apply later. She found it hard to accept that such knowledge would be all but forgotten in the future. In London, plantain had been considered an unsightly, unwanted weed. Yet here it had so many uses. She knew people put the leaves in their shoes when they were walking long distances. She had seen it used to ease the pain of a bee-sting and even toothache. Modern life had been so wasteful. She found herself becoming more and more ashamed at how her life had been. The only thing she missed was the written word. In London she had read so much. Here there was no time but often, like now, she found herself wanting to write something down. Anniel had seen her attempting to scratch words onto stones. He had laughed at the shapes he saw, not believing that they could actually mean words.

The next morning they left the area at first light, but the cuts on Carrick's inner thigh had rubbed on his saddle and soon began to bleed again. By midday, Kariss had insisted they stop. Carrick was furious with himself for letting them down. He would have argued to keep going but it made no sense. He knew that if they did, his leg would be unable to heal and it would end up infected. So he sat in a fit of self-recrimination by the fire, a sorrowful Cloud by his side, and watched as the two guards took Naraic to follow the fresh boar tracks they had found.

Naraic had brought his yew bow and half-a-dozen arrows. He really needed to make more. He had lost so many over the last few days. They could hear sounds ahead of them again now that they had moved from the heathland into the nearby deciduous wood. Naraic was pleased to see such a mixture of trees again after the tall red pines that had been so abundant further north. Here, hazel grew alongside holly and birch and even a few wych elm. He was so busy listening to the sounds of the boar that he failed to notice the lack of birds. The guards had not seemed to notice anything, either. All of a sudden he heard a yell to his left. He turned to see one of the guards grappling with someone. Behind them, three more men appeared. Naraic just had time to see the guard fall to the floor, clutching the blade in his chest, before he ran. He didn't get far. His ankles were kicked out from under him and as he landed face-down in the dirt, his shoulders were pinned and a knee rammed into his back. Naraic struggled with all his might, bucking against the man at his back. He managed to dislodge him and started to scrabble away, but with a blow to his head, his world went black.

15

When he came to, Naraic found himself slung over a horse's back. They were travelling quickly. From this angle he could not make out which way they were heading. Through the pulsating pain in his head he could hear men talking in a strange tongue. Panic fused with pain as he realised that the Romans had caught up with them. How much longer before Kariss was caught or did they already have her, too? He needed to escape, to get back and warn her. He wriggled, feeling for any bindings, and realised there was rope around his wrists and ankles. His heart sank; even if he could get himself off the horse, he would not get far.

More voices sounded up ahead and he felt the horse slowing. His stomach and ribs relaxed; he had not even realised how tense he had been holding himself against the discomfort of the ride. Maybe he would be able to get away now they had stopped? Twisting his head left and right, he made out another four horses and the sound of running water. The body of the dead guard landed close by. Naraic barely had time to register it before he too was hauled from his horse. The man who had captured him dragged him to the edge of the stream, pushed him down against a boulder, and walked away. The ground here was stony and the shallow water sang as it raced over its pebble bed but there were clear signs it frequently ran much deeper.

He found he was in the base of a sunken bowl, the sides of which were sheer and extremely high.

A few goats braved the slopes to nibble on the bushes clinging to the sides. It looked to be the termination of a narrow valley, through which they must have just ridden. Naraic groaned; even if he could get out of his bindings, his chances of escaping down the valley were slim. He wondered what had happened to the second guard. With any luck he had got away and warned the camp. These hopes were dashed a moment later when the missing guard was brought over and ordered to sit alongside him. His wrists and ankles were bound but otherwise he looked unharmed. The dead guard was flung nearby before the Romans returned to their comrades.

'Are you alright?' the guard asked him when they had gone.

Naraic's eyes refused to leave the lifeless, staring face of the dead guard. His head thumped with pain every time he moved it, and all he could think about was Kariss sitting at the camp, unaware of the grave danger she was in. He was far from alright.

'Do you think there is any chase of escaping?' he asked the guard, who let out a cold, derisory laugh.

'The only way out of here is past them.' He curled his lip up as he looked in the direction of the Romans. 'You were unconscious for most of the journey so you didn't see the number of men they have scattered down the valley. It is the only way in - unless you can turn yourself into a bird?' The guard shrugged at Naraic's lack of response, 'Thought not. This place is known as The Cauldron; even the goats have been known to fall down the sides and break themselves on the bottom.'

Surprised, Naraic pulled his eyes away from the dead man and turned to look at him.

'That bastard told me when he was bringing me over.' The guard nodded towards one of their captors. He was standing watching them with a sly smile on his face. There was nothing to show the men were legionaries. They wore no uniform, only dark clothing. It was only when they spoke they gave themselves away. Not that any of the men were wasting time talking to them. They appeared content to sit and wait. An ominous feeling filled Naraic as he wondered what they were waiting for.

'Do you think they have got Kariss?'

The guard fidgeted with his bindings. 'They didn't have to put them so tight,' he complained.

Naraic ignored the comment. 'Kariss?' he insisted. 'Do you think they have got her?'

The guard stilled his hands. 'If they had her, they would have no need to keep us alive, would they? With Kariss dead, Martaani has a straight road to the throne.'

A wisp of hope flickered inside Naraic.

'Do you know anything about her plans?' the guard asked. 'Will she stick to them once she realises we have gone? Or does she have an alternative?'

Naraic frowned at him but did not answer. If Kariss had not confided in him, he certainly wasn't going to.

The guard shrugged. 'I thought they might have told you,' he said. 'It might stop you worrying about her if you know what she will do.'

They were silent for a while. The guard

continued to fiddle with his bindings and Naraic found himself constantly dragging his eyes away from the dead guard, who was now attracting a quantity of flies. He looked instead at one of the goats bleating amongst the bushes. The sides of the valley end were sheer enough as to be almost cliffs but the goats seemed to be at home there. One had climbed almost to the top. If it hadn't been for the light patches in its long, scruffy hair, Naraic wouldn't have even noticed it. He watched it until it disappeared over the top, the shadows following it up the valley walls. Naraic wondered what time it was. They had been there for a long time now, yet the Romans had still made no attempt to interact with them.

'So why are they just leaving us here?'

'They are waiting for Martaani to get here. If ever there was a person who knew how to extract information...' The guard shivered. 'I just think about what happened at Dun da Lamh.'

There was no need to the notice the sun receding to feel a chill. Naraic threw a nervous look at the men, they were sitting talking with no sign of anyone approaching. The guard stretched out his leg and nudged the body of the dead man with his toe. A buzz of angry flies rose into the air. 'Looks like he was the lucky one.'

The flies landed again, crawling all over the man's face. Naraic's stomach churned. Would he be able to keep quiet when Martaani started on him? A vision of Inan lying with his innards pouring out onto the flagstones flooded his mind. He remembered the state of Anyetta's back and it was as if the wounds were suddenly there on his own body. He squirmed his back against the boulder to get rid of the feeling.

The guard didn't seem to notice. He was too busy wallowing in his own fear. His voice trembled slightly. 'Part of me even wishes I did know what Kariss's plans were.'

'Why?'

'Because, she will get it out of us one way or another. She isn't going to stop just because we say we know nothing; she will just keep going until there is nothing left of us to torture. Remember those children with the missing hands? If I knew something and told her straight away, maybe she would kill me quickly.'

Naraic bit back a sharp retort. He noticed the sheen of sweat on the man's face and the fidgeting of his body. The guard looked terrified. 'I thought we would be surrounded by a large troupe of men,' he admitted when Naraic asked him why he had volunteered to come.

For Naraic, the focus of his fear was his friends and Kariss. Every time he thought about what the Romans would do to him, he forced himself to concentrate on keeping Kariss free. It helped him conquer his nerves. He thought back to the day he was hunting on the hillside beneath Dun da Lamh fort with Tharain and Inan, when the Roman had come galloping through the trees with Kariss.

He had done something so immense that day, something that he had never thought possible. He had killed the Roman, the first man he had ever purposely killed. Today, when Martaani came for him, he would be strong again.

The men that had captured them stood up. The guard swore, he grabbed at Naraic's hands. 'Quick, tell me something just to keep her off my back.'

Coward, Naraic though in disgust, but he was worried. Something was not right. The guard knew enough to make Kariss's capture almost a certainty. It had been nagging at him ever since they had started talking. So why was he trying to get something more from him? He had no more time to think. The men had parted and a woman walked towards them. She walked with such purpose that he knew it could only be Martaani. He could feel himself start to shake.

She was dressed in dark clothing, just like her men. The only feminine addition was the strophium she wore tied tightly over her tunic, just under her bust. Other than that, only the rich Tyrian purple embroidery on a band around her dark tunic set her apart. She strode up to the feet of the guard and glared into his face. The air seemed to still. Even the birds were quiet. It was as if everything in the valley was poised, waiting.

'Well?' She flicked her hand towards him and one of her men dragged him to his feet. The guard was taller than Martaani; he kept his head down and looked at her feet, laced up in leather sandals. He mumbled incoherently and received a sharp slap across his face with the short strip of leather she was carrying.

'Well?' Like an insistent chick demanding food, her voice was determined and just short of shrill.

The guard shook his head. 'Nothing,' he said. 'He told me nothing.' Between his feet pooled wet.

Martaani saw and smiled. 'Your daughter wet

herself when I saw her, too. Maybe she already knew what a failure her father was?' She tilted her head slightly. She was enjoying herself. 'She will be the price of your failure.'

'No!' the guard cried. His knees buckled and he fell at her feet. 'Please, not her.'

'Would you rather your son? Or your wife?'

At her signal, two men dragged the guard away and Martaani turned her attention to Naraic. She exaggerated a sigh.

'I do so hate whining,' she told him. She cast her eyes around her. 'This is a wonderful place, do you not think? It is so well hidden, especially in the mornings when the mists rise up, making everything inside here invisible. Your friends have no chance of rescuing you. Especially now your tracker has so conveniently indisposed himself.'

She laughed at his shocked face. 'Oh, I know all about your journey,' she told him. 'I know exactly where your precious Kariss is, and I have for quite a while, thanks to your friend there.' She looked on as the guard was loaded onto a cart.

Naraic's mind was reeling but he held his tongue and waited. Martaani was equal in height to him and he refused to look down as the guard had done. She was a few years older than Kariss, with sun-kissed skin and rich dark hair, which she wore wrapped high on her head. A length or two of ringlets softened the sharp look, but nothing softened the coldness of her coal-dark eyes.

'I am sure you must be wondering why I have brought you here?'

Naraic waited.

Martaani smiled, 'I need you to tell me what her

126

plans are.'

'Her plans?' Naraic could feign ignorance as easily as she could feign friendliness.

'Obviously she has plans or she would have travelled with the larger group instead of trying to fool me with a cheap imitation.' Her voice had sharpened again, she paused to get herself under control. 'You are only a boy,' she stroked her hand down his cheek. 'I do not hurt boys. At least, not good boys who tell me what I want to know.'

Her hand smelled of leather and horses.

Naraic kept eye contact with her. 'I do not know her plans.' He willed his heart to calm down. It was thumping so hard in his chest that he was sure she must hear it. He could get through this, he told himself. Nothing has hurt too badly, yet.

'Pah!' Martaani's mood changed again, she twisted a large gold ring around on her finger as she glowered at Naraic. 'I do, however, have some very amusing ways to hurt insolent boys.'

Her voice was caustic and he had no doubt that he would not find them quite so entertaining. For a second he found he could not breathe, but then he pulled his shoulders back and lifted his chin defiantly. 'I do not know her plans.'

Martaani stroked her hand down his face again, pressing hard. Now the ring dug sharply into his skin. He felt it cut a line slowly down from his temple to his jawbone. Martaani watched him closely, her eyes lighting up as she saw blood appear. Naraic forced himself not to flinch.

In a voice like honey she said, 'Do you think you are tough little boy? Do you think you can withstand me?'

Despite his fear, Naraic found himself getting angry. He was stronger than she could ever know. The more she goaded him, the firmer his resolution to keep his silence grew.

'You do not know the kind of pain I can inflict.' She brought her hand down his face again. This time the pain was much worse as she worked her ring into the cut she had already made. Tears pricked at the back of Naraic's eyes but still he held his head firm.

Three times she dragged her ring down his face. When she could see it was not going to loosen his tongue she twisted the ring back into place and called for one of her men to produce his knife. Naraic gulped. *Kariss be safe, Kariss be safe,* he said silently to himself. Using the words as a mantra he tried not to focus on the pain as Martaani worked the knife's point into the soft part at the front of his shoulder. He cried out but still he kept chanting the words, over and over. The pain stopped and he opened his eyes to see her raise her eyebrows. 'Have you remembered anything?'

He shook his head, *Kariss be safe, Kariss be safe.*

'Maybe you need to start losing things before you will talk?'

Two men pushed him back to the boulder and pressed his right hand onto the stone.

Kariss be safe, Kariss be safe.

Fear was rising up his throat, he felt his insides turn to liquid, but unlike the guard, he maintained control of his bladder; even when pain tore through his hand as Martaani cut his little finger off. The fear exploded from him as he screamed. Blood spurted from the wound before he managed to twist his hands around and curl his fingers over the raw stub, pressing down hard. It oozed through his fingers and pooled into his palm, dripping onto the stones at his feet. He barely registered the sound of a horse galloping towards them or Martaani leaving to speak to the rider.

16

'Why are you being so stubborn, Taratus?' Faela threw up her hands in despair. 'Water will run uphill before you will ever listen to sense these days.'

Her older brother ignored the jibe. 'It is not I who needs to see sense,' he told her. 'We all know what happens when you trust our dear cousin. We watch her walk away from our home without so much as a backward glance, leaving us to face the consequences.' His dark eyes glinted in anger.

'Argghhhh!' Faela cried in exasperation. 'She was a child. It was not her choosing. We have been over and over this.'

'And yet you still cannot tell me why she has failed to contact us ever since that day.' He slammed his hand down on the table as his voice rose. 'Why she has failed to offer any message of remorse for our mother?' His other hand slammed down and his voice rose to a shout. 'And why it would appear that we, her own blood, were not the first people she sought out when she returned.'

Faela closed her eyes for a second and fought to keep her own voice soft and calm. She would not be drawn into yet another screaming match with him. 'We do not even know she is returned yet. The war bands could be gathering in preparation.'

'You did not used to be so stupid, sister,' Taratus spat.

'Yet you have always been stubborn about Kariss. Why is that, brother?' She glared at him, her eyes hoping to pierce through his outer layers to reveal the truth he held deep within.

He glared back, angry eyes shuttered against her probing ones. When she refused to turn away, he tried a different tack. 'Is this why Kydas left you? Did you drive him away with your infuriating questions?'

He watched as pain clouded her features and she turned and stormed from the hut. It had been a low blow, one he was not proud of. He slammed his hands down on the table again, sending a bowl clattering to the floor.

'Have you two been arguing again?' his wife, Shael, asked as she entered. She bent to pick up the pieces of the broken bowl, rubbing her back as she straightened. Her swollen stomach strained against her tunic.

He kept his back towards her. 'Do not start with me, woman. I am in no mood.'

Shael looked at her husband and shook her head. He had always had a cold edge to him, but for the last few months he had been much worse. Behind her, their two children pushed past the boarskin door-covering and ran into the room. Quickly she ushered them out again, grabbing the basket by the door on her way.

Faela could feel tears pricking her eyes. She dashed them away before they could fall. An image of Kydas filled her mind and for the thousandth time she wondered where her husband was, and why he had left. For the first two moons she had searched the woodland around Wendell, desperately hoping to find him injured and unable to make his way home, but all her searching was in vain. She went further and further afield, asking everyone she saw, but it was as if he had disappeared into thin air. Eventually, she had stopped searching, but he was never far from her thoughts. It had been over eight moons now and she had learnt to live alone again, but she had not yet learnt to forget.

The guards stepped aside as she left the fort through the massive in-turned entranceway.

'Would you have one of us accompany you?' one of them asked her as she passed.

She shook her head. 'I will not go far,' she promised. 'You will be able to see me.'

She found a spot on the sloped ground, hidden from the path but still visible from the gateway above, and sat down, gazing out over the surrounding landscape. Wendell was set on a low double hill, steep on the north and west where the entranceway was but almost level on the east where the fort was protected by a huge bank and water-filled ditch. Blackthorn with its long vicious barbs and Hawthorn with its shorter, more spiky, thorns gave further protection of both the spiritual and physical kind. In between these, bramble had been encouraged to grow, creating an impenetrable barrier for anyone seeking illicit entry. The south boasted the second hill where the ground rose sharply from the moat with no need for a separate bank. That was one of her favourite places to go when she wanted to get away from everyone. She would sit in the shade of an old weeping willow tree and watch the dragonflies buzzing around over the water.

Now was not the time to wander alone, though. Martaani's men had been in the area of late and no one trusted the foreign-tongued strangers. There was even talk that some Albion men were at her bidding; traitors from Votadini lands. No one could be trusted. Everyone was tense. The midsummer gathering was almost upon them. What would happen then was anyone's guess.

The air was filled with the sounds of insects, whirring and buzzing as they hovered from flower to flower. She plucked at a grass stalk and slid her fingers up the stem, stripping the seeds away. The stem became a blur as her eyes filled. This time she let the tears fall. Taratus had hit a nerve when he had accused her of driving Kydas away. Too many times she had wondered the same thing. Over and over, she had replayed the days and weeks running up to his sudden departure; trying to find something, anything, that could point to why he had left. No matter how many times she went over it all, she could not find the answer. The hollow space inside still gnawed at her whenever her guard was down, grinding at her resolve to move on and be happy. She rubbed at her belly, feeling the awful flatness beneath her hand. By now she should have been holding their babe, cradling it in her arms as it suckled from her breast. The longing for her lost child was almost as bad as the longing for her husband, even though she had only carried it for a few moons.

No one but Kydas had known it even existed, they had wanted to keep it a secret until the bump started to show. But as the first moon passed with no sign of Kydas, her grief had proved too much for the little one to cope with. Whilst she was breaking her heart under the willow tree after yet another failed search, her stomach had started to cramp, and the bright red life she had been carrying flowed out onto the cold, frozen earth.

Faela took a deep breath. Close by, she could hear the snapping noises of the broom seeds popping in the heat. She closed her eyes and turned her face to the sky, letting the warmth of the sun soothe her. She opened her eyes again and watched as a pair of ravens tumbled together overhead. Their raucous calls shattered the peace as they played.

'Two goddess symbols together in the sky, what a blissful symbol of balance.'

Faela jumped at the sound of the strange voice, her fingers instinctively grabbing for her small knife. Just below her stood a wild-looking druid in robes of bright madder-red, with deep purple borders where the edges had been over-dyed with woad. She eyed him warily before risking a quick glance up to the fort.

The druid held his hands up to show he was unarmed.

'I fear I walked a path less obvious than your guards are trained to see,' he told her, 'and I admit I have ensured they are distracted just now so we could talk, though I mean you no harm.' He slowly reached for a strap on his shoulder and sat the heavy, wet bag on the ground between them. 'I have been walking for many hours and the load gets no lighter. Forgive me for the intrusion.' He indicated the ground beside her. 'May I sit?'

Faela tightened her grip on the antler handle. It was only a small blade but it would give her precious moments until help could come. Did she dare shout? She looked at the bag. Whatever was inside was moving. The hairs on her arms rose up like tiny sentinels warning her of danger.

'What is in there?'

The druid dropped his hands and bent to tip the contents of the bag clattering out onto the grass. Faela jumped back in fright but when she realised what the jumble of shiny blue shells, huge claws and long antenna were she looked at the druid in disbelief.

He looked back and shrugged his shoulders. 'What can I say? I am partial to lobster and I miss it when I leave home.'

Faela laughed, her thumping heart calming quickly. Tales of Martaani's actions were getting everyone jumping at shadows. She pushed her knife back up into the leather case that hung on a long thong around her neck. Since when did druids do the work of the Romans? She quickly rubbed her tears away and sniffed, self-consciously, but the druid pretended not to notice. Once the shellfish were back inside their wet bag he dropped down onto the grass beside her and looked back up at the birds.

The ravens grasped talons as they rolled downwards through the air again, three, four turns before letting go, flapping their wings, and rising again.

'The balance is not a peaceful one,' he said as he watched them. 'See how they battle for supremacy? First one bird is on top and then the next, yet this

135

is no mated pair.'

Faela frowned. 'How can balance not be peaceful?'

The druid picked up a stick and set it over a round stone.

'See how the stick balances when there is the same length at either side of the stone?' He picked up a much longer stick that was twisted and uneven, and put on the stone. 'This stick will still balance but the ends are so different to one another, it takes time and patience to achieve it.' He pointed to the ravens. 'I believe we are looking at Kariss and Martaani here. Each balances out the other for now, but for some reason this dance is being played over your head.' He pointed the smaller stick at her. 'And I wonder what that signifies?' His eyes narrowed. 'Is there something important you should tell me?'

The temperature around her seemed to have dropped all of a sudden. Faela jumped to her feet and brushed herself off. She had no idea who this strange druid was but she certainly was not going to sit here and listen to his absurd accusations. He watched her as if studying her every move then just as she began to stalk away he jumped up, threw his arms wide, and spun in a circle.

'See all the land around you?' he whispered just loud enough for her to hear.

She stopped in her tracks and turned to glare at him.

'Martaani does not see it the same way.' He continued turning. 'She only sees land she can conquer, people she can master, and an area she can desecrate with her abominable and ruthless gods.' He abruptly stopped still and pointed his stick at her once again. 'But for some reason the gods have singled you out for me to find. You have an importance here and I mean to find out what it is.'

Faela stamped her foot in exasperation. This man was infuriating. She was not important, she could not save the land; she could not even save her own husband and child. Yet for all that she did not move, she remained rooted to the spot as the druid held his pose with his stick accusing her of keeping secrets. Eventually, she found her voice.

'Kariss was my cousin,' she told him, 'and my best friend.'

The druid let his arm drop and Faela felt herself able to move once more. 'But then she left and I have never seen nor heard from her since,' she finished before racing off up the hill to the safety of the fort entrance.

17

'You have been lucky.' Martaani's voice cut through to him, she did not sound pleased. 'Something urgent calls me away, but I will be back in the morning. If I were you, I would think long and hard tonight. Either you die slowly as I remove a bit more of you at a time, or you tell me what I want to know and I end your suffering quickly. Either way, you cannot help Kariss, but you can help yourself.'

She marched away, taking her men with her, snapping out orders. Not one of them looked back to him. It was as if he had been instantly forgotten. He waited until she had mounted her horse then he fell to his knees and vomited. His finger lay amongst the stones and he stared at it in horror. Shaking, he hobbled over to the stream. With teeth gritted, he thrust his hands under the water and held them there for as long as he could. The cold made the wound pulse with pain and streaked the water with red. He pressed back down on the cut and waited for the blood to start clotting.

Laughter made him look up. Martaani had left some men to guard him, they were looking his way. They made no attempt to come over and help. One of them drew his finger slowly across his throat, causing even more laughter. Panic welled again. Until today Naraic had had no idea what fear really was. He did not know if he could cope with any more. Still, he glared back at the men, defiant. They would not see his fear. They taunted him some more, but soon grew bored and turned away. Yet

Naraic's dread continued to build.

Breathe, a voice sounded in his head. *There is a way out for you.* The voice sounded almost like Dei, but with a deeper resonance. Instantly, Naraic felt calmed and wondered if this was what Kariss had meant when she said the gods talked to her. The men had turned their backs now and were busy preparing a fire. There was another boulder nearby. Naraic shuffled over to it. Something dug into his leg as he sat, and he remembered the stone he had hidden there. The men had obviously searched him when he was unconscious. His pouch, knives and amulet were all gone, but they had not thought to check his tunic hem. He worked the stone lose and stared at it, his distorted face reflected back at him from the shiny stone. Cobalam's words came back to him, *When you run out of options, this will be your last hope.* Well, he was certainly out of options now, but how could this be his last hope?

He held on to the stone for a long time but no ideas were forthcoming. Frustrated, he threw it forcibly onto the ground, where it broke. Naraic cried silently in disgust but then, as he moved his head, the light glinted off one of the larger shards. The stone was now in three pieces, each as sharp and lethal as a tiny blade. Naraic quickly checked the men, but they were not interested in him. He picked up one of the shards and tried to reach the rope around his wrists. The movement made his hand throb and the wound where his finger had been began to bleed again. No matter how he tried, he could not get any of the blades to reach. He tried a blade on the rope around his ankles. The fibres cut easily, though it would take a while to

139

work his way right through. He looked at the sky. Dusk was still a way off. He decided to wait until it was dark, maybe then he would be able to find a way out of the valley.

A mewing cry called from the sky. A buzzard flew out over the valley wall. It was the first sign of life he had seen since the goat had disappeared over the edge. Could there be a way up the steep slope? He leaned back against the boulder and concentrated on the lower part of the slope. He could smell food cooking and it turned his stomach. He realised he had not eaten since early morning. It was surprising how unimportant food seemed when you were scared.

By the water, a wagtail hopped from stone to stone, looking for food. He watched as it flitted a short distance away before resuming its search. The bird slowly moved further and further away until it was amongst the bushes at the edge of the valley floor, then it disappeared out of sight. Naraic smiled. He closed his eyes and let out a long, slow breath. *Thank you.*

Martaani rode as if her very life depended on it, out of the valley and into more open land. Her horse was soon lathered in sweat. Foam formed where the reins rubbed on its neck; she flicked her head out of the way as a large fleck flew past. There was no time to take in the beautiful scenery, the stunning hills surrounding them, which gradually formed yet another valley. No time to worry about the druid lair they passed on their way. Three men rode with her, each as eager as the other for this wild ride to be over. The men, at least, did not have long to wait. As they reached a small loch, they slowed. Four men were waiting with fresh horses. One of them was already off his horse and waiting. Martaani jumped from her mount and he hoisted her straight onto his. Without a word spoken they set off, the fresh horses and riders giving the journey a boost of speed.

The small loch ran into a longer one and they followed the curve of the bank. Moorhens wading in the grasses at the edge raced for cover. Over the water, an osprey hovered. Sighting a large fish, it made ready to dive, but the sound of the galloping horses broke the moment. Wheeling away, he flew off in search of safer feeding grounds. Martaani noticed none of this, her blood pumped through her veins as she pushed her horse ever faster.

'You must slow down,' The man in the lead called to her. 'You will break the horse's wind, either that or its legs.'

'There are always other horses,' Martaani snapped back.

One of the other men shrugged, 'Better to push hard now than in the dark.'

The lead man glared at him but said no more. He valued his life more than that of the horses, however concerned about them he was. There was another change of horses to come when once again Martaani would be the only one to keep riding. He kept his head down and hoped for the best.

Martaani showed no signs of exhaustion as they pulled up at the last changeover, though worry had furrowed deep lines on her brow. Her hair had long since lost its fastenings and she dragged her fingers through the tangled mess, shaking it down her

141

back.

She was relieved to see one of the new men was Proculus. He held out his hands for her foot and hoisted her into the saddle.

'Do you know what his mood is?' she asked him as they set off.

'He is… agitated.'

Martaani threw a look to the skies, 'Will we make it before we lose the light?'

Proculus shook his head. 'I doubt it, but if we press on hard we should not be too far off when it goes.'

Her fresh horse had already sensed her agitation and was eager to run, she only had to loosen her reigns and he was off. A further nudge with her heels and they were galloping along. The animal was as black as night and they made a fine pair, each with their hair flowing behind them. There was no further chance for talking. Proculus rode beside her, snatching a look at her every so often. He noted the higher than usual carriage of her shoulders and the stiffness in her neck. Her knuckles were white where they gripped the reins far too tightly. Her hand was well up the neck of her horse, giving it free rein to gallop as fast as possible. His horse suddenly lurched sideways as a partridge flew up from the undergrowth. His heart clamoured in his mouth as he twisted himself back into the saddle. Taking no more risks, he concentrated his attention on the ride once more.

The last of the weak evening sunlight was just fading as they trotted into Trimontium. Proculus dismounted at a run, leaving his horse to be caught by a stable hand. He was there to steady Martaani as her legs nearly buckled beneath her from the marathon ride. She gripped onto him for a moment before pulling herself erect. Falling back to his standard three paces behind, he followed her to where the Pontiff stood waiting. His face was a blank mask, they could read nothing from his eyes to forewarn them of what waited inside.

'He is busy with his meal,' the priest stated. 'You have time to make yourself presentable.' With that he disappeared into the Centurion's building, leaving Martaani to rush and change.

Inida did not rise as Martaani entered the room. Despite how she was feeling, there was not flicker of anxiety showing to mar her features, and no sign of the mad ride she had just endured. She walked tall and confident, her head held high. He pushed his plate away from him and let out a loud belch. Someone rushed forward to refill his goblet but he waved them away impatiently.

'My pardon for not being here to greet you,' Martaani said. 'I was detained elsewhere.'

'Courtesy dictates that it is polite to pay a visit to the king of the nation whose land you are staying in. Especially when you are relying so heavily on his help.'

Obviously courtesy did not extend to keeping the contempt out of his voice. Inida rapped his heavily jewelled fingers on the table top as he looked for any small sign of her discomfort.

Martaani frowned. 'Did I hear wrong, then?' she glanced pointedly at the Centurion. 'I had been led to believe that your wife was sick.'

Inida's fingers stilled and his eyes narrowed slightly. 'She is laid low with a fever.'

'In my culture it is deemed rude to visit a family when there is sickness in the house,' Martaani told him. 'I did not want to cause offence by interrupting. Naturally, I would have travelled to Dumpender Law to pay my respects again, had I known that it was not discourteous.'

The tension in the air evaporated as Inida indicated the chair next to him. He was a short man and did not enjoy looking up to people, especially those he considered beneath him. In his own fort at Dumpender Law he had his chairs set on a dais to avoid such problems. Martaani let out a quiet breath and called over one of the servants. She waited until he had filled her goblet with rich red wine and she helped herself to a handful of nuts from a bowl on the table. She used the time to further compose herself; Inida was not a man to cross.

She had first met him in Rome when he had been visiting Julia Domna, whose cousin Claudia he had married. Martaani had taken an instant dislike to Inida and his wife. Their air of superiority was overwhelming. Even the fact that Martaani was the joint heir of the Brigante nation, the largest nation in Albion, did not stop them from looking down on her. Inida had made sure to tell her that, of course, he had attained his throne down a direct line. It was implied, never directly stated, that to attain one any other way was somehow tainted.

Martaani watched him as she sipped her wine. He looked flushed, she hoped he wasn't starting with his own sickness. She made a pretence of stretching out her legs so she could move her chair slightly further away. Sickness was akin to weakness, Martaani abhorred it. It really was unthinkable that he had risked the chance of spreading it by coming here. In any other circumstance she would have said as much but in the stand-off between Kariss and herself, Martaani was relying on the Votadini. She would also need them after she won her throne.

All her life she had had it drilled into her how her ancestor, Cartimandua, had lost Brigantia because of the native nations joining together to rise up against her and the Roman forces. She planned to use the Votadini as her buffer to the contentious northern tribes. The Selgovae, who bordered them, were not fighting people, but their compliance could not be assured. To the west, the nations were unruly and rebellious, but it was not thought that they would interfere unless their borders came under threat. Some of the nations to the south should at least prove more amenable to a new Roman presence. They were more civilised, they had learnt a great deal from their earlier inclusion into the Empire and Inida believed they would be easily bought with promises of better trade links.

Inida waved his hand airily. 'I accept your reasoning,' he said, his voice back to its usual clipped formality. 'Though word of your arrival would not have gone amiss.'

Again Martaani looked to the Centurion, 'I was under the impression word had been sent.'

The Centurion took a step forward. 'A messenger was sent the day you arrived. I shall dispatch someone immediately to find out what happened to him.'

Martaani nodded to him and turned back to Inida.

'How is Claudia? I trust it is nothing serious?'

The Votadini King shifted uncomfortably in his seat, he glowered at a hovering servant who quickly stepped back out of earshot. 'She is failing,' he admitted in a low voice. 'I was hoping you could spare your physician to take a look at her.'

Martaani relaxed, this was not the disaster she had feared. His imperious attitude to everyone since his sudden arrival here was understandable now she knew the facts. Inida was a proud, conceited man with a temper that more than made up for his lack of stature. Yet for all his faults, he loved his wife.

'You shall have my best man,' she promised. 'And I shall ask my Pontiff to accompany him.' She smiled inwardly, that gesture would surely go in her favour. What the Pontiff had to say about it was a different matter, but she would face that later.

18

As soon as the light began to fade, Naraic started work on his ankle bindings. He kept an eye on the men but, apart from glancing over once or twice, they had shown no further interest in him. As darkness grew, they faded to silhouettes against the glow of their fire. Finally, the last fibre of the rope snapped. Naraic tucked the tiny blades into the hem of his tunic. He would have to leave his hands bound. His finger, or at least the place where it should be, hurt. Throbbing unmercifully, as if the digit were still there. A thought struck him, he had no idea what magic the Romans knew. He could not leave his severed finger behind in case they used it against him somehow. As quietly as he could, he crept over to the other boulder and tried to remember where it had fallen. He could smell vomit and knew he must be close. Not wanting to put his hands in it, he poked around with his foot.

'Oi. What you doing?' one of the men called.

'Trying to find somewhere comfortable to lie down.'

He got down on his hands and knees and felt about in the mess until he found what he was looking for. He tucked it into his hem along with the blades, and waited. The men seemed to be settling down for the night. He stayed put until he heard snoring then he tiptoed away, trying to locate the place where the wagtail had gone. The sky was dark, clouds must be covering the moon and most of the stars. Bodach was keeping him hidden. It seemed to take an age but finally Naraic found the place. Between the hawthorn and broom, he found a narrow goat path. Ducking under the bushes, he began to climb.

With his hands tied, it was hard going; there was no room to stand and he had to struggle along on his forearms and knees. Whilst the slope was not quite as sheer as it had seemed at first, it was extremely steep. Numerous times, he had to haul himself up using the shrubs. His hand burned with pain and his forearms and knees were soon broken and bleeding but he dared not stop. Eventually, he was forced to take a break; he cradled his hand as best he could and silently sobbed. When he thought back later, he could not say what exactly had made him cry: the pain from losing his finger, the shock at what he had been through, or just sheer relief at having escaped. All too soon he had to get moving again, he was still not safe. He was now well above the thick ground cover and was able to stand more often. He noticed a thick layer of mist rising from the valley floor and as the first rays of dawn began to lighten the sky, he felt panic begin to build. Looking up, he realised how close he was to the top. He had hoped to be over it before daylight could betray him but there was still an almost vertical section to negotiate.

Shouts drifted up to him from below. His disappearance must have been noticed. In his haste he took hold of a root to drag himself up and it came away in his hand, plunging him down the slope. He stopped abruptly by the trunk of a hardy birch, somehow clinging to the slope, the papery bark flaked around him like silver snow. *Breathe,* he heard again. With a huge effort, he stilled the rising panic and concentrated on slowing his breath. Up ahead to his left, he heard a goat bleating and quickly followed the calls, hoping the rising mist would keep him hidden from below. It beat Naraic over the edge of the slope, the wisps of white swirled about him turning the air damp and cold. The sound of the goat melted away and Naraic looked up to see a hand reaching down to him.

19

'Hurry,.' a voice called to him. 'They will be up here soon enough.'

Naraic found himself face-to-face with the wildest-looking man he had ever seen. His hair and beard were untidily plaited with bits of tree and vine stuck in them. His skin was filthy and all he wore was a poorly cured deer hide tied around his waist, barely covering him.

'Quick, there is no time.'

All around them was open moorland with pockets of marsh. Naraic's heart sank, there was no cover at all. The man led the way, dragging Naraic with him. They headed north over rising ground. Naraic's legs burned in protest but the man would not slow down. He kept throwing glances over his shoulder, not looking at where they had come from but further over, to the left, where the path led down the side of the valley.

Just as Naraic felt his legs would buckle, a small hollow appeared before them and the man pulled him to the ground. Though he was much older than Naraic, the man was barely out of breath, whereas Naraic gulped air as if he had been starved of it. A number of rooks flew overhead, cawing out to each other with their raucous cries.

'They will be here soon,' the man whispered. 'We must stay low and quiet; they won't come this far. This hollow cannot be seen until you are almost upon it.'

Naraic finally managed to control his breathing.

'Who are you?'

The man grinned at him, 'Men call me Torwain.' His voice was deep and lyrical. 'They also call me a druid.' He raised his head and peered across the moorland. On seeing nothing, he continued. 'I am here to lead you back to Kariss.'

Naraic could have cried with relief. It was only now that he realised he had no idea which direction he needed to take. He had thought no further than escaping the valley. 'But how?'

'Did I know?' Torwain interrupted. 'I have my ways.' The rooks called again. 'They are here.' His voice fell so that Naraic had to read his lips. 'Keep down and still.'

Tempers were rising amongst Martaani's men; her wrath would be immeasurable. Willing her to be delayed, they had searched every inch of the Cauldron floor. In their belief that no one could scale the sides of the valley, they had not bothered to look up. They suspected Naraic was hiding in the dense bushes on the lower part of the slope. A couple of men set about beating the bushes with their swords, to flush him out. The other three grabbed their horses; the only way out for them was back along the valley floor. They passed a second group of men, who also joined in the search. The valley was wider here, with more places to hide. The group split up, leaving one man to wait and give Martaani the news.

He was not a happy man. The giver of bad news did not live long in the Roman world. He had been at the village by the Tai and again at Dun da Lamh fort, so he was in no doubt what Martaani was capable of. The waiting only heightened his nerves, his mind playing ever more lurid scenarios of what would happen. Finally, he could take it no longer. Checking to see his comrades were out of sight, he fled.

The three men on horseback continued on to the valley entrance where a well-used track wound its way up the hillside. It weaved its way higher and higher. On a clear day the riders would have had a fantastic view into the picturesque glen but this morning the mist obscured everything. By the time they reached The Cauldron, it became clear how it had got its name. Mist appeared to be boiling up out of the hole in the ground, rising like steam from a cooking pot. They realised they would have to wait until the air cleared before they could check the top half of the slopes, not really believing for a moment that the boy could have got up that far but they would need to be thorough. A brief scan of the surrounding land was enough to confirm that he had not made it out. As far as the eye could see, the area was open, rolling moorland, rising even higher in places. There was the odd tree here and there but nothing that the escapee could use to hide himself. Besides which, his hands and feet were tied, so he could not run.

They settled down to wait. It was a relief to be in this group, they would hopefully miss the worst of Martaani's rage. The boy, though, would suffer when he was caught, and he would be caught. He could not possibly elude them for long.

In the hollow, Naraic had succumbed to sleep. Torwain did not attempt to look over to the waiting men. His beloved wildlife would tell him when the coast was clear. He lay next to Naraic, listening to his gentle breathing. It was strange but oddly comforting. He had not been in such close proximity to anyone in a long time. He closed his eyes and thanked the gods for bringing him there just in time.

Torwain had been waiting in the area for a while, knowing he would be needed soon. It was a place he knew well. There was a druid grove not too far away. It nestled close to a deep valley that ran south-east of here. The place was as dramatic as it was lonely. It was not Torwain's grove but many years ago, before he had turned his back on the world, he used to visit it often. The numerous hills and valleys in the area drew him in, like a moth to a flame, and he knew all about the secrets the area held.

There were a number of special springs in the vicinity that he visited whenever he was close. One, near the entrance to the cauldron valley, smelled of rotten eggs and tasted almost as bad but it did wonders for his health. The water rising through the rocks appeared in two places close to one another. On a warm day he would often sit massaging his bare feet on the rocks as the water flowed over them. His other favourite well was just to the east of The Cauldron, amongst the cloaking hills. This water was pure and clear, sent from the gods themselves. If Bodach kept the weather favourable, the views by the spring were breath-taking.

Torwain's connection with Cernunous was very strong. It was his guidance that had taken the druid deep into the wilderness, showing him how to read

153

the movements of animals and birds; and understand the delicate dance between hunter and prey. Lately, though, it had felt as if he needed guidance from someone else. The pull to visit the fresher of the two springs suggested Verbia or Nighean.

Torwain had stayed at the spring for three days. Patiently waiting for insights, all the while enjoying the rolling, open hills. A huge part of his life was spent in woodland, it was a pleasure to make the change for a while.

'You will need to embrace change,' Verbia had told him when she finally appeared. 'For your time now is changing. You must move back amongst mankind for a while and give up your solitary ways.' She knelt down beside him, bringing herself to his level to soften her words. 'It will be hard for you after all this time but we must each push ourselves beyond our limits now.'

'Is this why you are so far north?' Torwain had asked her. Verbia was a child of the Brigante rivers, especially the Weorfe. It was unusual to see her so far from home.

'This is a time of newness and beginnings,' she had told him. 'We each have our specialities and we must take them to where they are most needed. Cernunous is loosening his grip, you will not hear his voice as strongly for a while.'

Alarm had flowed through the druid. Cernunous was his life and his calling; without him he was lost, bereft.

'I am needed here to guide you now, just as you are needed back amongst your fellow men. Cernunous has not left you, he is just easing your

154

journey. He is letting you hear us, letting you remember what it is like to have others around you once more.'

Torwain had lowered his head. He had anticipated the need to make contact with people again. To this end he had fashioned himself the deerskin skirt to cover his usual nakedness, and practised using his voice for words rather than noises. He had not spoken to another soul for almost five years now and the words sounded strange on his tongue. He had known it would be hard to come back, but he had not expected the sacrifice to be so encompassing.

'It will not be so bad,' the goddess had told him, lifting his face in her hands. His scruffy appearance reflected in her green eyes and he had realised that he would have to try harder if he was to be accepted. 'Just wear this new life like a mask. When all this is over you can take it off, return to the forest, and never be seen again, if that is your choice.'

Torwain had nodded. He felt as if he were only just learning about the last few years of his life. He had thought that he had made the choice to withdraw completely into his wild state. Now it seemed that it had been his god calling him into the forest. Verbia had confirmed his thoughts.

'Cernunous needed you to learn. He needed to show you the hidden ways, the ways in which you can help Kariss and her friends. For that he needed to take you deep into his world. You did not disappoint him.'

A movement in the grass had made Verbia smile. She had reached out her hand and let the adder wind its way up, coiling around her arm and resting its head on her shoulder. Its skin was dark and its eyes had a cloudy film over them but the tell-tale X on the back of its head was still clearly visible. Torwain had watched as the goddess communed in silence with the snake. Cernunous also had a close affinity with the creatures; it was no mystery why he had chosen Verbia from all the maiden goddesses to be his guide now. She had run a finger lightly down the snake's back. 'Just like my friend here, you need to shed your old skin and start afresh. Once you do, you will find you can see clearly again.'

She had reached forward and touched him on the forehead. It had felt like a wash of light pouring over him, sloughing off his reluctance.

'You are needed. Urgently. There is a boy escaping the clutches of the Romans as we speak. They must not find him again. He is trying to make his way out of The Cauldron, but he is injured and weak. You must take him back to Kariss. Keep them safe from harm, guide them down the road. There is much to be done and no time to tell you anymore.'

In the hollow, Torwain watched as a solitary gull flew high overhead. The sky was watery blue, with hazy clouds scattered to the south. It was going to be a very warm day. A black bee hummed nearby and there was a constant drone from various flies hovering around the ground cover. Still he waited, not risking lifting his head and checking if the men had left. Eventually, he heard the bleating call of a male snipe and knew the area must be clear. He rolled over and looked out over the moor. There was no sign of the men, or the snipe, but he knew the bird would not be relaxed enough to call if the men were still anywhere near. Naraic was still sleeping, it was a shame to wake him. Torwain slipped out of the hollow and searched the ground. Finding the tell-tale delicate leaves he was after, he took a small stick and began carefully following the stem into the ground. It was not long before he had a collection of pignuts. A quick glance towards the hollow told him Naraic must still be sleeping. Even from here it was almost impossible to tell the hiding place was there. Only the sparse few gorse bushes that grew close by gave any indication as to where the hollow sat.

The gorse bushes were in bloom. Torwain pricked his fingers, gathering the yellow flowers. When he could carry no more, he returned to the hollow. His appearance woke Naraic with a start.

'I have food,' he told the boy. 'You must be hungry.' He dropped the flowers and muddy tubers. 'There is a stream nearby, when you need a drink.'

Naraic showed him his bound wrists. The rope had pulled and tightened during his escape. 'There are blades in the hem of my tunic,' he said.

Torwain's nimble fingers made short work of the rope. The chonchoidal fractures of the stone had formed curved blades that sat well, even in the druid's large hand. He admired the blades and noted how they fit together.

'This is fine work,' he told Naraic. 'I am very impressed. This stone is not from these parts. There is something very similar to be found just

157

north of here, but it does not break in the same way and is useless for tools.'

'My uncle had some old flint tools. They were good, but they were nothing like this stone.'

'No,' the druid answered. 'I did not mean flint. This is called obsidian, it is used overseas. Traders bring it to the south of Albion but it is very expensive. Not many people buy it because the flint is so easy to find.' He turned the pieces over in his hands one last time then handed them back to Naraic. 'I sense the gods have had a part in this. Can I ask where you got the stone?'

Naraic thought back to Cobalam, he must thank him one day. He secured the blades and picked up a pignut and squeezed. Underneath the chestnut-brown skin was a creamy white bulb the size of a large hazelnut.

'Cobalam the druid gave it to me.'

Torwain peeled a nut. 'I have met Cobalam, many years ago. I had need to speak to Dei, so I travelled further north than I usually do.'

Clearly he did not know. Naraic wondered if it was his place to tell him but Torwain had not spent years reading the subtle signals of nature to now miss the flicker of doubt that had appeared on his features.

'There is something you are not telling me.'

Naraic pulled a flower stem from his teeth and nodded. He explained what he knew about Dei. His words reinforced the reasons for all the gods' careful planning. They were not dealing with decent people. These Romans were a law unto themselves. They were a danger to them all. As Torwain listened, the last regret for his nomadic life fell from his shoulders. He was finally ready to face the world again.

The land rose higher the further north they walked. Moorland gave way to small pockets of woodland, and they took refuge in the trees whenever they could. No one followed them; Torwain kept an eye on the birds flying north. They would soon tell him if anyone was behind them. Midday came and went before Torwain realised someone was coming closer. The chatter of the small birds in the trees had stilled as the woodland paused. Suddenly, the silence exploded in a flurry of excited barks and Cloud burst through the undergrowth. He landed on Naraic's chest, sending him flying backwards into a tree.

20

Kariss carried a leather bag full of water back from the stream. At first everyone had tried to keep her in the camp but she insisted on doing her fair share of the work.

'What use am I to anyone if you have to fuss over me all the time?' she had demanded. 'I have learnt enough in my time here to know how to be careful. Besides which, I have my amulet.' She reached up and fingered the bronze hare. 'It has kept me safe so far.'

'Just make sure you stay within shouting distance and keep your eyes and ears sharp,' Anniel had insisted, realising that they were never going to get their way.

The water dripped from the seams of the bag, leaving a trail down her leg. She must remember to get some more beeswax rubbed on the inside as soon as they had the chance. She added the water to the pot by the fire and gave it a stir then hung the pot on the makeshift tripod Garth had erected over the fire. Not that any of them had much of an appetite.

'Where is Carrick?' Kariss asked Anniel.

He nodded towards the nearby trees. 'He went to be by himself again. He really is taking this badly.'

Kariss rested her head on his chest. Worry had turned her body to lead, her breath felt like it was being forced through a tight sieve of dread in her chest.

'Where is Naraic? All I keep seeing is him lying

with his insides pouring out like the blackbird in my vision. I cannot bear it.' Almost hysterical with remorse, she had dragged Anniel away from the others and told him all about her vision as soon as they realised Naraic was missing. Pushing back the memories of his mother's torture, he had hidden his own concerns and comforted her as best he could.

Anniel stroked her hair now and placed a kiss on the top of her head, willing his words to be true. 'Remember what Cailleach said. Visions like this are symbolic, not literal. Garth will find something today, keep strong. People cannot just disappear without leaving any trace.'

Kariss made her way through the trees, large oaks interspersed with hazel, birch and holly. At ground level, blaeberry bushes grew in abundance. Their waxy pink flowers were humming with pollinating bees and wasps. Carrick had not gone far. His cuts were beginning to heal but every movement caused the new scabs to pull. Too much and they broke open and blood would ooze again. At his instruction, Kariss had made a yarrow, comfrey and plantain paste, which was applied regularly. It stuck to his clothes, making him even more uncomfortable, so he had left his shirt off and cut the legs from his ripped trousers. He heard Kariss approaching but did not turn to face her, instead continuing to beat a stick against one of the bushes.

'That won't do you or the bush any good.'

'No.' He whacked the stick again and winced as the scratches down his back protested. 'But what else can I do? Garth was adamant I should not go searching.' He turned to face her, his face red with frustration. 'I know I could find him if only I could…' he threw the stick away in disgust and waved his hand to indicate his injuries.

Kariss perched on a rock and looked up at him. The ghosts she had seen behind his eyes when they first met were back. She wondered again what had caused them but she would not intrude on his privacy by asking. She had the feeling that he wouldn't tell her even if she did. 'This is not your fault. You must not blame yourself.'

Carrick made a noise of derision and looked away.

Kariss was silent for a minute. What she had to admit would not be easy but it would hopefully help him.

'I did not tell you something that happened earlier on the journey,' she said cautiously. Although she had overcome her earlier aversion to him, she was still not as comfortable with him as with the others.

Carrick looked back at her, his interest roused.

'I had a vision,' she continued. 'I saw that things were happening on this journey that were not safe.' She held her hand up as Carrick made to interrupt. 'I could not repeat the warning, not even to Anniel. To do so could have changed what would happen, take it out of the gods' sight. Cailleach was very clear about that. Each person would receive their own warnings, she said. If they were needed.' Kariss dragged a hand through her hair. 'I love Naraic like a brother. We have been through so much together.'

Carrick swallowed hard. 'So why are you telling me now?'

'To let you know that all that has happened was already foreseen. It was not your fault. You must stop punishing yourself. It is my fault. I thought I was doing the right thing. I thought...'

Anniel's call cut through the tension. Heedless of Carrick's injuries, they raced back to the camp, towards the sounds of Cloud's excited yelping. They found Naraic standing there, grinning at them. Garth was carrying Naraic's bow and, hanging back, looking like he wanted to fade into the woodland, was the most alarming man she had ever seen. She concentrated on Naraic, a vivid red cut marked the side of his face and a blood-stained cloth covered one hand, but he was alive. She smothered him in her arms, squeezing until he wriggled to be free. His face flushed with embarrassment. She hadn't noticed the wild man go.

'He will be back soon enough,' Garth explained. 'He is hiding our tracks whilst we break camp. Martaani knows where we are. She could be on her way here now, there is no time to lose.'

'His name is Torwain,' Garth explained to Kariss as they rode. 'He is a wandering druid who lives in the forest, do not be afraid of the way he looks.'

So this was the alarming druid Nectan had mentioned. Now that she had seen him, she was not so worried. He had saved Naraic, she could forgive him his unusual appearance. Besides which, she had missed having a druid to speak to. She looked at Torwain with interest. He was riding in front, next to Carrick, on one of the guards' horses. He rode bareback, his leather skirt barely concealing his dignity. She was relieved he rode in front.

'He came to the fort many years ago,' Anniel said. 'I remember thinking he was the most exciting person I had ever seen. He wanted Tharain to learn the ways of the druids but Mother could not bear to be parted from him. I remember being quite jealous for a while.'

Torwain led them north and then east, passing over the slopes of the highest hill in the area. It was far from an obvious route to take, the terrain was rough and extremely steep in places. Carrick's thigh was soon bleeding again, he lifted his leg and rested his ankle on the withers of his horse. It relieved the pressure on his thigh but made his balance precarious.

Torwain dropped back to have a quiet word with Garth, who was leading the spare horse, now acting as their pack animal. A quick shuffle round and one of the old guard's leather bags was emptied. Torwain borrowed Garth's knife, cut along the seams, and removed the strap. Once back with Carrick, he wound the leather tightly around his injured thigh, tying it in place with the strap.

'Try that,' he said. 'It should protect the cuts until we stop, but take it off when you are not riding. Your leg needs air to heal.'

There was plenty of time on the journey to find out what had happened to Naraic and the guards, how Torwain had entered the picture, and how Garth had finally found Naraic's bow lying in the grass where he had been captured.

They stopped next to a small loch. It was getting late by the time they had a fire lit and food cooking. Torwain tended to Carrick and Naraic, coating their wounds in the thick herb paste. He covered the stub of Naraic's finger with a plantain leaf and held it tightly in place with a strip torn from Carrick's ruined trousers. Cloud refused to budge from his master's legs. His tail thumped on the ground every time anyone spoke to him but he would not shift. His limpid eyes had a sorrowful look. He knew Naraic was hurt, he had tried his best to lick his wounds clean but the druid had pushed his nose away, rubbing some herb paste on the dog's scratches for good measure. With anyone else Cloud would have growled a warning but something about Torwain calmed him.

Talk had turned to the guard and how Martaani had managed to recruit him as a spy.

'I do not think he was a proper spy,' Naraic said. 'He was terrified of her. She said she had his family and that his daughter was going to pay for his failure.'

To everyone's surprise, Kariss was not angry. 'That poor man. How worried he must have been for them.' She shivered, it was an uncomfortable feeling knowing that someone had been passing information about her. 'We cannot blame him for what he did. He must love his family very much.'

'The bastard,' Garth cursed. 'I am sorry Kariss, but this is exactly why we are forbidden from marriage. I do not know how he managed to keep his wife a secret.'

She shook her head. Garth was a single man,

obviously he had never been in love. 'You are wrong,' she told him quietly. 'It does not matter if you are married or not, you will do anything for the people you love. Anyway, he failed, didn't he? He never gave Martaani my plans.'

'Only because he did not know them.'

'He should still have tried to warn you,' Carrick put in. 'Or stayed back at the fort.'

She let the men argue on. She could see their point, but she could not help wondering what she would have done in his place. Maybe the man had been relying on the fact the gods were protecting them? If she did become the Brigante ruler, she would have to ponder on the subject of guards and their loved ones. She could not risk the same thing happening again but she would not deny anyone the chance for love. Maybe the answer was to have them living in special quarters, where it would be noticed if anyone went missing.

'I sense you need to talk to me,' Torwain said later that night when everyone else was sleeping. Kariss had chosen to take the first watch and was sitting on a log next to the fire. The wood inside had a deep orange glow. She watched as dark patches appeared and disappeared, trying to find shapes or messages hidden there. Torwain sat down and looked into the flames with her.

'I had a vision,' she told him finally. 'I wasn't able to understand it all. Only the part that would keep me safe.'

The fire sighed as one of the sticks inside moved.

'I was too overwhelmed with worry about

Anniel. I knew that the vision indicated danger to the men.' She picked up a stick from the pile next to her. 'The thing is,' she placed the stick into the flames and reached for another one, 'Naraic wasn't included in the vision. Or I didn't think he was.'

'Did you have the vision after you had left Cobalam?' Torwain asked her. 'If so, Naraic was already being covered by the gods.'

Kariss looked at him. 'I had it the day we left him. It was Cobalam who asked Carrick to lead us through Cailleach's glen.' She explained the full vision to him and how she had interpreted it. When she finished, she showed him the bronze hare. He made no attempt to touch it.

'Keep it on you always,' he advised. 'Do not let anyone else hold it, the power there is intended for you alone.'

She tucked the amulet back inside her tunic. 'I feel so selfish. I was only able to keep myself safe. I didn't even think about Naraic.'

Torwain repositioned his deerskin slightly, giving himself a moment to get his words right. 'You have an excellent understanding for one not trained in our ways. You are open to signals and messages and your faith is as strong as any druid's. Do not be too hard on yourself for not understanding everything. Did you tell anyone about the vision?'

'Anniel knew something had happened, but not what. He also knew that Brigantia came to me when it became clear my fears were becoming a problem. I only told him the full details after Naraic went missing. No one else knew.'

'Then if you have spoken with the High One,

why are you asking me?'

'Brigantia did not talk to me about the vision. Only about my fears for Anniel; at that time they were threatening to overwhelm me and ruin the mission.'

Torwain patted the back of her hand. His skin was tough and calloused, his nails filthy with ingrained dirt. 'Love is the most powerful thing, but it can pull in both good and bad ways at the same time. Putting it in perspective so you can get on with your own life is not easy and many never manage it.'

Kariss smiled briefly at him. 'I have that under control now, I think,' she told him. 'But I'm worried. I failed. I could have stopped this happening if I had only understood the vision better.' She stared at the flames again. She had been wracked with guilt ever since Naraic had disappeared. Nothing anyone had said had lessened it.

'The vision was not about stopping what happened to Naraic. That was never in your power to do.'

Kariss turned her head from the fire and looked at the druid.

'You have to realise that you took the two most important messages from the vision and used them wisely.'

Her forehead wrinkled in a frown.

'You understood that at the time the message was for you and you alone. And you made sure you wore the amulet. Had you not done so, Martaani would have gained far too much information about you.'

'But what about the other parts? I never understood what they meant.'

'I suspect that this part of the vision was intended for me and not you. There is information there that you could never have understood, but which I need to keep you safe.'

A noise sounded from the loch, making her tense. 'A water dog,' Torwain told her.

'A what?'

'A water dog, a small brown animal that lives in lakes and rivers, though up here they are called Dobhran.'

Kariss realised he must be meaning an otter. She peered over to the water, but couldn't see anything. A quiet splash sounded and then nothing more. Torwain smiled at the relevance. Water symbolised emotions whilst the earth was grounding. The Dobhran lived in harmony with both and it was exactly what Kariss needed to do but as yet she had not managed it. He needed to choose his words with care. To help her understand, so that she could reconnect and achieve balance. Only then would she be able to stop her worries overwhelming her. He could see the strain on her face and the shadows under her eyes yet she looked at him with hope. She needed the truth, not placatory gestures. Torwain hesitated no longer; he explained everything, even the parts he would usually have kept to himself.

'The hand and the arrow indicate someone was leaving hidden messages. The fact they are marked by a cockerel feather makes it clear the messages are connected with the Romans. They have a god, Mercury. He is their messenger god amongst other things, and his bird is the cockerel. The Romans have a priest called an Augur, it is his job to read the signals of the gods using birds. Often it is the birds' flight they use, but they also read the entrails of living birds that they catch using bolas, the stones tied with a cord that you described.

'Your vision was a warning that someone was giving information to the Romans about you. That someone was one of the men in the group. The messages were then interpreted by an Augur, and only Martaani would have an Augur in Albion. The thrush set you apart from the others, indicating that you alone should know about the amulet and it would keep you safe. It did not mean that the others were not safe, only that what was sought was to do with you. The amulet would protect that information from being obtained.'

'How do you know all this? About the Romans, I mean?'

'When I learnt that they had a chance to return, I made it my business to learn all about their ways and their gods.' He looked down at himself and gave a snort. 'I do not look like a typical druid, so I was able to ferret the information out quite easily in Dumpender Law.'

'Cailleach asked me to learn as much as I could about the Romans when I was in London. But she told me to look for their weaknesses, not their religion. Maybe I got that wrong?'

'You are determined to find blame for yourself,' the druid said, with a rueful smile. 'It is honourable, but unjust in this case. It does not do a person any good to understand everything. If you had known information was being passed to Martaani, would you have acted any differently?'

'Yes.' Kariss was indignant. 'Of course I would.'

Torwain bowed his head respectfully, taking the edge off his next words. 'And that is what would have given you away. The spy would have realised something was wrong and Martaani would have found out how much influence our gods have with you. It is better she remains ignorant of that.

'You must understand, the gods do not give us tasks we cannot achieve. Cailleach knew you could not possibly know about the Augur but she knew that I could and that I was on my way to you. Do not forget, when Brigantia came to you after the vision, she could have explained everything.'

'Yet she only spoke about my concern for Anniel because it was affecting my ability to cope.' Kariss understood at last. 'I had wondered why I was sent the vision when she could have just told me then. Now I see that she only risked the visit because my behaviour was threatening our safety.' The realisation that she was not to blame for Naraic's abduction and the death of the guard was like a huge weight lifting from her. She felt lighter and able to breathe freely again. At the corner of her vision she noticed a movement. She turned her head just in time to see an otter trotting along the edge of the water. It lifted its head and scented the air, then it padded into the water and disappeared from view.

Torwain allowed himself a smile, 'I see why the gods have such faith in you.' Verbia had been correct after all. It would not be too bad mixing with people again. He had forgotten how enriching it was to connect with someone. He was beginning

171

to think he might actually enjoy being part of the group that saved Albion. He fidgeted with his deerskin again.

'I think we need to find you some proper clothes.' Kariss laughed. 'The guards must have had something spare with them, I am sure we can make a suitable outfit for you.'

'Do not worry, in the morning I will be leaving you for a while. I have brought us round in a big arc. Beneath here is a huge waterfall dropping down into a long valley, it is the quickest route back into Votadini lands. It is a very quiet route, I suspect Martaani has been using it to travel without provoking too much attention. There is a druid cell near the falls, I should be able to get news and a robe. If there is no news, I will work my way round to where Naraic was held.

'Fear not,' Torwain smiled, seeing the alarm on her face. 'I know this area very well. I will be quite safe. When I return I will lead us down the falls and back to your intended route.' He glanced at the others, sleeping soundly close by. 'Naraic could do with a day's rest and I suspect the rest of you could, too.'

21

The next morning when they woke, Torwain had already left. Carrick was on watch duty, he pointed to the loch.

'Apparently we will find good brown trout in there, and at the far side Torwain says there are plenty of straiph in full bloom, even though it is far too late for them, and close by you will find some stinging nettles. He asks that a strong tea be made, with the fresh nettle tops for everyone, to strengthen our blood. And that you, Kariss, collect enough straiph blooms for us all, to ward off the bad energies left by Martaani. Naraic especially needs these, though Torwain was also quite specific in stating that he must rest.'

'Have we not got enough injuries?' Anniel said, frowning.

Kariss racked her brains but could not remember what tree the straiph was. Nettles she understood all too well. She found it hard to believe you could eat them, surely you would be stung?

Carrick shrugged, 'As straiph is a plant of Cailleach's, he says Kariss will be safe enough providing she is respectful.'

'And I can manage the fishing,' Garth told them, coming over. 'There is some mending to be done as well. Carrick, could you manage that and keep an eye on Naraic?'

Carrick answered with a snort. 'Well at least I will be good for something.'

Garth pushed his good shoulder. 'Oh cheer up,

grizzle guts, or Naraic will wake up and think he still has ugly Martaani watching over him.'

There was an uncomfortable few seconds of silence, whilst the words sank in. Carrick had been short-tempered ever since the incident with the lynx, and they had all been treading on egg shells around him.

Suddenly, he burst out laughing and sent a well-aimed stick in Garth's direction. It hit him smartly on the arm. 'Get on with yer,' he said.

Garth rubbed his arm and grinned. Carrick was alright really, he just needed to stop moping Now that Garth knew he had a sense of humour, he would not let him hide behind his grumpy nature any longer.

The loch sat in a natural bowl, the sides of which rose in undulating hills covered by rocks and heather. Large boulders stood proud in the shallows, along with water-loving grasses poking their tips above the rippling surface. Anniel and Kariss made their way around the shore to the far side. As they did so, they disturbed a huge dark bird nesting on a small islet. Its great wings flapped laboriously as it hoisted itself into the air. The eagle's body was dwarfed by its wingspan, the head barely showing once the bird was high enough to start its customary soaring. To Kariss the sight was unbelievable, even Anniel gasped at the close encounter. He was used to seeing the magnificent birds quartering the hillsides in search of prey but they were notoriously shy of people and rarely let anyone close enough for such a view.

A bounty of white came into view as they

reached the far side of the loch. Blackthorn bushes clung together in a craggy cleft in the hillside, their branches weighed down with the multitude of May flowers covering them. It was indeed very late to see them. Kariss remembered collecting sloe berries with her mother every year. She understood immediately why Anniel had been anxious. Most people had worn thick leather gloves to protect their hands, but her mother had taught her to respect the tree's defences and pick with care. She knew that if she was respectful the straiph would allow her to harvest what she needed without injury. If she was impatient or greedy she would be rewarded with a sharp stab from the multitude of vicious thorns, a cut that would be slow to heal but quick to attract infection.

They had brought one of their food bags with them to carry the harvest. The weave was made from loose linen fibres that would allow the contents to breathe.

'Let's find the nettles first,' Kariss suggested. 'They will crush the flowers if they go on top.'

The calls of a yellowhammer filled the air as they passed the blackthorn: 'little bit of bread and no chee-eese' it sang, over and over. The nettles were only a short distance away, growing up through a cluster of small rocks.

'We need the fresh tops,' Anniel told her. He pulled his hand inside his tunic and reached for the nearest plant. He winced as the stinging hairs found their way through the cloth. Kariss searched the ground for plantain leaves to help the pain but found none.

'Do not worry about that,' Anniel told her. 'I

will sort it in a minute, just let me get a few more tops. Can you find me a decent-sized stone?'

When the bag was just over half-full, he picked some larger stems and scrunched them up onto a flat-topped rock. By now, tears were leaking from the corners of his eyes as the vicious stinging hairs worked their way through to his skin. He held his hand out for the stone and crushed the nettles until the sap ran free. He rubbed his stung fingers in the juice and sighed with relief.

'I never knew you could do that?'

Anniel laughed and wiped away the last tear. 'It is not for the faint-hearted,' he admitted. 'Those old stalks really have some kick to them. Most people prefer to use something that does not increase the pain first.'

It was good to hear laughter again after the tension of the last two days. Kariss took a deep breath. 'We haven't been alone like this in a long time,' she said, a mischievous glint lighting up her face.

Anniel smiled. 'I am sure we can find a secluded spot before we get back.' He looked over the water. He could make out their camp and Carrick sitting on one of the boulders in the shallows. He stroked his hand through Kariss's auburn hair; it had grown again and was now almost at her shoulders. He could feel his arousal growing. Pressing himself against her, he kissed her firmly before groaning and pushing her away. 'Can we hurry, though?'

Back at the blackthorns he hung back and let Kariss collect the flowers. She hung her head and closed her eyes. Communing with the straiph was a bit like communing with gorse; it had to be done at a distance, not touching as with every other tree.

Blessed Straiph, she began, speaking the words slowly in her mind. *Please gift me your flowers this day to aid us in rebuilding the protection around our group.* She paused, waiting patiently for an answer, feeling with her mind for any indication that the tree was relaxing its guard. Despite Anniel's urging, there was no rushing blackthorn. Behind her she could sense Anniel pacing. Without turning, she stamped her foot and he stopped. 'Sorry.'

Forgive him, he means no disrespect, Kariss said to the straiph.

The air was filled with birdsong and the sounds of the water lapping the shore. She could feel the warmth of the sun caressing her back but inside her head there was silence. The straiph were making her wait. Kariss's mind began to wander. She thought about the path ahead of her and how hard it was going to be. Flashes of her journey north came to her, interrupting. She remembered how daunted she had felt when Naraic and Brigantia had first told her why she was in Albion; how much stronger she had felt day by day. The desperate cold she had felt when her horse had stumbled in the river and the loving face of Brigantia when she had come to her aid.

Faces drifted in and out of her thoughts. Seula, the tavern keeper who had been so friendly when they had become stranded at Ad Gefrin amidst the Roman-friendly Votadini. Dei, the arch druid who had appeared out of nowhere in the middle of a snow-filled ravine and led them to the safety of the nemetons. Cobalam, who had saved her life and given her the strength to continue, and Raien, the younger druid who had looked after their horses. All these people who were strangers to her yet had offered friendship and help, enabling her to complete the first part of her task.

So you know how to face adversity. The collective voice of the trees filled her head. *You have been tested and tried and you let the experience strengthen you.*

Kariss could feel how impressed the straiph was. She fought back a smile.

Thank you, she bowed her head *We would like to have some of your flowers to help us keep the strength we need to face our fate.*

She filled her mind with thoughts of Martaani and what she knew of her cruelty.

Do not fight your fate, flow with it. There is always a way through, if you can find it. You are welcome to my blooms but I warn you, my thorns are sharp. Do not ever take your safety for granted. You may be watched and aided by the gods but you still have to take responsibility for your actions.

With that the straiph withdrew from her mind. Kariss took a deep breath to steady herself; she had not expected to feel such respect from them. It moved her more than she could have imagined. She blinked her eyes slowly, thanking the trees in her mind, then carefully she began to pick the delicate flowers. Using only her fingers, she eased her way to the base of their stems and used her nail to snap them from the thorn-riddled branches. She chose her flowers with care, taking only a few from any one place. Her bag was almost full, only a few more handfuls of flowers would fill it. She reached for another bloom but had the overriding feeling that she had taken enough.

She pulled back her empty hand and nodded her head to the trees, thanking them for their kindness.

It was mid-afternoon by the time they returned to the camp, having found a secluded spot to spend a couple of hours alone. Torwain had still not returned so they set about preparing a tea with the nettles. The leaves soon lost their sting as they stewed in the boiling water; they left them steeping there for a long time to get the maximum benefit. The resulting tea was very bitter, but its effects far outweighed the bad taste.

Here by the loch they were sheltered by the surrounding hills from worst of the wind. Even so, the horses, excited by the sudden change in the weather, stamped their feet, wanting to run free. Anniel checked their tethers and brought them closer. Overhead, clouds chased each other across the sky, morphing quickly from one shape to another.

'The weather is coming in,' Naraic said, concerned eyes on the sky. He had been jumpy and distracted all day. His hand throbbed constantly and a number of times he had been brought to tears with the incessant pain. The thought of a wet night was almost more than he could bear.

'It might just blow over,' Anniel told him, 'The weather changes quickly up in the hills.'

High-pitched squeaking calls floated over the water to them. They turned to see one of the golden eagles returning to the nest. In its talons it carried prey of some sort. The parent bird let out a series of yelping calls in answer to the chicks' cries.

'And to think, I always thought they were silent birds,' Anniel said.

'They usually are.' A voice answered him and they turned to see Torwain carrying a handful of bark and some meadowsweet. It was a relief to see that he now wore a brown druid's robe. He looked over to the eagle. 'They spend most of their lives in silence. Sometimes, though, they make those funny yelps when talking to each other but you only really hear it if you are close to a nest. Occasionally, they will screech if they are being mobbed by ravens, but that is all.'

Anniel shook his head. 'We are not much good at setting a watch, are we? One bird flies by and we all look away.'

'Well, it was a very majestic bird,' Torwain said. 'And I am not one to make a noise when I walk.' He looked at the pot by the fire. 'Can I use this?'

Kariss nodded, tipping out the remains of the cold nettle tea into a bowl.

'I found some willow and meadowsweet,' he said to Naraic. 'A decoction of these will soon help with the pain.' He placed half the herbs and bark into the pot, tucking the rest in a bag for later. 'It just needs to simmer for a while.'

22

The dull thump of hooves could be heard in the distance. As they came closer, the sounds echoed round The Cauldron. One of the men crawled back under the bushes, slipping and sliding in his haste to reach the bottom. He scoured his face across a gorse bush and winced in pain but it was nothing compared to what Martaani would do to him.

At the bottom she stood beating her short horse-whip against her leg, her face as hard as iron. At least she should know by now, the man thought as he forced his way down the last few feet, and he wouldn't have to be the one to break the news. The men down the valley would have had that thankless job. He emerged dishevelled from beneath the bushes and stood facing her.

Her voice was a whisper, barely audible in the misty morning air. 'Where is he?'

'We have found his trail. We are just following it now.'

'Who removed his bindings?' Her voice was precise and clear. The words seemed to hang on the air, hovering close as if tethered by the rage she was somehow managing to contain.

The man, relieved by her quiet demeanour, should have known better, should have guarded his words more carefully.

'We found his bindings cut where he was left.'

'Cut? How did he get a knife?' her voice was rising, she did not turn as the second horse rode into The Cauldron.

The man shook his head. 'We found shards of

obsidian, he must have had it on him… hidden… somewhere…' His voice trailed off as he realised his mistake.

Martaani's face was stone, 'I said he was to be searched and all his possessions removed. How could he have had something hidden?'

'We must have missed it.'

With a roar of frustration, she brought the whip across him with such force that it broke, and the man staggered backwards. From above there was a muffled shout then the sounds of the second man coming back down.

'The men have ridden to the top and found where he got over. His trail then vanishes on the moor. Should they keep looking?'

Martaani spun round and faced the Augur. The ride had added some colour to his pale cheeks and for once he looked almost healthy. 'Show me the shards.' His voice was ice. He rolled them carefully in his hand, taking care not to cut his skin. 'This stone is alive with vibrations,' he told Martaani. 'He had a druid's help.' He let the shards fall to the ground, shaking his hand as if to rid it from the taint. He readied his bolas and looked up at the sky, waiting. No birds flew over, even in the bushes they were silent. His horse stamped a hoof and the silence was broken. 'There is no point in remaining here,' he said. 'We will not find him.' He looked to the men. 'The next time you search someone, do it properly or it will be your entrails I use next.'

They left the valley in silence, each dealing with the defeat in their own way. The Augur watched the skies in earnest, hoping to read something vital in the movements of the birds, but they stayed ominously away. The Albion gods were still guiding their actions; he might very well catch the next one and split it neck-to-tail just to annoy them. He did not like being thwarted by these uncouth and unruly gods. He felt their negative presence around him like a cloak, even his very breath felt tainted by them. He thought of their shadows hanging over him and felt his anger boiling and knew he must regain control of himself. It would be a long day in the saddle. He would take control later, for now he wanted to bury himself in his feelings.

Martaani rode at his side, trying to ignore how much her body was protesting in pain from the gruelling few hours she had put it through. She should have used a chariot to return but that would have slowed her down and shown weakness to her men. She focused on what had happened, searching for a new way forward. Defeat was not accepted in the Roman way of life. When one scheme failed another, better, one must be sought. She kept coming back to the founding of their foiled plan.

A rider had galloped into Trimontium the day after they had arrived, seeking the Pontiff. He had listened, barked a few questions, then dismissed the man with a flick of his hand. With slow, thoughtful steps he had made his way to where Martaani stood conversing with Proculus and the Augur. He had looked pointedly at the former, who had nodded to Martaani and stepped away.

'Kariss is heading south in a small group, using quiet pathways.'

Martaani remembered the rush of adrenalin she had felt at the news. The men she had left further north had given her no joy. They had ransacked small forts and terrorised outlying villages, but so far there had been no news of her foe. Now, finally she had the chance to act.

The Pontiff went on: 'She has sent a decoy with one of the warrior groups heading towards Brigantia.'

'The messenger is with Kariss?'

He had nodded, 'One of the guards.'

She had been impressed.

'One more thing.' The Pontiff's lip had curled as he had spoken. 'She is travelling with her new husband, Anniel. He is the eldest son of Lord Alpin, the one that he called his "blessing".'

Even now, Martaani could feel the fury that had coursed through her body at those words. She glanced sideways to where the Augur rode, tight-lipped and grim-faced. Then she let her mind take her back to that day, when they had thought the answers were all appearing before them.

The Augur had paced up and down, his mind working furiously as he had digested the news. 'She has a plan,' he had told them. 'She thinks to outwit us.'

'He must not kill her,' Martaani had insisted. 'That is my right, I will not be denied it. He must kill the son.'

With a shake of his head, the Augur had dismissed the idea. 'The prophecy was clear. Kariss was to obtain the blessing, there was never any mention of her keeping it. He is of no consequence to us now. But if we kill him, we risk uniting the tribes even more strongly.' His pause had lasted only a moment. 'Her plan is the key; why else would she choose not to travel with a full

contingent of men? We need to find out what it is.'
He had looked to the Pontiff. 'Who else is with
her?'

'They have a guide, he is a tracker and a spy. A
man to be wary of. Other than that she only has
her husband's private guard, a boy, and two further
guards. One of which is my man.'

The Augur had rubbed his face. 'So she has no
druid with her, she is unprotected.'

He had strode away without another word and
the other two had watched him leave before
Martaani had called to her serving woman, ordering
wine and food to be brought to them inside. There
was no knowing how long the Augur would be
gone and she had been hungry. The food was much
better in Trimontium than Stanwick, they had
regular supplies from the continent. The wine was a
rich, deep red and tasted of sunshine. She had
savoured the taste, swirling it around the inside of
her mouth.

'So,' she had said to the Pontiff, enjoying the
warmth of the wine as she swallowed. 'Are you
going to tell me how you managed to get a spy into
Kariss's inner circle?'

The priest had calmly helped himself to another
olive before answering. 'A man must have his
secrets. How else could I keep my position?' His
eyes had flashed, wicked and sharp. 'So many
would love to take my place.' He had turned his
nose up at the floor with its shattered mosaic,
broken and missing tiles making the pattern hard to
discern. 'Of course they do not envy me this.' His
arm giving a brief wave at his surroundings. He had
paused for maximum effect. 'But they will. Just as

185

soon as they see how we have beaten and tamed the beast.'

Martaani remembered how she had sipped her wine, thinking, *Oh yes. You do so love your secrets.*

A light breeze had made the door-covering shift and scrape on the floor. Outside, the sun had been warm and the Augur's skin had shown a sheen of sweat as he had swept the cover out of the way and entered the room. He had thrown two live birds down onto the table. He had broken their legs and wings and they had cried out as they lay, unable to move.

Deftly, the Augur had sliced the belly of the blackbird open. The insides had stayed firm and the Augur had been forced to use his blade to release them, spilling them out onto the table. After a quick glance, he'd pushed the empty carcass to the side and lifted the second bird. The thrush was sliced open as well, but again the bird's innards had refused to slide out without help. This time the intestines had remained closely packed, rolling onto the table in a ball, telling the Augur nothing. He had stabbed his knife into them, impaling them onto the wood. Martaani had scowled at the Pontiff, the Augur was not known for displays of temper. In fact, Martaani had never known him to display anything other than silent disgust at being in Albion. The Pontiff's shoulders gave the barest hint of a shrug in return. Now Martaani wondered if they should have seen it as an omen.

The Augur has said nothing, returning his attention to the blackbird entrails, studying them carefully; looking at them from every possible angle, even asking that the door-covering be pulled back to allow more light onto the table. His forehead had creased as he had worked, furrows appearing between his eyebrows which deepened the longer he looked. Finally, Martaani had run out of patience.

'Well?' she had snapped at him.

At her words, the Pontiff's expression had changed from detached calm to amused interest. Martaani had ignored him. The Augur had raised his head slowly. Only when his face was vertical had he lifted his eyes from the table to look directly at her.

'Very well.' The boredom in his voice contrasted sharply with the fire blazing in his eyes. 'If you wish me to tell you what the birds have to say.'

'It would be nice if you shared what you see with the rest of us, yes.'

Martaani had never had any tolerance for self-important priests. Religion was a means to an end, a necessary tool in the fight to achieve control. It was not a ladder priests could climb in order to look down on the ruling classes. She deferred most of the time, as the Empire demanded that she should, but she wanted action, not restraint, and her frustrations had got the better of her.

The Augur had been sizzling with indignation, yet his eyes had never left Martaani's face. His control had been exemplary. Waiting for a few more breaths he had then held his hand out over the thrush.

'This bird represents Kariss.' He had pulled out the knife. She remembered how the intestines had remained tightly packed, even whilst the Augur flicked them across the table with the tip of his blade. 'I can get no news of her. Her gods have her well protected. We will get nothing if we go after her now.'

He had then moved his hand over the blackbird. 'This bird has a lot to say.'

The Pontiff had almost smiled at the pointed words but Martaani had remained oblivious.

'There is information to be had from someone else in the group. We must get them alone. In such a small group this will not be easy. All their movements are intertwined.'

'Then how?' Martaani had demanded impatiently. She had looked at the mess of entrails and wondered how on earth the Augur could discern anything from them.

'The boy is the key. We need to get him away from the group, but first we need to take out the tracker so he cannot follow.'

The Pontiff had taken a step forward then. 'The boy also has a dog with him, I suggest we get rid of it too.'

The Augur had tilted his head and stared at the entrails. After a moment he had nodded. 'That would indeed be wise,' he had agreed. 'Though the presence of a dog will make getting close enough that much harder.'

'I shall see what I can arrange,' the Pontiff had said. 'Fauna would be the one to seek for assistance.'

'The goddess of animals, I like that,' Martaani had said. 'Make it so.'

The Pontiff had bristled at the demand; he was not as good as the Augur at hiding his contempt, but Martaani did not care.

'I will consult Fauna and see if she will oblige us,' he had told her. 'I do not presume to command the gods.'

Even now, Martaani seethed at the slight, but she shook it off, she had got to the part she was trying her best to remember.

'There is the hint of a shadow hanging over this reading.' The Augur had interrupted then. 'It may be more prudent to investigate it further before we do anything.'

Martaani had looked from him to the mess on the table and back again. 'What kind of a shadow?'

'It is not definite,' the Augur had answered, 'The merest suggestion of something, no more. I would need to study the bird for much longer.'

Martaani had snorted. 'I expect you have found a speck of dust.' She had lifted a bowl that sat on the table and slammed it down on the entrails. 'The time for stalling is past,' she'd said, swirling from the room.

A cold shiver brought her back to the present. She glanced again at the Augur riding stiff-backed beside her. Everything about him said he was livid with anger. The set of his shoulders, the stillness of his body. Usually he rode as if he was a loose sack of apples. Arms and legs wobbling around, head bobbing as if it would fall off. Now his elbows were fixed firmly into his sides, his knees gripping the sides of the horse so tight not even a flea could crawl between them.

She had thought they had everything taken care of, that nothing could possibly go wrong. Even the gods had helped them. Fauna had advised the

Pontiff to the whereabouts of a lynx with cub. It had been easy for Martaani's men to inflame its temper, using blow pipes to shoot small stones at the animals from a distance. Not only did this keep the men out of harm's way, it also left no tell-tale footprints close by for the tracker to notice. The Pontiff's spy had distracted Naraic, taking him off to hunt without his dog. Everything had worked perfectly, but they had still been thwarted. The druid had arrived to take them all unawares. That must have been the shadow the Augur had seen. Only a fool overruled the seers of the priesthood. She glanced at the Augur again. He would probably not speak to her for days.

Their route took them along a wide valley, the sides of which gradually became narrower and steeper. The riders felt dwarfed by the sheer scale of them. Only the dark-haired goats scattered around the slopes seemed oblivious to the sheer majesty of the area. A shout came from the front riders and everyone quickened their pace, urging their horses into a canter. The animals sensed what was coming and pulled at their reins, tossing their heads to be free of the bit. Another call came and the horses needed only a slackening of their reins to lengthen their strides. At full gallop, they neared a wooden palisade surrounding some buildings. It was hard to make out how many were inside but two high conical roofs could be seen over the wooden staves.

This was believed to be the seat of the Selgovae druids, who gained their powers from the mighty waterfall that crashed and roared its way down the hillside behind them. Hidden from their view, the water pooled before forming a fast-running river that crossed the roadway at an angle, heading back the way they had come and widening out into an innocent river. It was known that the waters were swift to change at the druid's whim. Some days there was only a moderate flow of water coursing down the falls, and the river was barely a hand's-breadth deep; whilst at other times the falls could not even be seen through the amount of water spray that misted up from the volume of water raging down the crag. Then the river became dangerous, pulling stones and rocks along with it to trip any unsuspecting rider.

Even with the Augur amongst them for protection, the Romans were taking no chances. No one trusted what a druid would do, or could do; even the Votadini turncoats were wary of them. The Roman religious figures were, if anything, more scared than anyone. Their own knowledge came from trusted schools of learning. The druids, however, disappeared for years into hidden nemetons; groves where no one could find them. It was a mystery what went on inside them. This place was the only one to be open to passing travellers, being on the direct route through the range of hills to the Votadini lands. The Augur was not convinced that this was the true nemetons, he could see nothing especially sacred about the palisaded buildings.

The waterfall was special, that he could not deny. Even from the brief glance the road afforded them as they passed he could accept how important it was. Yet the openness of the place went against everything he knew about the druids. They were sly, dangerous men who preached free will and independent thinking. There was no control of the people, no mastery of the populous. Everyone was free to worship in their own ways, with only guidance from the druids, although the power these men held was legendary. They could change the tides, whip up storms, and call down great ice balls from the heavens if they chose. They could disappear into the wilderness, leaving no trace of their passing, only to appear almost by magic at another place. The Augur shivered at the thought and glanced nervously about him as he clung to his horse's mane and begged the gods not to let him fall. His horse had dropped back a little and there were soldiers on either side of him now, but still he felt vulnerable. He hated this feeling of weakness. These people and this abomination of a religion were an anathema and they were starting to get under his skin.

They had reached the river now. Some of the horses thundered through the water, sending up plumes of spray to soak their rider's legs. Others took the water at a leap, hoping to clear the river in one go without wetting their hooves. The Augur's mare crashed headlong into the water, the shock of the icy flow took her by surprise and she cat-leapt the rest of the expanse. The sudden lurch threw the Augur up onto the horse's neck and she responded by flinging up her head. The impact from the poll into the Augur's cheek almost lost him his grip and he slid sideways, only to be held in place by the closeness of the rider next to him. Pain banged through his head as he struggled to regain his seat.

The valley floor narrowed after the falls, the

ground rose as the road wound its way between the hills. On each side, water cascaded in small rivulets but the Augur barely noticed. The horses kept on galloping, spreading into a line as the road turned into a path. He could imagine eyes watching them from secret places, hidden amongst the craggy, uneven hills. To their left the ground began to fall away into a gully before the hill rose sharply upwards. Scree covered the lower slopes and it clattered down in showers as the grazing goats ran from the horses.

This place was auspicious. The Augur could feel the gods' presence here, just as he had on the outward journey. He was not as worried about them as he was the druids. They would be easily tamed by the Roman gods. In all honesty there was not that much that separated some of them, from what he could make out. He had discussed at length with the Pontiff about the possibility of combining some of the gods' names to make it easier for the local people to accept the superior Roman religion. It would not take long then before they would be able to drop the Albion gods' names altogether and let them fade into the obscurity they deserved. Of course they would need to get rid of the druids first, and do it better than Suetonius Paulinus had done at Ynys Mon all those years before. The foolish man had let some of the druids escape to find refuge in the northern regions.

As if the sun had suddenly dawned on his thoughts, he realised the way the gods had guided his mind. He sent up his thanks to Apollo. The deity always guided his prophecies, even when he was not looking for them. The druids were the biggest problem they faced in Albion. They were sneaky and dangerous. He saw now how the boy must have escaped - with their help; and he saw why. It was all to help him realise the greater picture, the vision of a world without druids. A world where the Great Roman Empire ruled all, and no one stood in her way. The boy was forgotten, as was Martaani and her conquest of Brigantia. They were but minor parts of the main event.

The ride back was completed in silence. The soldiers were afraid to speak, the Augur was lost in his thoughts, and Martaani was busy overcoming her recriminations and preparing herself for her next step. They had been unable to stop Kariss from returning to Albion, they had been unsuccessful in finding out her plans. Everything pointed to the fact that they should be preparing for a battle. Maybe she just needed to concentrate more on that.

They had only one Centuria at their disposal. The Emperor had refused to sanction any more men to be led by a woman. Still, they had the auxiliary recruits from the Votadini lands and they could always encourage more to join their ranks. The Brigante nation was one of the largest in Albion, any fighting force they mustered would be a force to be reckoned with. It was for this reason that her men had been busy causing mayhem around the region. Fires had destroyed homes, presumed 'accidents' had killed key family members and caused families to disintegrate into destitution and despair. Discordia was one of Martaani's favourite goddesses, she favoured the disruption and chaos brought by her interventions. Her men had just added fuel to the goddess's fire. Martaani was hoping to make Brigantia's people so distrustful of each other that they would never be able to hold rank in a battle.

The triple peaked Eildons came into view, rising high above the surrounding landscape. Beneath it, she could see Proculus waiting at the gates. She half smiled to herself. She needed to master someone after the failure of today, she was looking forward to slipping into bed with him tonight. He would enjoy letting her take out her frustrations on his body until they both collapsed into an exhausted sleep. In the morning she would tell him what had happened and listen to his advice. Until then, he would have to succumb to her dominance.

23

'Did you see Martaani?' Kariss asked.

The druid shook his head and pulled at his neckline. He looked so much more approachable now he was dressed, even if the robe was irritating him.

'I went down the waterfall and found the druids. Martaani had indeed been using the valley as a route back and forth. They said a large group galloped through a little before midday yesterday.' He chuckled, his voice cracking at the unusual exercise. 'Apparently they always go past fast and in as tight a formation as possible. It is as if they fear the druids will pick them off one by one.'

Anniel handed the druid the bowl of may flowers, 'We have each had our share. These are for you; I will heat up the nettle tea again once your medicine has finished boiling.'

Torwain took the flowers and gave a rueful smile. 'I had not thought to include myself as one who was in need of them but perhaps I was wrong.' He put a flower in his mouth, savouring the almondy taste. 'We are lucky this year that the trees are still in bloom, though I imagine Cailleach has had a hand in that.'

'Have all Martaani's men gone?' Naraic asked. There was a slight wobble to his voice. Kariss sneaked a good look at him. She had noticed he was looking pale but had put that down to shock and blood loss. Now, though, she wondered if there was something else.

Torwain swallowed another flower. 'I made my

way round to the valley where you were held. There was no one in sight. I found a local man who confirmed that everyone had left. The Selgovae are no friends of the Romans, they were the first to stand firm with the Brigantes when Queen Cartimandua was overthrown.'

'Then why did they let them use the valley?'

'They are hunter people in the main, they returned from a hunting trip to find the valley occupied and no sign of the few people left behind to watch their homesteads. They chose to watch and wait in the hope that their folk were still alive.'

'And were they?' Carrick asked.

'They found their bodies in a shieling towards the end of the valley, along with that of a stranger. I believe he was the guard you lost, they have agreed to give him a decent funeral. I also asked that word be sent to the Segovae King. I am hopeful that a messenger will meet up with us tomorrow.'

The next morning, they broke camp and followed the burn that ran out of the loch. Torwain had warned them the going would be hard and to lead the horses but even so they were surprised at the treacherous path he had chosen. The gentle burn soon changed into a noisy waterfall, crashing over the rocks to a deep pool just visible over the edge of the rocky ravine.

'Do not try and get too close to the edge,' Torwain warned them. 'It is not stable and you will not survive the fall, especially further down.'

The water continued its descent in a series of small waterfalls before finally plunging 200 feet down the ravine in a magnificent white cascade.

'It looks as if a giant white horse has galloped into the hillside and become fast,' Naraic said as they paused to look at the falls. 'Leaving its tail for us all to admire.'

'You are certainly not the first to call it such,' Torwain called back. 'It is known here as The Grey Mare's Tail.'

A flash of blue-grey diving down the gully drew their attention. The peregrine falcon twisted, bringing its yellow legs forward for the kill. Pigeons flew out in all directions but one was not so fortunate. The falcon retired with its kill to a stunted hawthorn clinging to the hillside. It was soon out of view as the path took them further away from the water. Small stones on the steep path made the going precarious. More than once they slipped and almost fell. Carrick cursed under his breath as he skidded on a loose stone and the skin on his back pulled tight against the healing cuts. He found the pain of his other, deeper, cuts easier to bear. The pain felt more honest to him being ever present and not hiding, waiting to strike the moment he put a foot wrong. He had never been one to accept limitations and he had never shirked responsibility. No matter what Kariss had told him, in his mind he was the one responsible for Naraic's abduction. If he had not been stupid enough to get hurt by the lynx, Naraic would not have been hunting with the guards.

At the very least he would have been able to find their tracks and follow quickly before the boy had been hurt. The relief, when he had seen him back at the camp with the druid, was like a weight being thrown forcibly from his shoulders, but now he found his concerns building again. Naraic was clearly not coping as well as he pretended. He was jumpy and nervous and Carrick strongly suspected he was not sleeping well. He watched the boy trying to negotiate the path in front of him, holding the horse in his uninjured hand. Cloud was close to his heels and every few steps, Naraic would reach out and touch the top of his head with his fingertips as if seeking reassurance.

Carrick sighed. Tonight he would sit down with the boy and have a talk. He needed to drive his fears out so they could not linger and fester. He had seen men suffer from this sort of thing before and watched as it ate them up inside.

He was so busy with his contemplations that he did not see Torwain hold his hand up in front and walked straight into the rear end of Naraic's horse. The horse's tail swished in annoyance and a rear hoof lifted from the floor. Carrick slapped its flank and the horse put the foot back down and shifted its weight across both hind legs.

Two druids stood on the path in front of Torwain. Their bare feet were white, with thickened skin.

'Your journey is safe,' the younger man said. 'No one has used the pass today and there is no sign of anyone further up or down it.'

Torwain nodded his head. 'I thank you, Rurann.'

Rurann and his fellow druid turned and led the way. He was young for an arch druid, but Torwain had known him for many years and had nothing but respect for him. The Grey Mare's Tail was a place that roared the power of the gods to all who came near. It needed a druidic presence, but it was unusual for them to live in such an open manner. Of course they still had their retreat, but there always had to be druids at the falls.

The water crashed into yet another deep pool, this time hidden from view by the turn of the path. From here it flowed on as the beginnings of a lively river. The ground evened out and the travellers were happy to find themselves at the bottom of the valley. The path terminated by a wooden palisade, inside which were two buildings. Numerous hens scratched at the ground for food and goats wandered about freely. The beginnings of a thick stone wall were noticeable just inside the enclosure; clearly the druids were reinforcing their security.

'We have prepared a meal for you,' Rurann said once they were all inside. The horses were led to the other end of the enclosure where grass grew in abundance. 'I know you need to be moving on very quickly, we will not delay you long. However, there is one in your midst that is in need of help and your time will be well spent in resting here a while.'

Rurann led them to the larger of the two huts, the smell of roasting meat wafting out of it soon put paid to any complaints about the impromptu delay.

'Thank you,' Kariss said as they each took a seat around the large central fire over which a young druid turned a small spitted boar. 'This is very good of you, however Torwain here has been very good at tending to any injuries.'

'I am afraid this is help of a deeper nature,' Rurann said. He stepped towards Naraic. 'Would you mind coming into the other building with me?'

The boy's eyes grew wide with alarm, his good hand tightening on Cloud's neck until the dog yelped in pain.

'There is nothing to fear,' Rurann said in a soft voice, 'you can bring your dog with you if you like.'

'Could I come with him?' Carrick asked, surprising them all. 'He has been through quite a trauma lately and it would be good for him to keep someone he knows by his side.'

Rurann tilted his head to one side. 'Of course you may.' He turned back to Naraic. 'Would you prefer that?'

Naraic nodded his head and looked gratefully at Carrick. They followed Rurann out of the building and into the smaller one. It was also circular in design but without the central hearth. The air was chilly and the druid handed them some skins to wrap around their shoulders.

'If you want to wait here, I shall return for you shortly.' He smiled at Naraic. 'I promise you, you are safe here. No one will harm you and I shall make sure there is plenty of food left for you.' He backed out of the door, pulling the covering in place.

No sooner was he gone than Cailleach appeared, bringing with her a soft glow of light to banish away the darkness of the closed room.

'Hello Naraic.' She sat down on the hard earthen floor and indicated that they should do the same. 'And Carrick, it is good to see you too.'

Carrick fell to his knees and bowed his head. He had never been in the presence of a god before, but even to his untrained eyes, there could be no doubt that this was Cailleach. Her skin was carved with wrinkles, furrowing her face in deep lines. Her long grey hair reached down to her waist and was held neatly in a loose plait. She had a stoop to her back but she moved with an ease that belied her age. She focused her eyes on the tracker; they were deep with the knowledge of time, yet they had a twinkle to them, making them shine like emeralds in the dim room.

'There is no need to bow, Carrick,' she told him. 'It is I that should be bowing to you both.'

Carrick lifted his face in shock. The crone's lips pulled at the corners in a concerned smile, her head nodded gently. She turned her attention to Naraic. Reaching out, she took his injured hand in hers. He flinched and Cloud gave a low warning growl.

'Oh, hush,' Cailleach scolded the dog.

There must have been more to her demeanour than the others could tell because Cloud immediately stopped and laid his head on his paws. Naraic sat silent. Inside, his emotions were at war with themselves. On the one hand this was Cailleach, wise goddess of the land and grandmother to all, but on the other she had let Martaani threaten and maim him. He may have dealt with the situation at the time but in the short while since, hindsight had crept in and festered. It heightened his fear, darkened his dreams and tied his mind up in terror.

Gently, the goddess peeled away the plantain leaf covering his finger stub. The wound beneath was tinged green from the herb paste. Carefully, she wiped it away. Naraic winced and almost pulled his hand away but Carrick touched his elbow. The reassurance stilled his reaction but his eyes filled with tears.

'I am so very sorry I could not prevent this,' Cailleach said. 'And this,' she stroked the side of his face where Martaani's ring had cut into him. 'But there are times when I cannot intervene. I can, however, help now.' She leaned forward and blew on the raw stub. Her breath was a warm relief, taking the pain and the incessant throbbing away.

'You must keep letting Torwain treat this,' she warned. 'It may feel like it is healed, but the wound is still the same. I have only removed the pain, though it will heal much faster now.'

Naraic felt his body lighten as the pain left him. His mind cleared a little, but he still felt angry and very scared. Without the pain to overpower his thoughts, the feelings of hurt and resentment were escalating. The nausea caused by the constant fear increased and he began to shake. A tear escaped and rolled down his cheek.

'I understand the feelings that haunt you,' Cailleach said. 'You feel betrayed by me after all you have done.'

More tears followed until they became an unstoppable stream. Naraic couldn't bear it anymore and a sob tore itself from him. He yanked his hand away from Cailleach's and shrugged off Carrick's, his eyes wild with emotion. Then he threw his head back and let out a heart-rending cry. Carrick looked helplessly at the goddess. He had no idea what to do. He had suspected Naraic was suffering more than he had said but this was so much more than he expected. The boy was broken.

The goddess moved swiftly. In less than a heartbeat she had gathered Naraic up in her arms.

She looked at Carrick and said only one word.

'Wait.'

Then she was gone, Naraic with her. Darkness was upon Carrick in an instant, wrapping itself around him in a cold caress. Cloud jumped up and started to whine. No reassurance from Carrick would settle him, he raced around the room, searching. The dark was no barrier to his movements. Carrick preferred to remain where he was. Concern making him fret. Despite his best intentions, he had come to care deeply for the boy. He had only begun to see the warning signs today. Yesterday, Naraic had been quiet and withdrawn but that was only to be expected after his experience. Torwain had given no indication that anything was amiss. He began to wonder if they had told the full story about what had actually happened in the Cauldron Valley. His mind raced with possibilities, each one worse than the last. Time became a blur, he was just about to stand and pace the floor when the pair reappeared. With one look from the goddess, Cloud immediately resumed his seat next to Naraic and again lay with his head on his paws.

Cailleach released Naraic and he calmly sat down next to Carrick.

'Are you alright?' Carrick asked him, glancing between the pair.

Naraic nodded looking slightly abashed, 'I am now, yes. Sorry.'

'Yer have nothing to be sorry about,' Carrick reassured him. 'I just wish I had realised how bad yer were feeling so I could have helped.'

'There is nothing you could have done,' Cailleach told him. 'I believe the ring Martaani used to inflict the cuts down Naraic's face was imbued with some kind of spell. I think she became angry when it did not work fast enough to loosen his tongue. No matter how she may portray herself, she is very scared of our powers and what we can do. She must have realised that we were protecting him and cut off his finger in the hope that fear would make him talk instead.'

'I feel much better now,' Naraic said. 'Like I did before.'

Cailleach looked steadily at him. 'Always remember, you are protected even though we may be restricted in what we can do. This time, the obsidian Cobalam gave you provided the means to escape and inadvertently protected you against the poison, slowing it down. Torwain, guided by Verbia, sent the birds to show you the way and led you back to safety. Now I have banished the poison inside you and you are free to be yourself again.'

Cailleach smiled, the wrinkles around her eyes upturned at their edges mirroring her mouth. She turned to Carrick. 'I have only one more thing to say. This attempt by Martaani was guided by her gods and priests. Nothing was left to chance, including the riling of the lynx mother shortly before you made camp. It was no simple act of fate that ensured you were the one to follow the concerned Cloud. They needed to ensure both tracker and dog would be out of the way when they took Naraic. Do not doubt your actions or sway in your convictions. You are a victim of a higher power, just as Naraic has been. Shame and recriminations have no place here.'

Carrick dipped his head in thanks, through his closed eyes he sensed the darkness return. They were alone again. He moved to the doorway and lifted aside the covering. Sunlight flooded the room and they stood, blinking.

'Where did you go?' Carrick asked.

Naraic frowned. 'Go? I never went anywhere.'

'Naraic, you and Cailleach were gone for ages. She held you in her arms and you both disappeared.'

Naraic had no recollection of going anywhere. As far as he was concerned, the goddess had held him in her embrace until he had sobbed his grief out. It had never occurred to him that she had taken him somewhere to cleanse his body of the corrosive spell Martaani had inflicted him with. He looked around the room as if to find something that would confirm it, his eyes wide in relieved amazement.

'We should get back to the others,' Carrick said, suddenly aware how long they had been.

'I hope there is some food left,' Naraic said. 'I am famished.'

Carrick was pleased to hear how much lighter his tone was.

A wonderful aroma of freshly-cooked food wafted across the courtyard towards them. Rurann appeared at the doorway and welcomed them inside.

There were a few more people in the building than when the pair had left. The Selgovae King,

Galan, had arrived with a handful of guards. To everyone's shock, he stood to welcome the pair.

'I gather you have been something of a hero,' Galan said to Naraic. 'Not everyone has a run-in with the Romans and lives to tell the tale. As many of our tribesmen have found out to their cost, both the last time they came to Albion, and this.'

Naraic bowed his head in respect. The King's words were a boost to his lightened spirit and he struggled to keep from grinning. He held up his maimed hand.

'Not all of me survived, my Lord.' He took his seat next to Torwain and sat unflinching as the druid redressed the wound.

'I was just hearing the full tale from Kariss,' Galan continued. 'I want you to know that I have ordered a small fort to be built close to the end of the Cauldron Valley. There will also be a number of outlying houses scattered along the valley length to ensure nothing of this nature can ever happen there again.' He spat on the floor, then remembered where he was and apologised to Rurann. 'I am so angry and ashamed that this has happened in Selgovae lands. You should have been safe here, all of you.' He pulled a silver cuff from his wrist and held it out to Naraic. 'Please take this as a token of my sorrow.'

Naraic looked up with widened eyes. He glanced around him at the smiling faces of his friends. Kariss nodded her head, encouraging him to take it.

'Thank you, Lord,' he said before placing the band around his wrist. It was too big and slipped down over his hand, so he tucked it further up his arm until it stayed in place. Galan roared with laughter and ruffled Naraic's hair.

'You will need to grow into it, lad,' he said, 'but it will not take long. Already, you are almost a man.'

The smell of the roast boar was making everyone's mouth water. One of the druids began to carve pieces off, laying them on a platter so that everyone could help themselves. Cups of mead followed and soon everyone was too busy eating to talk much. Even Cloud got his share. It was a happy group that left the palisade when the feasting was finished. Rurann and Galan rode with them. Before long, Rurann said his goodbyes.

'I have been away from the nemetons for too long,' he apologised, 'or else I would ride further with you.' He turned his horse up a barely perceivable track.

'Oh, the palisade does not protect the nemetons,' he explained, seeing Kariss's look of confusion. 'That is just our ceremonial area, where we worship the power of the Grey Mare. You could not have such a feature in the land and fail to worship it.'

'But why then are you starting to replace the wooden staves with a stone wall?' Anniel asked him.

'Romans and druids are not friends. I felt it would be prudent to make the buildings more secure, though it appears we were too slow in our work. So far, they have not tried to cause the place any harm. Rather, they gallop past as fast as they can, fearing that we may contaminate them by our very presence.' He chuckled again. 'It suits us to let them think we live there whilst they walk sedately past the path to our real home as we watch from the trees.' He winked, held up a hand in farewell, and was gone.

The group rode on, easy in the company of Galan and his guards. The valley began to widen out, as did the river they had been following all the way from above the waterfall. It was midday when they came to a small settlement.

'I must take my leave of you now.' Galan said. 'The Cauldron valley is just a short ride north of here. I want to see for myself where the fort will be. Have no fear, though. Although we are not fighting men, I will be at your side come midsummer with an army of men. If you require my help before then, you need only send word.'

They separated into two groups, one going north and the other south.

24

It was late when Carrick finally arrived back from his scouting trip to Stanwick. They had expected him four days earlier and the worry had stretched them all taut. They dared not send anyone to look for him yet, lest Martaani realise they were hiding in the Carvetii lands. It was after all the most obvious place for them to be hiding. Venutius, hero of the Brigante nation and leader of the uprising which had ousted his ex-wife Cartimandua and her Roman allies from Albion all those years before, had hailed from here.

Carrick was tired and hungry, he sat before them with a haunch of venison and a jug of wine and proceeded to tell his story between mouthfuls. Martaani was unfortunately back in Stanwick with a small number of men in attendance. It looked as if she was making that her base until midsummer. Her men were keeping a very close eye on everything that happened in the capital, including the gateways.

'I stayed only long enough to speak with Hightern and his advisers' he said. 'Basically, Stanwick is out for us, if we want to remain out of Martaani's reach until midsummer. Her men are watching everything that goes on there. Lord Hightern even finds his private meetings constantly interrupted. As soon as she learns something is happening that might interest her, Martaani shows up for an impromptu visit. All conducted friendly enough, but he is in no doubt she is spying on his every move. Even my visit gained her attention, though I was gone long before she showed up. It was lucky that I took the precaution of leaving by the eastern gate, though. As I suspected, there was a man following me. I led him all the way to the east coast before finally giving him the slip and making my way back here. That is why I took so long.'

'But what could she do if we went?' Naraic asked. 'Surely she would not risk attacking Kariss there?'

'Your naivety does you credit, Naraic,' Garth answered. 'Especially after all this woman has put you through. If she has men and priests with her, I am afraid there would be no safety in Stanwick for any of us. Quite apart from accidents or poisoning, imagine what would happen if Martaani managed to, say... set the inner rooms of the fort alight, and kill both Kariss and Lord Hightern at the same time?'

Naraic blushed. 'She would have a straight walk to the throne,' he muttered.

'Precisely, and there would not be a thing any of us could do, apart from outright war, and then who would lead us?'

Brigantia's words came haunting back to Kariss's mind. *Anniel's role is far more than just your husband... he is a key part in the saviour of the Isle of Albion. Why else would we have had to put you through so much to get to him?* Was his role to unite the tribes, not behind Kariss but behind himself? Was he the only one able to take over and defeat the Romans if Kariss should fail? Could their marriage have only been to serve as his gateway to the throne?

A hand covered hers on the table. No words

211

were spoken but a feeling of calm came over her and the vision she had been given when she had awakened back in Albion that final time filled her mind. In it, she was leading a host of warriors, with Anniel at her side. A golden torc around her neck indicated that she had assumed the throne of Brigantia. All thoughts of her early demise fled. Relieved, Kariss looked to her side to where the Carvetii druid, Darnus, sat smiling at her. He leaned closer and whispered, 'I have been waiting to give you that message. I trust I got the timing right?'

She lay her free hand on top of his. 'Yes,' she answered. 'I believe you did.' She kept his hand sandwiched between both of hers for a moment, before releasing it and focussing her attention back to the subject at hand. She asked Carrick about Lord Hightern. She was very concerned to hear how surrounded and vulnerable the old king was.

'Lord Hightern is weak in body but not spirit. He is nobody's fool and has good advisers with him.'

'Is Martaani making things difficult for him?'

Carrick started to laugh but choked on a piece of meat. He wiped his mouth on his sleeve and looked around the startled faces. 'Oh, she is trying to, but like I said, he is nobody's fool. He is managing to frustrate her actions in as many ways as possible.' He paused and took a long drink. 'She tried to infiltrate herself onto his council, insisting he must not hesitate to seek out her help in any matter, however small. He thanked her for her kindness and said he would indeed find work for her men to stop them from being idle.'

Anniel raised his eyebrows. 'I am sure that went

down well.'

'She could hardly admit how busy they really were,' Carrick agreed. 'Hightern now has them guarding the eastern gate and escorting nobles around the region because of all the troubles and unrest there has been lately. It hopefully slows down their ability to interfere.'

Laughter rippled around the table. Lord Hightern was obviously a very canny man despite his age.

'Did you get to see Corio and Bodvoc?'

Carrick looked at the man who had spoken, he had not met Darnus before he left for his reconnoitre at Stanwick. Plump for a druid, he carried the usual air of calmness with him. Unlike Torwain, he kept himself smart and well-groomed. His dark hair, flecked with a smattering of grey, was cut short and kept neatly trimmed, as was his beard.

'I did indeed,' Carrick said. 'Corio speaks highly of you. He has been forced to lay low for now. Martaani has both an Augur and a Pontiff with her and in such close proximity they are blocking his abilities to hear the gods' voices.'

Darnus shook his head. 'That is grave news, I must find out what is to be done. I will wait to hear the rest of the news then you must excuse me.'

'Of course,' Kariss told him. 'It is good we wasted no time in getting here, we can wait a day or two longer to make our plans.'

'You are welcome to come with me,' Darnus invited Torwain. 'Though maybe it would be prudent to keep a druid with Kariss at all times.'

'Agreed,' Torwain said, rubbing his jaw thoughtfully. 'You can easily send a message to me if I am needed, though I am loath to use the birds for help, knowing the Augur's propensity for slitting them open.' A visible shudder ran down his body.

Carrick finished his food and tossed the bone to Cloud. Gnawing noises rose from under the table, along with the occasional crack as the bone splintered. 'Corio asked me to tell you that he is the only one being blocked. Bodvoc, it appears, has been spared. The Romans do not think him worthy of their attentions.'

Darnus and Torwain exchanged puzzled glances before Darnus jumped to his feet.

'I am afraid I must leave you,' he told the group. 'This raises questions I feel cannot wait any longer to be answered.' He looked at Carrick. 'Is there anything else I should know before I take my leave?'

'Corio said you would know what must be done. He gave no other message.'

Darnus voiced his thanks, gave a nod of respect to Kariss and Anniel, and left.

As they waited for the room to settle again, Anniel spoke quietly to his wife. 'Is everything alright, you went very pale?'

'It is fine,' she assured him. 'Just my imagination running away with itself again. It is alright now.' She gave his arm a squeeze and smiled.

To everyone else she said, 'I agree. It would be suicidal to have both Lord Hightern and myself in the same place right now. The Carvetii have offered us safe shelter until midsummer and I intend to accept it. We have half a moon until then, that gives us more than enough time to arrange what needs to be done and plan our response if Martaani refuses to accept defeat.'

'That is exactly what Hightern himself said,' Carrick told her. 'He advises that you do not arrive at Stanwick until midsummer morning and that you arrive with a full guard.'

Kariss looked at Anniel, 'Can you arrange the guard?'

He nodded.

'Lord Hightern has his old head of the army, Cartivel, as his close friend and adviser,' Carrick went on. 'Cartivel asks that you keep the gathering warriors away from the fort until such time as they may be needed. He is concerned that unnecessary fighting may break out. Already, there have been rumours of Roman groups camping out in the nearby woods. He suggests your early warriors remain where they are now, camped on the northern border, but that any following men wait the time out further away. He suggests that it would be better to keep the numbers of tribesmen who have come to your aid as difficult to gauge as possible. There is still time for Martaani to send for more men, should she feel she will be outnumbered.'

'That makes sense. I must send word to Uurad and Tholarg.' Kariss frowned, 'I would really like to speak with them in person but I suspect that would be a foolish thing to risk.' She realised she was finally starting to think like a leader. 'Carrick, can I ask you to be my voice? After you have had sufficient rest, that is.'

Carrick looked pleased, 'I would be honoured.'

It was good to see that the ghosts had retreated again, thought Kariss. He was becoming more and more amiable the longer he was with them. 'Is there anything else you can tell us tonight?'

Carrick thought whilst he took another long drink. 'Stanwick is a place of tension,' he told her. 'The Romans are tolerated but the people are uncomfortable with their presence. The arch-druid, Corio, is watched like a hawk, the older druid not so much. Martaani's men consider him too senile to be much of a threat. Corio's hands are tied, he is unable to leave the fort without being followed and will do nothing to attract suspicion. They are all biding their time until the meeting. One thing of interest, though. It appears Martaani has a strong connection with her chief guard. They try to keep the relationship secret but it is clear that it is more than an official one. The Romans appear to form strict groups in their military, only the group forming Martaani's personal guard are with her. The rest, Dainarr, the current head of the Brigante warriors, believes to be either camping out in the woods or lodging at the Votadini fort at the triple hill known as Eildons, four days to the north.'

They spoke for a while longer, going over the news from Stanwick before retiring to bed. Kariss was the last to leave the room; she blew out most of the candles, taking the last one with her to light the way. A low whistle caught her attention as she crossed the muddy yard. In the shadows, Carrick was waiting. She blew out her candle and hurried over to him.

'I have a message for your ears only,' he told her. 'It is from Corio, he had only a moment to speak to me so it is brief.'

'Go on.'

'He told me to tell you to ask Darnus about the meeting at Barmr Craggs. You are to trust those present as if the gods themselves had spoken to you.'

Kariss lay in bed thinking about the message. She had never met this Corio but she trusted his word implicitly. He was the arch-druid of the Brigante nation, her nation. He would not have reached such a position without the respect and love of Brigantia herself. As soon as Darnus returned she would find a quiet moment to speak with him.

Next to her, Anniel's breathing told her he had fallen asleep. His hand still held hers on his chest and her head rested on his shoulder. She was safe and loved but she could not sleep. Her mind was a turmoil of thoughts, each one rolling over the others, tangling themselves up disjointedly inside her head. She was here, so close to Brigantia, waiting for the midsummer celebrations and the election of the next leader of the nation. She had warriors lining up along the border, waiting to fight at her command, to push Martaani and her Roman supporters out of Albion. Martaani had effectively shut down Stanwick with her presence, people were afraid of her. They had good reason, Kariss thought, but this would not aid her. When it came to an election, people would vote with their hearts, they would not give in to intimidation. Or would they? Was Martaani short-sighted enough to not see that problem? She would not bother with the common person, they would not have enough influence, but the leaders of each family would be the ones to target.

She sat bolt upright in bed.

'What is it?' Anniel mumbled, his voice still thick with sleep.

'Martaani took Drost's wife and daughter to make him do her bidding. She took the family of the guard's as well. Who else has she taken? What if she is taking someone from every family in order to get their vote?'

All signs of sleep fled and Anniel jumped out of bed. Pulling on a tunic, he hurried out of the door. He returned moments later and climbed back into bed. 'I have told the guard to find me the best Carvetii spies and to have them come to me as soon as possible tomorrow.' He pulled Kariss down to lie beside him again and kissed her. 'I was proud of you at the meeting this evening,' he told her. 'I am even prouder of you now. You will be a great leader.' He kissed her again. 'But now you must sleep. It is late and we have much to do tomorrow.'

25

Darnus sat amongst the stones. The god Maponus had just left him and he was contemplating their discussion. At first the god's words were frustrating but the more he thought about them, the more he understood. Maponus was the son, the hunter and the warrior. His weapon was the bow and he was worshipped by archers all over the north. Though he was a warrior god, he understood more than just aggression. He was clear-thinking and tactful, knowing where to place his feet so as not to cause any disturbance. He guided his archers, not only in this but also in learning about their prey, be it animal or foe. Then he helped them read the wind, the land, and the probable route of escape before they released their arrow. Many was a time they would need to still their action and wait for another time and place. It took patience to be a hunter, and inner fire to be a warrior.

Now, he had told Darnus, was not a time for action. It was a time of waiting, watching and preparing. The midsummer gathering and its vote for succession must happen before any action could be taken against the Romans. Kariss's whereabouts must stay a closely-guarded secret, whatever the cost; and as he had just found out, that cost would be great.

Darnus looked down at the stone head between his hands, the hollowed top of which still contained the wine he had placed there earlier as an offering. He lifted the head and drank the wine, it tasted strongly of blackberries. His mouth pulled at the tartness. He lifted the head and looked at the face, the bulging eyes stared blankly back at him. He inhaled deeply as panic started bubbling deep within him. The stone eyes never flinched and neither should he. *What will be will be,* he thought. The panic settled to a lump of sadness which would have been greater had it not been for the honour of being trusted with the truth. He closed his eyes and felt a hand caress his cheek. Calmness overwhelmed him. The goddesses had never appeared for him alone but he felt them in other ways, such as this. He had seen them at the gathering at Barmr Craggs but other than that, they were mainly just emotions for him.

He placed the stone head back on the ground, the youthful image of Maponus still staring out at him, reminding him of the job at hand. He needed to take his news, at least some of it, back to Kariss. He stretched out his limbs and stood. His main centre of worship lay further north; it was the place Darnus would ordinarily have gone had there been time. Here, he made do with the stone head and an old stone circle. He tucked the head neatly into the small hole at the base of one of the stones then scanned the surroundings but saw nothing amiss; he already knew there was no one about, the gods would never appear if there was. Instead, they would send a warning of the danger at hand. The thought made the druid shiver. He wondered if Dei had been given a warning.

A buzzard mewed overhead as it scoured the countryside in its search for food. Darnus watched as it was joined by its mate. The pair circled overhead, calling every now and then before moving further away. Again, he thought of Dei. Was he here, in the ether? Would he come when it was time? He shook away such thoughts, they did him no justice. Taking his blackthorn staff, he began his slow walk back to the small collection of huts making up the village that was to be home until midsummer.

When he got there, the place was a hive of activity. Kariss had called another meeting, this time a few of the Carvetii who were there to protect them were also included. In the dirt on the ground was a rough map of the area drawn by Torwain. The five Carvetii men, dressed in unassuming clothing, stood looking at it. Darnus recognised them. They were part of the select group that Kinithu, ruler of the Carvetii people, usually kept close to him.

Kinithu himself was staying far away at the western end of his region. He wanted Martaani to overlook him as any kind of threat. He was not classed as a king and this went in his favour, as did the fact that his nation was not a large one. It also helped that he walked with a pronounced limp, something he had made sure the Roman spies watching him had noted.

Martaani did herself no favours discounting him. Whilst it was true that he would be of no use in a battle, his nation was a proud one. They had been at the root of the previous uprising and were determined to have a part in the second one. All of the Carvetii warriors were fully prepared in case they should be needed, but there was no gathering of the troops to be seen anywhere in the region. Instead, the whole nation was complicit in the mock ignorance of any issue developing in their neighbour's land.

Darnus had met up with Kariss and her small band of people with the full support of Kinithu. Through Darnus, he had made it clear that his people were at her disposal. The borders were all being watched, and his guards knew where all the Roman soldiers were. In short, this was the safest place Kariss could possibly be.

Darnus rushed over to Kariss. 'We need to talk.'

Kariss stepped to the side with him so they could speak in private.

'You must take no action,' Darnus told her, glancing over to the map. 'It is vital that you stay quiet and hidden.'

There was a tone to his voice that had not been there the day before. It set the hairs on Kariss's arms on end. She held up her hands to stop him. 'We are not taking action as such,' she explained. 'I remembered in the night how Martaani likes to force people to do her bidding by kidnapping members of their families. She took a lord's wife and child in the north and sent back the body of the wife to ensure he would betray me. The druid Dei intervened and saved the daughter and kept me safe. It cost him his life.'

A strange look flashed across Darnus's face but it was gone as soon as it appeared. 'The news of Dei's passing was a great shock to me,' he said.

'I had no idea you knew him.'

Darnus nodded briefly, 'We only met the once.'

'Would that be at Barmr Craggs?'

'How did you hear about that?' He looked shocked. 'Torwain?'

Kariss shook her head. 'No, Carrick gave me a private message from Corio; he said I had to ask you about Barmr Craggs and trust all who were there as if the gods themselves were speaking through them.'

'I see there is much I need to tell you, Kariss.' Again, he glanced at the gathered men. 'But here is not the place or the time, I am worried about what you are planning.'

A couple of the men's voices rose above the general hum of conversation; an argument was brewing. Kariss could hear Anniel trying to calm them, then Carrick's voice interrupted. 'He was at Stanwick just before I was,' she heard him say. 'One of the guards told Lord Hightern that he had just left the fort when I was there.' The argument subsided, Kariss pushed it to the back of her mind and turned back to Darnus.

'Martaani also took the family of one of our guards. That was how she was able to get hold of Naraic on our journey here. It seems to me that this is a method that she uses a lot.' She waved her hand towards the men and the map. 'We are trying to arrange areas for each man to cover. They will try to see if there is talk of anyone disappearing since Martaani arrived. If we know who has been taken, if anyone, then we can plan accordingly.'

Darnus looked impressed. 'That is a good idea,' he said. 'I was instructed to tell you to use this time to hide and watch, to learn all you can, to plan for every possible eventuality. You are indeed a wise woman.'

Kariss flushed, 'I don't know about wisdom, but I do know that twice Martaani has come closer to us than is comfortable by using this method.'

'May I speak with the men before they leave?'

They made their way back to where the map was now divided into five areas. The spies were gathering their things together, ready to leave.

'You must ensure that no action is taken,' Darnus told them. 'The word from Maponus is to watch and learn. No more. The information you gather will be used when the time is right. But that time is not now. However hard it may be, you must not make your true reason for travelling known to anyone, or help anyone who has had someone taken. You are the best that Kinithu has. Make us proud. Be invisible and be alert to the fact that Martaani will have her own spies out as well. Her gods have been active here. They are invoked daily, just as our own are, but we do not know the extent of their powers. Trust no one, even those you have trusted before. Brigantia has been rife with troubles and accidents these last moons. I am certain these Romans are at the heart of it all, yet no one has been able to catch them at it. I am sure Carrick has already explained to you that Cartivel of the Brigantes has sent his best spies out. Do not interact with them, it may bring unwanted attention down on you.' He moved around the men, touching each on the shoulder and the forehead. 'Maponus guide your journey,' he said quietly to each in turn.

As soon as they had left, he turned to Kariss. 'Now we must find Torwain and talk.'

They made their way into the woods surrounding the village. As soon as Torwain gave the word, they sat amongst a patch of wood sorrel, whose flowers were just at the end of their yearly display. In companionable silence they waited whilst Torwain circled wide around them, Kariss watched him in fascination. He seemed to be inspecting every inch of the land around them. Darnus smiled, he was used to Torwain and his ways. He had gone deeper into the mysteries of the natural world than any other druid known. Of course, it was not unusual for a druid to go into retreat and see no one for an extended period of time, but Torwain had become almost feral. Even now it was clear he was still struggling to come to terms with being back amongst people. He did not sleep in a hut like everyone else but out here in the woods. Whilst he was making a valiant attempt to keep the matts from his hair and the worst of the undergrowth from his clothing, he would never fit in with what was considered normal again.

Finally, Torwain came and sat with them. 'We will not be overheard or interrupted here now,' he told them. 'And I will know should anyone attempt to draw near.'

Darnus took a few deep meditative breaths before he began, holding each a little longer than the one before.

'Nine years ago, seven druids were called to a natural temple in the heartland of Brigantia. Each druid was to play a major role in the saving of Albion. Six gods were represented, those who were to be the key gods in this fight.'

'Six? Why not seven?'

'Dei came late to the meeting. Cailleach had hoped to spare him from the troubles but as his grove lay at the heart of the northern lands, it was clear Martaani would target the area no matter what other plans the gods preferred.

'The druids present were Dei and Nectan, both of whom you have met already. Also Torwain and me. The others were Corio and Bodvoc of Stanwick and Umar of the Parsii nation to the East of Brigantia. The first two representing Cailleach and then in turn: Cernunous, Maponus, Brigantia, Verbia and Belatucadros.'

Kariss considered his words. 'I have met Verbia, Brigantia and Cailleach. Naraic has spoken of Maponus to me but I have never met him or any of the other male gods. I do know that Bodach has been helpful to me, he has helped guide me and aid others. Why was he not represented?'

'Clever,' Torwain said, his voice laced with respect. 'It is wise not to forget those who have helped you. Bodach is ever-present and always will be, but he is a god of the sky. He is not connected to the earth in the same way the other gods are. His strongest connection is through Cailleach so he is represented through her, too.' His eyebrows raised and he looked sharply at Darnus. 'I never realised before, that would be why she had two druids present.'

His friend nodded his agreement. 'Neither did I. Yet now it has been spoken, it seems obvious.'

'What about Nighean?' Kariss asked. 'She appeared with Cailleach and Brigantia at my wedding.'

'There are many maiden goddesses,' Darnus

explained. 'All over Albion and further afield. Maiden goddesses tend to be closely connected to their local areas. Nighean and Verbia are either one and the same or else very close sisters.' He shrugged. 'The gods do not reveal everything to us. I am sure Cailleach and Brigantia will have other names in other places as well.'

Kariss remembered the shrine with the many stone Nigheans. *Even the gods must have their mysteries,* she thought.

'So does this mean the gods know what is to happen?' she asked.

Darnus laughed. 'If only things were so easy.' He looked to Torwain but the other druid was standing stock-still, staring into the trees. His hand lifted slowly, hovering in mid-air, warning them to be quiet. His head turned as he followed whatever had taken his attention but his feet remained rooted to the spot. Suddenly he relaxed and turned back to them, lowering his hand.

'Problem?' Kariss asked.

'Someone was walking through the trees but they were a long way off and not heading this way.'

'How can you tell?'

'Cernunous is a great teacher,' he answered, mysteriously. 'As for the gods knowing what is to happen, that would make life far too easy. They have a very good idea of what could happen but nothing is certain. Each of us has our own independent will.' He bent and lifted a large stone, pointing to the insects crawling desperately to find shelter from the sudden light. 'I could have told you that the bugs would scurry away quickly and hide under whatever is nearby, but I could never have accurately predicted which bug went where. I could have set up a few more obstacles to try and guide them to the places I wanted them to go but still nothing would have been certain. Added to that is the fact that the Roman gods are also in play, they will be guiding their own people and putting their own obstacles into the mix. It is like an ever-growing circle, full of layers. Who knows if there is yet another layer above the gods?' He placed the stone back in its place and sat down on it.

Darnus sat deliberating his words. For all his focus on planning and looking at all the angles of a problem, he had never considered another layer above the gods. Who on earth would that contain?

'I think I understand,' Kariss said. 'So the gods believe that you seven... six now,' she corrected herself, 'are all important in what is to come. Does that mean that you are the obstacles?'

'In a way,' Torwain answered, 'but it is more that we are the tools the gods are using to guide things in the right direction. Rather than us being obstacles, think of us as help.'

Darnus dragged his mind back to the conversation. 'For instance,' he said, 'it is no coincidence that Torwain here has dedicated the last nine years to living in the wilderness and learning all there is to know about reading nature.'

'Already your skills have saved Naraic and led us to safety,' Kariss agreed.

'Now that Stanwick is out of bounds for us, I can be of even more use,' he said. 'I can move about this land without anyone knowing I exist. I can map out where all Martaani's men are for you and I can take messages to people.'

Kariss shook her head. 'I don't know why, but the thought of you leaving us just now fills me with dread. I want to keep you close by, Torwain. For some reason it feels important.'

'Then that is what I shall do, but permit me to still sleep out in the trees,' he shivered involuntarily, 'I cannot bear the thought of being shut up inside.'

'Of course, you need your own space and I feel safer knowing that you are out here. The huts will only confine your abilities.'

Torwain gave a deep theatrical bow. 'Then I shall become your shadow in the woods, the guard that no one else will ever see.'

Darnus nodded. 'I agree. The gods guided each of us nine years ago to grow into the person we need to be now. Torwain is probably the one druid Martaani knows nothing about, if she has bothered to learn of us at all.'

'Without Dei, Naraic and I would never have reached Dun da Lamh,' Kariss said, 'and from what I understand, many people would have died if he had not told Martaani how I was hiding. Being blocked from returning here forced me to face my greatest fears and find a way through them. It made me strong enough to fight whatever battle lies ahead. His part in this is clear.' She jumped as a blackbird flew scolding through the trees, her eyes shot to Torwain but he shook his head and smiled. There was nothing to worry about.

'Nectan was able to confirm to Lord Alpin that I was indeed myself and not an impostor. He helped me to believe in myself and to find deeper understanding in my trust of the gods, but I believe his role was more important to Lord Alpin and

Anniel than it was to me. It was Brean and Cobalam who helped me more, yet they were not at the gathering.'

'Brean and Cobalam are not druids I have heard of,' Darnus said, 'though I have no doubt Torwain will have met them at some point.'

Torwain nodded.

'They helped you by healing you, did they not?'

Kariss agreed.

'There are many great healers amongst our kind. In these cases, the individual was not as important as their abilities.' He held his hand up as Kariss made to object. 'I know they are good men; I would struggle to believe any druid was not. That is not what I meant. Their roles will have been guided just as those of us present at the gathering have been, but they as individuals were not integral to the picture the gods could see.'

'I do indeed know these druids,' Torwain said. 'Brean, I have only met a couple of times but Cobalam is well-known to me. He has now taken over Dei's role of arch-druid in one of the most important nemetons of the north. He is a great man, but his main role was to support Dei and pick up the pieces when he was taken. He has much work to do to right the wrongs his people have been subjected to. His main path was to be ready for this, not to be ready for you.'

The complexity was not lost on Kariss. She had heard talk of the weavers of fate. As Darnus and Torwain were explaining everything, it was as if she could see threads stretching back from everyone, crossing and re-crossing, creating a spider's web of intricate design. She could lose herself trying to

230

untangle all the threads.

'So what happened at this gathering?' she asked.

'I am afraid I must disappoint you there,' Darnus said. 'For there is nothing really to tell. The gathering was at Barmr Craggs, a safe and holy place for us. Our gods had guided us there, none of us knew that the others would be present. There our gods appeared, Cailleach told us there was a great plan to protect Albion. That each of us had been guided in our actions over the years to reach this moment in time precisely as we needed to. She warned us of the immense danger to our kind especially, and gave us a final chance to turn back, to give our place to another. None of us flinched. Then our gods spoke privately to us. I could not tell you what anyone else was told, nor can I tell you my message, for it was for my ears only.'

Kariss felt the blood drain from her face, only to be replaced with a deep, heartfelt shame. She reached out her hands and grasped Darnus and Torwain. 'I am so sorry,' she said, her voice dampened with sorrow. 'I have been focusing on my part of this plan and on Martaani so much that I forgot just how dangerous the Romans are for druids. You are in far more danger than anyone else here. We can all be forced into being their subjects but you...' she could not say the words. An image of the defiled druid left sprawled across the standing stones on their journey south flashed into her mind.

'We are in no more danger than you are, Kariss,' Darnus said, his eyes clouding as he spoke. Torwain looked sharply at him but let the moment go, there would be time later to ask what was amiss.

Darnus continued, oblivious to his friend's concern. 'We know that the Romans will target us, they must eliminate us if their rule is to be successful. They do not understand our gods and their powers and so they fear us more than any other. You they fear, because they know you are the one that can unite the north against them. You are the one the prophecy called.'

'The fear they have of us serves only to show our strength,' Torwain added. 'Remember that. People do not fear the weak, they only fear the strong. So they wish to kill us.'

Kariss stiffened her back. This talk of death had been alarming until she realised that she had already died once, at her own hand. Yet here she was in another land, amongst friends. Death was not the end of living; it did not quell the soul. She squeezed their hands and let go.

Darnus continued, 'The gods gathered us at Barmr Craggs so that we could be aware of each other. To know who else was key to your quest and who we can trust if things go awry.'

'But what of the other druids, they are all in danger? Why not involve them all?'

'They will be involved in their own ways and be given their own warnings as needed, but the fewer druids that know of the bigger picture, the safer we will be. We have already learnt that Martaani likes to torture people to get the information she wants. We have been tested and tried many times by the gods over the years to ensure that we are strong enough. Yet even then she found a way around Dei's defences.'

'Dei was right to tell her what he did,' Kariss

said immediately. 'I would never have been able to continue if all those people had been burnt to save me. Plus, it forced me to find my own way back here.'

Darnus held up a hand in peace. 'I do not know the story of how Dei died, only that he did so under great duress and with Cailleach's blessing. Your defence of him is admirable but unnecessary.'

Torwain suddenly looked up, his eyes scoured the trees.

'We are about to be disturbed,' he warned them. 'We should head back.'

They stood to leave. 'Is there anything else I need to know?' Kariss asked as they walked.

'I have told you all I can,' Darnus said. 'I would only say that such a gathering is unprecedented and gives weight to the threat we are facing.'

'I do have one more question.' She looked at Torwain. 'Is it safe?'

'We have a few moments still,' he said, glancing behind him.

'Who is Benakuradros?' she struggled with the unfamiliar word. 'I have heard Cailleach mention him before.'

'Belatucadros,' Darnus corrected, 'is the god of war and battles.'

They had almost reached the safety of the huts before one of Kinithu's spies caught them up. He was out of breath from hurrying. 'I had to return to warn you.' He panted. 'There is a band of Martaani's soldiers heading this way. They are not far behind me.'

26

Torwain grabbed Kariss by the hand and ran.

'Darnus will warn the others,' he told her.

They hurtled through the trees, twisting and turning, following no direct path. Torwain was muttering something under his breath but Kariss could not make out what he was saying. She tried to glance over her shoulder to see if their tracks were being hidden but she stumbled over a root and almost fell. Torwain dragged her on, not stopping his chant.

He stopped before a huge oak tree and pushed her up into the branches.

'Climb,' he ordered.

Behind them, the sounds of distant shouting had started. Kariss climbed. The branches were sturdy and easily held her weight but the height was unnerving. About two-thirds of the way up she found a large hollow in the trunk.

'Get in,' hissed the druid.

There was only just enough room for both of them to fit and they sat squeezed tightly together, catching their breath.

'Keep your head well back,' Torwain warned. 'We will hear if anyone gets close.'

Kariss's heart was pounding, she could feel it almost bursting through her chest. It reminded her of her flight from the burning flat in London.

'What about the others?' she whispered.

'Darnus knows what to do. He had already prepared a plan before we arrived.'

A raven flew onto a branch just visible from

their hiding place and called out a raucous warning. Almost immediately came the sounds of men moving through the wood. Torwain held up a grubby hand, spread wide. Five men, he signalled. The raven called again, agreeing.

They stayed silent as the men passed beneath them. They heard a few words spoken but they were in a strange language and they could not understand. They could hear the frustration in their voices, though, and it gave them a feeling of hope that the others had got away safely.

In the tree, Torwain and Kariss sat silent. Torwain held up a finger and pointed to the ground. Then he held up four fingers and waggled them to mimic walking away. Kariss nodded, she glanced up to the raven. This high, the sunlight reached easily through the canopy and shone down on the bird's feathers, releasing an iridescent sheen of green from its wings. The bird was watching the ground intently, its beady eyes never moving from one spot. Kariss could feel her heart hammering, even with Cailleach and Torwain's protection. She knew she was safe enough, but her concern about the others was intense. She forced herself to breathe calmly, counting slowly to four on every inward breath, repeating it on each exhale.

She glanced at the bird again, watching as she opened her wings, stretched her neck forward, and let out another jarring cry. The sound echoed through the woodland. Beneath them, a twig snapped. Satisfied, the bird casually folded back her wings and shuffled her feathers, stamping her feet on the branch for good measure. Turning her head, she looked Kariss full in the face and winked an eye. Kariss smiled and answered with an almost imperceptible nod of her head. She could recognise Cailleach in any of her forms now by her eyes. That piercing green was never quite hidden.

Her smile was soon gone as the raven snapped her head round to look at the sky. A faint mewing cry carried over the tree tops. Kariss felt for Torwain's hand and squeezed it tight as the sound came again. The raven hopped to a higher branch and watched the eagle.

In the hollow, Kariss could only wonder at what was happening. All sorts of scenarios ran through her mind, each one worse than the last. She felt Torwain nudge her side with his elbow and she realised how tightly she had been gripping his hand. Her nails had dug deep cuts the shape of crescent moons into his palm, two of which were now starting to bleed. Torwain smiled at her and shook his head. He took a deep breath and let it out slowly. Kariss followed suit. Gradually, she calmed down again, refusing to let her mind run away with her. Instead, she concentrated on the intricate web the gods had managed to weave around her. She was starting to realise just how complex their plans had been. The druids who were always in the right place at the right time; the people she needed most who had happened to find their way to her side; even down to the hiding places they had always managed to find. All of it, she was in no doubt, had been carefully orchestrated beforehand.

She wondered how many different plans the gods had made. After all, she was always being told that nothing was certain. Was there another druid who could have taken Torwain's place if something had happened to him? Or another man who could have guided them south? It seemed such an impossible task, weaving the threads of fate. She had tried weaving cloth on one of the many looms at Dun da Lamh. At first, all she had produced was a tangled mess. Her warp threads were a mixture of tensions, making it almost impossible to work the weft between them. Eventually, though, with much guidance, she had managed to thread the loom correctly and learnt how to pass the weft thread backwards and forwards to create an even weave. Once she had the knack, she had found the work to be almost hypnotic. Whilst the other women could weave and chat, she needed to concentrate fully on the process. She wondered if the spinners of fate chatted whilst they wove, or did they concentrate on the lives they were playing with?

She looked up again, she could just see the eagle as it swooped down into the distant canopy. For a long while there was nothing more to see but then it rose silently out above the trees and circled slowly. Cailleach called again, loud and defiant. Then she resumed her watch on the man below. A shout echoed through the trees, agitating the silence. Overhead, the eagle swooped lower, also watching. More noise sounded from afar, Kariss tensed. Torwain lifted a hand in warning. The men were returning. This time their voices sounded angry. There was a short exchange between the waiting man and the other four, then they were gone, stamping back through the trees.

The raven called after them, then she hopped down into the hollow and began to peck Kariss and Torwain. Over and over the vicious beak jabbed, driving them from their shelter.

27

Umar followed Faela up the slope, taking his time, letting her raise the alarm. When he arrived at the entrance, the gateway was barred by a handful of guards with more arriving to stand firm behind them. He held his hands open and skywards in a submissive gesture.

'I come in peace,' he told them. 'Your druid Kel will vouch for me. Please tell him that Umar of the Parisii is here.'

At Kel's insistence the guards ushered Umar inside the fort and took him to the great hall to wait. Two guards stayed with him, watching him warily as he ran his hand up one of the huge oak posts holding up the roof. Umar murmured to himself; a low, undulating sound that seemed to echo in the stillness of the place. He moved around the hall, feeling all the posts. All the while, the bag over his shoulder wriggled and clicked, making the guards even more nervous. All of a sudden, he stopped murmuring, threw his arms wide and spun around in a circle before stopping to sniff the air. The guards looked at each other, confused. The druid pointed to a spot above his head, staring intently at it, though there was nothing obvious there to the men watching. After a few long moments he dropped to his knees, left his bag, and began crawling around the floor, sniffing. The guards shifted uncomfortably, but they made no move to stop him.

Eventually, Kel shuffled in, using two staffs to

aid him. One was a gnarly old blackthorn stave that he had carried for as long as he had been at Wendell; the other a holly stave he had acquired a few years ago, after a fall had left him with a permanently painful hip. He was an ancient, bent, and almost broken man, but he refused to give in and accept assistance. The only other concession he allowed himself to ease his burden was the cloak he wore to keep the chill from his bones, even in the height of summer. His face creased into a myriad of amused lines as he saw his visitor on his hands and knees. 'You do not change,' he said, his voice soft and husky with age. He lowered himself shakily onto a stool.

Umar jumped to his feet and bowed his head in greeting. For a moment he looked taken aback at the frailty of the man before him but then he favoured him with one of his brief, rare smiles.

'The guards looked bored,' he answered, shrugging his shoulders. 'I thought I would entertain them. Do you think they would bring a bucket of water for my bag? It is beginning to dry out, I fear.'

'Lobster, I presume?'

'But of course.' Umar nodded. 'They are the ugliest of creatures, but the taste…' He broke off to nod his thanks as a bucket of water was brought in for him. From inside his robes he produced a lump of salt and crumbled it into the bucket. One of the guards gave a sharp intake of breath as he saw the precious salt dissolve. Umar looked at him with a frown. 'Does your bucket leak?' he demanded.

The guard looked taken aback. Umar continued

to glare until he shook his head.

'Then all you need to do is place it in the sun until the water dries and the salt will be left at the bottom, it will not be lost.' Umar waved a hand dismissively in the air. 'Better still, find a shallow indent in a rock and put the water in there. It will dry all the quicker.' He plonked the bag of lobster into the bucket and turned his attention back to Kel.

'I am afraid the process of producing salt is not something most inlanders are aware of, Umar,' the old man told him. 'So far from the sea, it is an expensive luxury.'

Umar looked contrite. 'Forgive me,' he told the guard. 'I forgot myself. Have you ever tasted lobster?' Again the guard shook his head. 'Then I shall cook one when we are finished here and you shall see why I bother so.' With a brisk nod of his head the subject was closed. The guards took their leave, relieved to be away from the mad man.

Once they were alone, Umar looked back to his elder. 'It is good to see you again, it has been too long.'

Kel nodded, fingering the long, straggling wisps of white hair at his chin; all that was left of his once magnificent beard. His pale, watery-blue eyes were failing, and what little hearing he had left was distorted by a constant high-pitched squealing, which only he could hear. His hidden senses, though, were still as strong as ever, and he could perceive no such weaknesses from the druid before him. The years since they had last met had not taken anything away from Umar, rather he seemed... stronger... harder, for all his dry humour

241

taunting the guards with his antics.

'Has your time been well spent?' Kel asked him, his voice now stiff with formality, for all that his heart had raced with joy when he heard Umar was at the gate.

'It has ...' Umar cut off abruptly as Kel held up his hand and gave a quick shake of his head. Not now, not here, his eyes seemed to say. Umar hid a grimace at his slip and quickly rushed on.

'It has.' He reached inside his robe and pulled out a ram's horn talisman carved into the likeness of a horned man. 'Our Shining One, Belatucadros, has been a faithful guide and teacher. He inspired me to take a voyage overseas, to view the might of battle and see its face for myself.'

Kel realised his palms were sweating and for a few short breaths the building swam before him.

'I learnt a great many things and came back much the wiser for it,' Umar continued, oblivious to the distress of the man to whom he spoke. 'In the very heart of a battle, I felt the battle-rage warriors talk about. The red mist that takes over and makes it possible to face the fiercest of opponents time after time and feel no fear at all. I come now to help Brigantia in her hour of need, to aid Kariss in her war. For there will be war, of that there is no doubt.

Kel closed his eyes as the words tore at him like unforgiving barbs.

This is the way it must be, my friend. The soft, fluid voice filled his mind, flowing between Umar's words and soothing their effect. *Light and dark take equal measure. Be proud of him and what he has achieved, without you it could not have been possible.*

Did it have to be him? Kel asked, never taking his attention away from the other druid's words. This ability to talk with the gods and still hold a conversation with the living was a fundamental ability of all druids. For all Kel knew, Umar could very well be talking with Belatucadros even as he spoke to him.

Kel's answer was felt rather than heard, the deep-seated shame needed no words for him to understand that this was yet another form of his punishment. The feeling passed through him like a wave. Behind it was the usual calm serenity his goddess, Nantosuelta, always inspired in him. She was the goddess of the hearth, of peace, and of passing; though it was natural, not violent, death that she was associated with. Her druid was as peaceful as she was, abhorring violence of any kind. It was hard to hear Umar talking of battle with such pride.

Umar had stopped speaking. Kel opened his eyes and nodded his head. 'War,' he sighed. 'I had hoped that would not be so, but I fear you are right.' He stamped his holly staff onto the floor, symbolically cutting through his inner pain and allowing him to focus wholly on the love he bore for the man before him.

The action was not lost on Umar, who bowed his head in recognition and flushed slightly at his lack of tact. He had known his actions would be an anathema to the old man but as always happened when they met, he had felt the uncomfortable fluttering of nerves. They were compounded by the fact that Kel had deteriorated so drastically since they had last met. It had shocked him, though

243

Umar was in no doubt as to his age.

'And now arch-druid of the Parsii,' Kel continued, his eyes glinting in the dim light. 'You have done well for yourself. For that reason alone, I have no doubt you already know that Kariss is not here, nor do I think will she come.'

Umar let the topic of war fall away. He had relished the expectation of a debate about the differences in their respective gods' methods on his way here, but it was clear that Kel had no energy for such a conversation now. 'In truth, I had no idea why I found myself heading here instead of to Stanwick.' He glanced to the doorway and lowered his voice. 'But I found my reason at your door. Tell me about the woman I frightened.'

'Faela? She is one of Kariss's cousins. Why would she interest you?'

Umar frowned, 'I do not know. Is she a warrior? She did not seem like one.'

The old druid sucked in a sharp breath and Umar realised he was laughing. 'She is a fierce one, of that there is no doubt, but she is no warrior. Still, I would not get on the wrong side of her if I were you.' He gestured to a stool, 'Do not make me look up at you. There is nothing makes me feel older than a crick in my neck.'

Umar pulled the stool closer and sat whilst the older man continued. 'Kariss and her three cousins were inseparable when they were young. It grieved them badly when she left, especially Faela and her older brother, Taratus. They have struggled since to get along. Dimmi was too young at the time, he is now a druid and returns here regularly, but he spends much of his time trying to keep the peace between them.'

'I felt much pain from her,' Umar said, 'much more than I would have expected after all this time.'

Kel frowned, his eyes almost hidden beneath his wrinkles. 'Faela's husband went missing early last winter and despite everyone searching, he was not found. She grieves for him still.'

'She is young enough to find someone else,' Umar said, 'she is not bad on the eye and she has good connections. Surely men must be lining up for her.'

Kel looked at him sharply. For the first time he saw his own nature reflected back at him. He too had failed to understand the depths that love can run to, and it had cost him dearly. He hoped Umar would never make the same mistake. 'Faela has not looked at another man since she met Kydas,' he told him. 'It will take someone very special to turn her head now.'

For almost 30 years, Kel had been the druid at Wendell, yet even those long years could not go anywhere near righting the wrong he had once done. Druids were not permitted to marry, but they were not immune from desires of the flesh. Kel had always been a devoutly committed druid, fiercely loyal to the gods, yet his carnal desires had always run strong. He would regularly leave the Parsii nemetons where he had lived before, to lie with Tchara, a woman from the nearby village. To Kel, these desires went no deeper than fulfilling a physical need. Love was something that he felt only for the gods, so it never occurred to him that the woman he lay with loved him just as deeply as he loved Nantosuelta.

From time to time, he would also lie with a woman from a different village and it was she who provided him with a son. As an orphan, Kel had no recollection of his own parents. He had been raised in the nemetons and taught to love the gods from the moment he was old enough to learn, but from the very moment his baby boy had squeezed his finger and looked into his face, he was smitten. For the first time in his life, Kel learnt what genuine love for another person was.

For the first few years, his life did not change much, lying with both women as and when he felt like it. When the baby" mother got sick and died, however, his life turned upside down. With no one to care for the baby, Kel took him to Tchara. Even now, all these years later, he shuddered at the thought of it. She had not yelled or hit out at him, there was no tantrum or hysteria. Instead, her face had drained of all colour and she had simply turned and walked silently away, leaving a puzzled Kel behind. Later that evening, her body had been found by the side of a small pond in the woods. It was so badly mutilated that it was still hard to believe anyone could have inflicted that much harm on themselves, but in her hand the knife she had used to gouge at her flesh was proof enough of what had happened.

Umar was certainly not the first child to be born of a druid, but the manner of Tchara's death could not go unpunished. Druids were supposed to tend to the people they served, not cause them so much pain that they tried to tear their own hearts out with a dagger. Kel had been banished to Brigantia and the fort at Wendell. Umar, though, had been kept behind in the Parsii nemetons. They allowed Kel to see his son once a year but in between times not even the gods would give him news.

Umar had grown up much as Kel had, with only the druids in the nemetons as his parents. Initially, he would be excited at their yearly reunions, but as he grew, the meetings became harder. There was a strain between them that each tried their hardest to pretend did not exist, but guilt was a heavy burden to bear, and it weighed their scant relationship awkward and heavy.

Kel looked again at his son, there was not much of a physical likeness. Where he had always been slight of build, Umar was muscular and athletic. He had his mother's height and eyes, with only his jawline resembling Kel's own. Umar's nature, too, was at odds with his father's. Kel had always been reserved and quiet whereas Umar could only accurately be described as an eccentric. Kel wondered what impact, if any, he had ever had on his son's life.

'Is there a reason you are so interested in Faela?' he asked

'I wish I knew,' Umar answered. 'The gods have indicated that she has a role to play in up-tipping the balance between Kariss and Martaani. I must find out what that is, and soon. Midsummer is almost upon us and I must be at Stanwick for the ritual.'

28

The sun was directly overhead as they neared the ravine. The wide floor was dominated by the river rushing its way over the stony bed, the sound peaceful and soothing. After two and a half days with barely any time for rest, they were travel-sore and exhausted.

Forced out of hiding by raven Cailleach, Kariss and Torwain had crept to a place where they could look down on the village. Above them the raven had croaked, keeping up her guttural cries until the trees below them had begun to rustle. Dragging her eyes from the scene in the village, Kariss had almost wept with relief as Garth broke through the undergrowth, closely followed by Anniel, Carrick, Naraic and Cloud. Their clothing had been torn and they were covered in briar cuts, but they were safe.

'They have found the map,' Kariss had whispered to them, nodding towards the village where they had been able to make out legionaries grouped around the drawing Carrick had made on the floor.

Anniel had not turned to look as he had thrown Kariss's bag to her.

'We need to leave. Now,' he had hissed, without stopping to embrace her. His words had been unusually curt.

'What about Darnus? And the others?'

A strangled scream had rent the air just then, followed by the keen, clear sound of druidic chanting. Naraic had gripped Cloud so tightly that the dog had let out a yelp. Kariss had turned back to the village, shocked. In full view, Darnus had stood with one of the Romans held tightly against his body. Face to the sky, he had called out his prayer. Kariss was about to cry out but Anniel had clamped his hand down on her mouth.

'Now!' he had hissed as the raven had barked her agreement. Anniel's face had been unreadable but something in his voice had stilled any argument. Horrified, Kariss had followed him through the trees and away from the blood-curdling sounds which filled the air.

Trapped in the thick tangle of undergrowth, Darnus had been unable to get everyone away to the safety of his bolt-hole. The tracker's warning had given them enough time to grab their things and flee the village but the legionaries had been too clever in their surprise attack. They had sent a splinter group into the surrounding woodland to pick off any escapees. Keeping each other in sight, they stationed themselves at intervals around the village.

As they cowered in the briars, the hard-to-hear words of Maponus came back to Darnus. With a sigh, he realised that the time he had been dreading was here. He closed his eyes and inhaled deeply. Above him, the cry of an eagle told him that Bodach had come to lend his support. The sound filled him with courage; this was what his life had been leading him to. It was his privilege to be of such service to the gods and in particular his own. Maponus, the god of hunting and battles, was today, through the sacrifice of Darnus, saving the hunted to let them fight their battles another day.

Darnus looked to his new-found friends and smiled sadly. With barely a sound, he whispered his plan to them. Before they had a chance to stop him, he bolted from the brambles and crept back towards the village. Alone, he had no trouble keeping silent. He neared one of the roundhouses and ducked under the overhanging roof. His legs remained exposed, but it gave him enough cover to creep round behind the solitary legionary scanning the edge of the clearing. Before the man even realised he was there, Darnus came at him from behind and wrapped his arms around him. With a finger and thumb pressed deep into each side of his windpipe, he slipped his blade underneath the apron on the legionary's sword belt, and tucked it under his mail shirt, to press against his manhood. The legionary froze, dropping his pilum. The spear clattered to the ground, alerting the nearby militia.

Darnus pressed on the blade and relaxed his other hand long enough to let the man's scream escape. Drawn from their stations, the outlying legionaries raced to the village. The way was now clear, but Darnus needed to keep attention away from the woods for as long as possible. He threw his head back and cried out to the gods.

The power of Albion's druids was legendary, and Darnus in full chant was truly terrifying to the Romans. The legionaries from the woods joined the other soldiers in a semi-circle in front of the druid, and stood aghast, waiting. In the centre of the group Martaani's face was a mask of pure hatred. To her right Proculus was torn between anger at the druid, and anger at his legionary for getting caught. Anger at the legionary won. His life was now forfeit, his ineptitude costing him no further protection. Proculus grasped his short sword, but Darnus had been waiting for such a move. With a speed that belied his appearance, he turned to face Proculus. At the same time he grasped the legionary by the hair and dragged his dagger across his exposed throat, screaming obscenities at the praefectus as he did so. Blood sprayed the ground between them, splattering the bare legs of the Romans.

Proculus roared in anger, but the shock stayed his hand for a moment longer. Time was now against Darnus, Maponus had promised him that his sacrifice would not be made alone. So now he let the head fall from his hand and turned his thoughts inward. Focusing only on the calming presence of the god within, he put up no struggle as the legionaries moved in. They dragged him through the houses to the map.

Without the benefit of the Augur and Pontiff, Martaani was unable to comprehend his lack of fear. Where she saw only a defiant druid glaring back at her, her religious leaders would have immediately suspected more. They would have cautioned her to tread carefully, to give them time to invoke their own gods for protection. Martaani, however, saw no need for stealth.

'Strip him,' she demanded.

Her eyes took in his naked body. She noted the excess flesh around his waist, the greying hair covering his chest, and she curled her lips in amusement, thinking him unmanned.

Darnus held his head high and smiled back.

There was no shame in the body the gods had bestowed upon him. He watched as she flipped her hand out. Proculus removed the dagger hanging from a jewelled sheath on his left hip and placed it onto her palm. Long fingers curled slowly around the handle. Maponus spoke in Darnus's mind and the druid took a deep breath, shuddering as the god deepened his possession.

Martaani saw the shudder and stepped forward in delicious anticipation. She revelled in her power over others. Proculus too mistook the shudder as one of fear. He nodded to the legionaries holding the druid and they tightened their grip on his outstretched arms.

Slowly, the point of the pugio pierced the skin just below Darnus's collar bone. He flinched as the blade sunk to half a finger's depth. As Martaani sliced the blade down towards his chest, he screamed. She stilled her hand, smiling at the sound.

'Where are they?' she asked, her voice light and conversational. 'I see you have been planning something here,' she inclined her head to the map. 'What was it?'

Defiance returned to Darnus's eyes and he smiled back at her. The blade moved again and pain lanced through him, tearing another scream from deep within. His breathing shortened, sweat beading on his brow as he bucked against the dagger. He could feel it all, burning so deeply that it turned his stomach. There was, however, no fear. Maponus had taken it from him by loosening the connection between his soul and his body. This action filled Darnus's mind with a calm detachment that he didn't think to question.

Again, Martaani stilled the blade and again Darnus smiled as he caught his breath. He looked her straight in the eye, proud and unrelenting. The longer he could distract her and her guards, the more chance the others had of escape.

'I will take that look from your eyes, druid,' she spat. 'And you will not keep that smile on your face.' She nodded to a guard Darnus had not noticed before. He handed her a fire brand. The air shimmered around the glowing amber tip. She pressed it to his wounds.

Pain such as he had never known existed blanked out everything. He came to on his hands and knees, gasping for air. He must have screamed to make his throat hurt so much, but he had no memory of it. He could smell his flesh cooking and feel the charred skin tightening. They gave him a few moments before hauling him back to his feet.

'You are not smiling now,' Martaani gloated. She pushed the point of the pugio onto the fresh burn.

Darnus vomited on her feet. She slapped him hard across the face. He looked up and smiled at her.

Again and again the brand and the blade took their turn but each scream that tore from Darnus was always replaced by his contumacious stare until Martaani could stand it no longer. She put out his eyes but still she could not stop his smile.

Her patience snapped. 'What is it with you druids?' Martaani yelled at him. 'What will it take to make you yield?'

Darnus turned his head towards her voice. Maponus was pulling him away now, taking him into the ether where he would be forever safe from harm. He just had time to tell her:

'Albion is not yours to take.'

Without horses, the journey to the ravine had been exhausting. They had not dared use any of the bolt-holes Darnus had prepared for them lest Martaani managed to force the information from him. Instead, they had followed the raven as she led them safely away. Just after midday, the bird flew down to land on a patch of strange rock rising from a bed of boggy orange coloured mosses. The rock spread out to the south, forming a deeply cracked pathway amongst which a variety of plants clung to life. They sank onto the rock, grateful for the rest.

Their initial fear had gradually given way to shock and it was a few moments before anyone spoke.

'How did they know?' Garth said at last. He looked towards Carrick.

'I was not followed. I swear it.' The tracker looked worried, 'I have been thinking about nothing else. There is no way anyone had time to follow me, find our hiding place and then organise such a strike.' He paused and looked around the group. 'Someone must have betrayed us.'

A frisson of alarm ran through everyone. Anniel nodded his head. 'Carrick is right. That was a well-planned attack, not a rushed one. So one of the Carvetii must have given us away.'

'What about at Stanwick?' Garth insisted. 'Could someone have got hold of the information there? You said that you were followed when you first left. You led them off the wrong way, but could that have just been a ruse? Maybe Martaani was already preparing her soldiers as you left.'

Carrick jumped to his feet. 'Are you so convinced that I am a spy?'

Garth held his hands up in a peaceful gesture. 'You misunderstand me, Carrick. I was not suggesting you. For sake of the Goddess, man, you are one of the most trusted men of the Vacumagi, and my friend.' He paused, choosing his next words carefully. 'I meant that someone at Stanwick could have found out where we were, somehow, during the time that you were there. Martaani could have ordered her men to follow you so that you would believe everything to be safe. Meanwhile, she was readying her men and setting off.'

Anniel nodded. 'You came a different way back, so you would not have seen them on the road.'

Carrick sat back down, the ghosts returned behind his eyes. He looked at Garth with half a smile, then round at the rest of the group. 'If I did anything to lead them to us I could not be more sorry. I keep hearing Darnus screaming, and know it should have been me.'

Cloud gave a whine and crawled over to him, forcing his nose underneath his hand and thumping his tail on the rock. Everyone was silent for a moment then Kariss spoke up. 'Remember the message you gave me, Carrick, when you returned from Stanwick?

He looked up and frowned.

'I know the message was private, but we are beyond that now.' She looked to Torwain, who nodded. 'You told me that I should trust all those who were at Barmr Craggs as if they were the gods themselves. I cannot tell you all that happened there but I will tell you this. Every druid present was there for a reason; they each have a key part to play in all this.' She sighed and for a moment her eyes flooded with unshed tears, but she blinked them fiercely away. 'Dei saved Naraic and me on our way to see Lord Alpin, he had already completed his task by the time he was killed. I think it was different with Darnus. I could have learnt about Barmr Craggs from any one of the druids who were present there, it did not need to be him. So I think…' she gulped down a breath to steady her wobbling voice, 'I think Darnus's task was to give us time to get away.'

The raven tilted her head to the side, watching Kariss. Unseen in the nearby woods a youthful face looked out from behind a silver birch.

'I think he knew,' Torwain added. 'There was something on his mind this morning when he returned. I had meant to ask him about it but…' His voice faded away.

'So you must not think you should have given yourself to Martaani,' Kariss told Carrick. 'You are needed to get my message to the waiting warriors. There is no one else I would trust for the job.' Her initial reservations about him had been shed slowly on their journey south. There was no doubt that he was a prickly, reserved man, but he had proved himself faithful. She would not be without him now.

Torwain lifted his head, he had felt Maponus's presence. Scanning the treeline, he saw him standing watching them. The god inclined his head in greeting, smiled at the raven, and melted back into the wood.

29

'These rocks have given me an idea,' Torwain said a short while later. They had been discussing what their next plans should be. They were no longer willing to trust anyone else; not only were they afraid of spies and informers, they were also reluctant to put any more lives in danger.

'This rock forms a huge pathway around some magic springs,' he continued. 'It is a sacred place and many people live close by, too many for us to stay here, but it brings to mind a similar spring. This one is hidden away in a deep ravine. The locals are scared to venture near, believing it to be a dark place, full of the gods' wrath.'

Naraic looked concerned. Torwain put a reassuring hand on his arm. 'You have nothing to fear, trust me, Cailleach will not let us go if it is wrong.' He turned to the raven, but she was nowhere to be seen. From high above a black feather fell, twisting and dancing in the air to land at Torwain's feet. He picked it up and smiled. Naraic was instantly pacified. The sound of Darnus's screams had brought his own meeting with Martaani flooding back, rattling his calmed nerves. As he put his hand down to push himself up off the rocks, it closed over something hard. Picking it up, he found it was a small black hag stone. He rolled it around in his hand. It was smooth and warm, and felt like it belonged to him somehow. A hand reached out to him, holding a strip of leather.

'You have your own amulet now,' Kariss told

him.

They set off again, keeping to the top edge of the stony pathway. The strange rock formation covered the ground as far as the eye could see. In the distance they could see smoke rising from one of the many homesteads. Further away still, the ground rose to a small peak. It was too far away to make out the walled settlement that covered the summit, but Torwain assured them it was there.

Stunted hazel and hawthorn trees, interspersed with the odd ash tree, gave them their only cover. Apart from that, the area was bleak and windswept. In a few places the pathway stretched out like long fingers reaching ever outwards. Here they had to traverse the rock, stepping across the deep fissures filled with eyebright, heather and ferns. The air was filled with the calls of wheatear and meadow pipit, overhead they could see plovers and hovering kestrels. Clearly the birds did not find the area bleak.

The sun was almost directly overhead when they reached a well-trodden path heading due east. Carrick took his leave of them then. It should take a day and a half to reach Tholarg and Uurad, but the way would be fraught with danger. It was one of the few routes across the spine of Albion, so-called because of the line of craggy hills dividing east from west. Martaani and her soldiers would be all over the road, trying to block Kariss from reaching Stanwick. The way was full of peaks and deep valleys, with boggy moorland in between. Not much opportunity to stay hidden for long. Carrick had refused to hear anything of the whereabouts of the spring the others were heading to.

'This way is safest for all of us,' he said. 'We have no way of knowing where the informer came from. If it was a Carvetii then Martaani will already know of the scouts we sent out this morning, and the amount of warriors we have hiding near Stanwick.'

'I think we must also assume that she has leverage on many more people,' Anniel said. 'Though our scouts will not be able to find us to confirm that now.'

Carrick thought for a moment, 'I will keep an eye out. They know where the warriors are gathering. When they see we are gone, that should be where they head for, but I no longer know if it would be safe to trust any news they might have. We must doubt everyone now.'

'Take care Carrick, my friend.' Kariss gave the tracker's hand a squeeze. 'Stay safe.' She longed to throw her arms around him and hold him tight, but she felt certain that he would have recoiled had she tried.

'This is what I do best,' he said. 'I am a spy and a tracker and I am very good at it. On my own I can move quicker and quieter than almost anyone.'

Torwain grinned and clapped him on the shoulder.

Carrick rolled his eyes, 'Apart from a druid, I know.'

'You can call upon the gods anytime you need them. Cernunous will be a great help to you in moving unseen.'

Carrick clasped his arm then turned to Naraic and ruffled his hair. 'Remember all I taught you, and keep this shaggy hound by your side at all times.' To the others he grinned, raised a hand, turned and headed away, with only his ghosts for company. He had never been any good at farewells.

Only a short distance on, the group came across a small cluster of roundhouses. Sounds of hammering could be heard, rhythmic and numerous, though they could not see where from. A small distance away from the houses, a number of small chimneys with fat potbellied bases were smoking away merrily, attended by three men. As they crept closer, the air took on a strange smell.

'It is a copper mine,' Torwain whispered. 'Hopefully they will be too busy to notice us, but we should keep to the cover of those trees over there just to be safe.'

They passed by without mishap, and shortly after they left the strange rock formation behind. The trees grew taller again and dominated the land, which folded down into a steep-sided gill. Beneath their feet the grasses were full of clover. Bees hovered amongst the flowers and their droning gave the area a feeling of peace and safety. They stopped for a short rest near the base of the gill. A small lively brook gave them their first sweet water since they had fled the village. They did not dare linger, though. Whilst Cailleach had led them safely out of Carvettii lands, and Torwain had covered their tracks as only a druid could, they knew Martaani would not take her failure easily. She would be sending out soldiers in every direction, trying to find them.

Hawthorn leaves had sustained them most of the morning, but by late afternoon hunger forced them to stop. Once again they found themselves up on high land. The trees had given way to open moors and rolling hills spreading out in all directions, offering breath-taking views. Garth and Naraic soon caught a brace of woodcock, which Anniel roasted over a small fire. They ate them with ramsons and pignuts. They were uncomfortable; the moorland had few enough shrubs for cover, so they doused the fire, covered the burnt ground with torn-up clumps of wiry grass, and began to walk again.

They stopped only when the sun had set and the cloud-filled sky allowed no light through from the hidden stars. Unsurprisingly, Torwain knew this area well; he regaled them with stories of the many natural wonders the land had to offer. Shafts opening up in the ground, like rocky chimneys taking rivulets of water down into the earth. A dangerous place in the dark, he told them. Each opening was deep enough to ensure anyone falling in would not be able to get back out. Further on, he said, was a fall of water that cascaded over a cliff face and plunged straight down into a deep pool. He had often swum there, letting the sacred water cleanse him.

He spoke of the land as if it were an old friend. His words conjured up clear pictures of the places he described. If the circumstances had been different, they would have taken the time to detour and visit them. But even though swimming in such a pool could only be beneficial to them right now, they simply could not afford the time. Kariss hid a smile as she watched the druid speaking. It was very clever, she thought, to fill their minds with such tales. To encourage the magic of the land to chase away their fears whilst they rested.

The following morning, Anniel woke them just before dawn. No one was happy about rising, they were aching and foot-sore, but they were still too frightened of being caught by Martaani to complain.

'Who were you arguing about when the spies were getting ready to leave yesterday?' Kariss asked Anniel as they followed a stream down into another gill.

He glanced over to Garth, who shrugged his shoulders. 'She will have to know sooner or later.'

Intrigued, Kariss prodded her husband. 'Tell me.'

Anniel sighed. 'Alright, but you're not going to like it.' He helped her over a fallen log and waited until the others were over.

'Your cousins have not all been as loyal as we would have hoped. The eldest one, Taratus, has given people cause to worry.'

Kariss remembered a boy not much taller than she was, though a few years older. He had a crop of tight, dark curls and dark, intense eyes. Apart from an annoying habit of thinking he was always right, she couldn't think of anything that she hadn't liked about him. As children, they had played together all the time, along with his sister Faela, and quite often their younger brother, Dimmi, as well. It all seemed so long ago now.

'It seems that he has been seen talking with a number of Votadini, known to be friendly with Rome over the last few months, and he had been seen in Stanwick just before Carrick arrived.' He paused for a moment and watched as the sky grew ever lighter. 'Word is that he will be bringing men from Wendell to the Gathering to support you, but no matter what he says, we cannot trust him.'

Kariss looked at the others, and back to Anniel. 'But he has spent all his life in Brigantia, surely he cannot side with Martaani?'

'Kinithu's spies have been watching him for a long time,' Garth told her, 'ever since he was seen in Traprain Law meeting with Inida, the king of the Votadini.'

'What about the others, Faela and little Dimmi? Have they turned against me too?'

'We simply do not know,' Anniel said. 'It is one of the things we were hoping to find out when the scouts returned.'

That day had been long and hot. Kariss could not remember much about it besides the relentless walking. She didn't even have the energy to worry about Anniel's words. It was all she could do to keep putting one foot in front of the other.

The moon was just returning from her dark phase, but the stars provided enough light to keep going long after night fell. The high ground was well behind them now, though the land was still dominated by low, rolling hills. Large rocks started to appear, looming out of the darkness. Stars blinked in and out in the distance as yet more craggy shapes seemed to move eerily across the horizon. A white shape swooped. Right above their heads it let out a screech that sent their blood cold. Torwain laughed, 'Screech owl,' he told them. 'We are being welcomed.' He pointed to a sheltered area where one of the rocks formed an overhang that was almost a small cave.

'This is Barmr Craggs,' he told them with a grin.

They looked around in awe as Torwain reached into the back of the shelter and brought out a pile of dry kindling.

'Of course, this is only the very outskirts of the craggs,' he explained. 'I cannot take you into their heart.' He set about laying the fire. When the flames were cracking nicely, he stood.

'I have to leave you here for tonight, I must go into the craggs and speak with the gods, but I will be back in the morning with food. You need have no fear. You will be safe enough and will need no guard tonight, no one can approach here without the gods' knowledge. You must promise not to wander until I return.' He waved a hand at them, 'Sleep well.'

The weary travellers were not sorry to stay put and rest. Tawny owls hooted from the cover of nearby trees, and screech owls flew low over their heads, searching for voles. Nothing could make them feel safer. As hungry as they were, they lay down around the fire and slept.

30

Torwain made his way into the heart of the craggs. He had not expected to hear the call of Cernunous yet. After what Verbia had told him he had assumed, regretfully, that his god would stay silent for much longer. So it was with some trepidation that he made his way into the heart of the rocks. The moon was only the merest sliver in the sky, so he had only the stars and his senses to guide him, but he knew this place well, and the darkness did not deter him.

Deep within the mysterious towering rock formations, the gods could approach with ease without the risk of interruption. Torwain had never learnt the reason behind their preference for stone but all across Albion, caves, rocky outcrops and such-like were known to be magnets for the gods. Many hundreds of years ago, man had learnt of this connection and had moved huge boulders into circles, shaping the rock to suit their needs. In these places, the people worshipped in ceremonies as old as time itself, celebrating the spiritual connections they could feel, even if they could not see them.

It did not take long for Cernunous to appear. The faint shadow of his antlers stretched out across the earthen floor, reaching towards Torwain like fingers. The druid nodded in greeting, conscious now of his clothing. In his haste, he had forgotten about it. Quickly, he shrugged himself out of his robe and faced Cernunous as naked as the god himself was. For Cernunous was the god of nature and he delighted in each creature's pride in their own bodies. He saw no sense in man's growing discomfiture of his nakedness. Clothing was merely for warmth. In the summer, therefore, there was no need for it.

He waved his hand, indicating that they should sit. Cross-legged, they faced each other. As ever, Torwain was filled with awe. Cernunous was as virile as any man could wish to be. Even the atmosphere around him seemed to crackle with power. His head was adorned with a set of antlers that would make any stag proud to bear them. Amongst the tines hung a pair of golden torcs, symbolising the wealth he also represented. Around his waist, two-horned serpents coiled themselves. They were not snakes Torwain had ever seen in Albion but then Cernunous was known to inhabit many more lands than just this isle. When he spoke, his voice was deep and resonating. Torwain could never be sure if his ears actually heard the words or if his body simple felt them.

'You have done well, my friend,' the god said. He reached up and unhooked one of the torcs. Placing it around the druid's neck, he smiled. 'There is much to be proud of, but there is much yet to come. You are being hunted and will need all your wits about you if you are to survive.'

The metal sizzled with energy, Torwain could feel it tingling on his skin. He had never heard of such a gift given before. He was not convinced that he had earned it but there was no time to worry about that now. Cernunous's words were all that mattered. As usual they were puzzling, wrapped up in the lesson he needed to work out. This god was not one to give everything that was needed, nor was he one to listen to idle questions. It was up to the listener to work out the whole story. Life was a lesson that never ended.

Torwain thought long and hard. He knew they were still being hunted, Martaani was never going to give in and wait to meet Kariss at the midsummer Gathering. So why would his god have called him here to tell him something that he already knew? It came to him in a rush. Cernunous had never mentioned Kariss, or any of the others. It could only mean that Torwain was the one now facing the net closing in around him. The others were not the ones in danger here. For that at least, he was grateful. He wondered if this was how Maponus had told Darnus or how Cailleach had told Dei.

Death did not frighten Torwain, he knew it was simply the gateway to ultimate peace. It was the end of living that he feared. He felt so alive, so connected to the countryside and all the beings around him. He had no wish for that to end any time soon. In his desperation to cling to life, he went over what Cernunous had said once more. Two words echoed loudly in his mind: *to survive*. Those words were not there by accident, Cernunous had been giving him a lifeline.

The god waited patiently, watching the bats as they flitted around them. The interplay of the hunter and the hunted, the stillness of caution and the flight of fear; these were all things that the god understood well. The bats were adept at finding food, using skills far beyond the understanding of their prey. Torwain now faced similar unfathomable skills. Cernunous only hoped he had learnt enough in his years alone in the wilderness, because there was only so much help he could give him now.

'It is no coincidence that I am speaking to you here, is it?' Torwain eventually asked.

Cernunous smiled. 'It is not. This is the only place safe enough to give you this information now that the Roman gods have been invoked in Brigantia. They are getting stronger day by day. The priests with Martaani have performed a number of rites and increased their gods' powers here.'

'That would mean Cailleach was waiting to lead us to the water-rock springs, all the while knowing that I would make the connection with the one south of here.'

Cernunous nodded. 'And in doing so, you would have to pass by the craggs and I would be waiting to give you the news you needed to hear.'

Torwain's mind was reeling. How could the gods be so sure of them?

'Because we know you better than you know yourselves,' Cernunous answered. 'You talk to us all the time in your mind, is it so hard to believe therefore, that we know what you are feeling?' He paused. 'I know you did not want this task, Torwain. I know you wanted to stay out in the wilderness, living like an animal. I believe you also know that you could have indeed done that. You were not forced to take this path, only guided to it. Even now you could choose to walk away, though I do not know if that would save you.'

Torwain shook his head adamantly, he would never walk away. He was almost offended at the suggestion until the god's last words sunk in. 'Then the priests have me in their sights?'

Cernunous nodded, his eyes full of concern. 'We believe so. Their spies have told them that a wild druid is helping Kariss. They know you have powers beyond their abilities, and they are very frightened of you. For a while they believed Darnus was the one, but...' he let his voice trail away. After a moment he added: 'He did not disgrace himself. He died well, and gave enough time for Cailleach to lead you all away.'

Like a stab from an icy spear, fear launched itself through Torwain. The god pointed a hand and one of his serpents unwound itself from his body and crossed over to Torwain. The touch of the snake's skin on his own brought such an overwhelming calm that Torwain was no longer afraid. He let the snake wander unchecked over his body, finally settling around his upper arm. Torwain now found he was full of self-reproach.

'There is no shame in fear, Torwain,' Cernunous scolded. 'Fear keeps you sharp: without it, you would never survive. You must feel it again before too long, but for now let it rest. You are still important to this quest, you will be needed again before it is all over, but your way ahead is no longer clear to us. It is a problem we had not foreseen. I cannot tell you if you will live or if you will die.'

Far away, a wolf cried, the haunting sound echoing amongst the rocks. Torwain listened for replies. Was it a lone wolf, or one of a pack? For a long time there was silence then another wolf answered, quickly followed by two more. The calls rose and fell on the night air as the young family sang together. It gave Torwain an idea.

'If the way ahead is not clear, it suggests I need to stay hidden. It is the most sensible thing to do, and the one thing that everyone will expect.' He toyed with the torc as he spoke. 'I may be the hunted one, but I can use that to our advantage, and keep their eyes away from Kariss.'

Cernunous listened carefully, his head tilted slightly to the side, causing the one remaining torc in his antlers to catch in the starlight.

'I can find Martaani's men easily enough, they have no idea how to traverse our woods. They are noisy and unafraid of the people they believe to be beneath them. I will let myself be seen, or at least let my presence be known. While they waste time searching for me, thinking Kariss will be close by, I will be gone, on to the next place. They will be so busy chasing ghosts that they will not have time for anything else.'

'That is a courageous plan, my friend, and it could well be why we could not see your path clearly. But it will be fraught with danger, are you really prepared for that?'

Torwain gripped the torc, a sardonic smile spreading across his face, 'And which path won't be?'

Cernunous laughed; a low, throaty sound that resonated through the enclosed space. 'You have seen right through me, I have indeed given you this torc so that I can keep a closer eye on you. No matter which path you choose to take.'

'You have taught me well all these years, so this is the path I choose. If I hold their eye, then let me take their vision far from Kariss; if I am to be hunted, then let them hunt me where I am strongest; if I am to be the next one killed, then let it be on my own ground.'

Cernunous bowed his head to his druid, hiding a proud smile. Torwain still had the power to surprise him. Torwain noticed that the snake was no longer around his arm. He had not felt it leave yet there it was, back around the god's waist. Its unblinking eye was watching him as they turned to mist, and vanished from sight.

All at once, the air seemed lighter, empty. He closed his eyes and went over the conversation once more. His fear was still there, like a dusting of snow on an early winter's morning. Now, though, it was tempered with an intense excitement and he wondered if Verbia had some connection with the serpent. Maybe it had even been her in disguise? He smiled to himself. He would not be a victim to the Romans and their iconoclastic ways. He was going to be as much of a nuisance to them as he possibly could.

The only thing to vitiate his enthusiasm was the worry about what would happen to Kariss now. He had developed a lot of respect for her in the short time he had known her, and he had grown especially fond of Naraic. The boy would have made a great druid. Whilst he knew he had to leave, surprisingly, a part of him wanted to stay and keep them safe. It was not his place to question the gods, but he regretted not asking what the plan now was to keep them safe.

Sometime near dawn, Kariss woke with a start. Her heart was racing, and she was trembling. Her dream faded quickly. Try as she might, she could not recall what had caused the fear. Unable to lie there any longer, she crept out of bed and tiptoed to a nearby slab of rock. The air was still and warm, it was going to be another muggy day. She sat looking at the horizon for a long time. Focusing on her breath, she forced her worries away from her. Telling herself that all that mattered was this moment, this breath. She was aware of the air in her nostrils as she inhaled, and felt her chest rise and fall. Gradually, her body calmed, her mind stilled, and the stresses of the last few days fell away. In this meditative state she found her peace, and she let it fill her with its restorative glow.

The sounds of the countryside coming awake eventually filtered into her consciousness. A little way off, by the edge of a small copse of hazel trees, a white shape flew close to the ground. The screech owl was hunting in the faint dawn light. She watched as it hovered for a second before diving headfirst. Just before it reached the rough grass, it thrust its legs forward and plunged onto its prey. From this distance it looked virtually all white. It took to the air, a vole dangling from its talons. Kariss smiled, he must be hunting for his family.

Suddenly she was a young girl sitting atop the protective earthen bank on the eastern side of Wendell Fort with her cousin, Taratus. They had sneaked out of their respective houses early to watch the sunrise. They too had seen a screech owl hunting.

'See how light it is,' he told her, 'that means it is probably a male bird.'

'How do you know?' she asked, full of awe.

'There was a dead one in the spinney down by

the river a while back, Kel showed it me, and told me all about them. Look, he is catching food for his family.' Taratus took hold of her hand. 'I will always look after you, too,' he said, with the seriousness of a child.

A hand touched her shoulder and she jumped, brought back to the present with a jolt. Torwain stood there, looking concerned. She smiled, dashing away tears she hadn't realised were falling.

'I was thinking about my cousin, Taratus,' she said quietly. 'Something just reminded me of him.'

Torwain laid the dead roe deer he was carrying on the ground and sat down beside her. 'Many years have passed since you last saw each other. You cannot know the things that may have changed him.'

'We always talked as if we would be married when we grew up. Silly children's stuff really, but I was thinking about the day he promised to always look after me.' She managed a weak smile. 'I never expected the marriage, but I did think we would still be friends.'

31

The deer made for the best food they had eaten in days, and they set off for the last leg of their journey in fine spirits. The rocks grew larger the further they walked. Some of them seemed to defy all logic as they took on the strangest of shapes. Torwain led the way, steering clear of the sacred inner temple. Even this outer area was normally taboo for non-druids, but there was no time to take a wider route.

Kariss could feel how charged the air was; she thought back to the rocks in the park where she had met with Cailleach and then ended her London life. They had held the same feeling; it was as if the place knew magic. The huge waterfall where they had met the druid Rurann had felt the same. It was much stronger than what she felt every time she went near a stone circle. That reverence was more for the ceremonies that went on there, rather than for the place itself. These wild places, though, were full of natural power and it was breath-taking. She felt for Anniel's hand, and grasped it firmly.

It was just after midday that they reached the ravine. Torwain had led them a circuitous route to avoid passing any of the local inhabitants. Soon enough, though, he led them down through the dense trees to where the river flowed freely over a gravel bed, burbling pleasantly. Tired feet rejoiced at the cooling water, which came no deeper than mid-calf height as they crossed to the far bank. Back into the trees they were soon hidden again but they kept the river in sight as they followed its course. The trees on the far bank began to be dominated by patches of dense shrubbery and here and there the reddish rock of a hidden cliff face showed through.

'You will be safe enough here,' Torwain explained. 'So long as you are careful. There are forces here, too strong to ignore.'

Anniel looked sharply at him, 'Are you not staying with us?'

To everyone's dismay the druid shook his head, 'Alas, I cannot. The news I was given at Barmr Craggs makes it too dangerous for you to be near me just now.' He pointed up into the trees, 'We are here.'

Ahead of them, they could just make out an area of rock. Dominating it was a massive patch of smooth stone forming an overhang. Water poured over it from above, gathering into a small pool where it met the ground.

'Not much of a cave,' Naraic said, looking at the wet space behind the falls.

Torwain laughed. 'That is the reason you will not be disturbed here.' Turning to the side, he pointed to a small cave opening in the dry rock nearby. 'The water here is magic, it makes stone. When the stone builds up too much, the water diverts elsewhere.'

The cave was dark but dry inside, with plenty of room for them all, though the roof sloped down sharply towards the back, making standing impossible. A fire could be lit by the entrance when it grew too dark to see so even if the nights were chilly, they would not suffer.

'How on earth did you find it?' Kariss asked him. Torwain was full of surprises, she was sorry he would be leaving them.

'Many years ago a family from a nearby village came to live close by. The parents would collect water from the well on the top of the rock to drink, but their young son did not like the taste and only drank water from the river, which is known as the Brilliant River. They had been here for a few moons when they noticed the bucket they left in the well was starting to turn to stone. Soon after, the parents grew sick and died. The villagers saw the stone bucket and they thought the well was cursed. They gave the boy to the druids and fled the area. After he had grown and left the nemetons, the boy, now a druid, came back to see if his memories were true. He recognised the magic of the place and stayed. When the waters moved away from the cave, he made it his home. He lived a great many years, but he never drank the water from the spring. I met him the first winter I followed Cernunous into the wilds; he was very old then and did not have long left to live.'

Naraic shook his head in disbelief. 'Water cannot turn to stone,' he said. 'That is just a story.'

Torwain walked back to the pool. A branch was poking out of the water, he pulled it free. The part that had been immersed was now stone. 'The druid used to put all sorts of things into the water and they would all turn to stone sooner or later. It is not the thing that changes, but the water around it. Otherwise, this whole branch would be stone now.' He shrugged. 'Then again, who knows. Maybe there is still a wooden branch inside the stone one, maybe not.' He glanced up at the sky, the day was marching on. 'I must leave you now, but I will see you again at the Gathering.' He turned to leave.

'Wait!' Kariss ran after him. Of the seven druids that she had been told to trust, two were now dead, two were trapped in Stanwick, and one was far away in the north and goodness knows where the last one was. She was not going to let Torwain go without good reason. 'I know I shouldn't question the gods, but why must you leave? What is so important that you cannot stay? We are all in danger, why not face it together? Let us help you.'

Torwain took her face in his grubby hands and lightly kissed her forehead. 'I am afraid Martaani's priests have me in their sights. They are going to tear this countryside apart looking for me, so I am going to make it easy for them.'

Cloud whined and jumped up at the druid, standing on his back legs as he licked at his arms. Torwain gave his ears one last scratch. 'Stay out of danger,' he told him, 'and keep an eye on this lot for me.' He pushed the dog gently down and began shedding his robe. Once it was gone, he stood before them wearing nothing but the golden torc around his neck. It was the first time the others had noticed it. Torwain explained why Cernunous had given it to him. 'I am going back to the wilderness. I am going to haunt Martaani's men until they do not know where to turn. I will keep them so busy that they have no time to hunt for you.'

There was nothing any of them could say to change his mind. Kariss stood with tears in her eyes. 'Promise me you will stay safe.' He smiled at her and winked.

Anniel stepped forward and grasped his arm. 'Stay safe, we do not want to lose any more friends.'

Garth in turn said his goodbyes then Naraic, tearful and trying hard to hide his misery, came forward and hugged the man who had saved him from Martaani. Torwain had not hugged anyone since he was a child. He was more touched than he could ever have imagined. He found himself blinking hard, and had to force himself to pull away.

'Keep to the ravine until the last moment, unless you hear anything else,' he told them all. 'You will make Stanwick in two days, easily.' Glancing up, he saw Cailleach, perched on a high branch in her raven guise. Relieved to know they were still being watched, he hardened his heart and turned his thoughts forward. 'Until then you should be safe here.' He smiled at the sorry faces looking at him, a wicked gleam now in his eyes. 'Cheer up, I am going to have fun.'

With that he was gone, blending in with the woodland in a trice. Cloud whimpered and curled up on the pile of clothes Torwain had left. It was a subdued group that set about making the cave a home for the next half-moon.

32

The overnight rain had refreshed the landscape. It had been almost a moon since the last rains had fallen, and the earth was cracking in the heat. A layer of dust had built up over everything, plants had drooped, and the smaller streams had been slowly drying up. Now the land was vibrant again. The wilting plants reached once more towards the sky, the streams ran with renewed vigour, and everywhere was washed clean of dust and grime. Kel sighed. This used to be one of his favourite times. In his younger days he would go out into the woods, shed his clothes, and dance as the rain fell around him. He would imagine that he could hear the land drinking its fill. In later times, he would be happy just to be outside watching as the earth woke, replenished. This morning, though, the sight did not move him as it should. It served only to reinforce how decrepit he had become. He had struggled out of his hard bed to stand as he always did and greet the dawning of the day, but each day was getting harder and harder. Air hunger made his breathing laboured; stiffness made his movements awkward; pain ate away at what little energy remained to him. The rain held no rejuvenating powers for him now, and he was too tired to even be sad about it.

His watery eyes took in the sights of Wendell one last time. It had been a good home. He was about to turn and go back inside when a movement caught his attention. Umar and Faela were walking the boundary, deep in conversation. Kel sighed again, but this time there was a smile playing on his lips. Knowledge was a wonderful thing; it could add purpose to defeat.

Last night, his final night, Nantosuelta had blessed Kel with the truth. Everything that had happened to him over the last thirty-odd years had been directly orchestrated by the gods. They had needed the child of a druid to be raised as a disciple of Belatucadros. That child must be tormented by events beyond his control, and strong enough to use that pain to drive himself far beyond that of an ordinary druid. For this, they had kept Kel on the edge of Umar's life, creating an awkward relationship that never had the chance to develop fully into either love or hatred. Umar had developed exactly as they had hoped. When the time came, he would not quail at his task. Kel, Nantosuelta had told him, should be immensely proud of his son.

Kel had always been proud of Umar. He would have been proud even if he had failed at everything he had tried to do. He watched his son now, taking in the familiar gait of his walk, and the wild gesticulations he made as he talked. Even at this distance he could make out the usual seriousness of his features. Umar was not one to smile easily, for all his eccentric behaviour.

Until this moment the old druid had always held conflicting emotions where his son was concerned. Whilst he loved him dearly, and found a certain amusement in his comedic behaviour, he also felt an uneasy shame at his son's unconventionality. It stabbed at his conscience, because he had viewed it as his failing as a father. His son would not have been the eccentric that needed to set himself apart from his fellow druids if only he had had his father around to nurture him as he grew. Now, finally, his guilt was gone, and he could look at his son with unblinkered eyes. Years of shame had given way to the comfort of knowing just how important his sacrifice had been.

He took a deep breath, dragged his eyes away from his son, and shuffled back inside. The dimness blinded him for a few moments and he leaned on his sticks, waiting for his sight to adjust. The centre of the room was taken by a small hearth, the glowing embers sat waiting for more fuel. Using the last of his energy, he bent and added a good helping of sticks. His breathing was becoming laboured, there was not long to go now. By the side of his bed, a box sat ready. It held his few precious possessions: a clear quartz point, wrapped in a fine bronze wire; a stone carving of his goddess, Nantosuelta, holding her tall staff upon which a tiny birdhouse sat; a small kidskin, grown grubby over time, that Umar's mother used to wrap him in as a baby; a short length of willow, which had been Umar's teething stick; and a lock of downy fine hair, that Kel had taken from his son on the day they were parted. Kel stroked the lid fondly, knowing everything was safe. He lay down on the bed and pulled a blanket over him. Despite the warmth of the morning, he was feeling chilled. Casting another look around the room, he nodded in satisfaction. There was nothing more to do except wait. She would be coming for him soon.

On the east side of the fort, an elm tree had

come down in the night. The huge trunk now spanned the moat, giving easy access for anyone wanting to get inside Wendell's defences unseen. Taratus and a group of men were hard at work, trying to clear the moat whilst trying to save as much precious wood as possible. They had already removed all the upper branches and those on the top side of the trunk. Now they were attempting to split the bole. The sound of them hammering in the wedges echoed up to where Faela and Umar stood watching.

'Of all the times for this to happen,' Faela said.

'Have no doubt, gods had a hand in this.' Umar looked up at the calm sky. 'The weather last night was not bad enough to bring down a sapling, never mind such a mighty elm. Let us hope it was our gods' work and not the Romans.'

Faela looked sharply at him, 'Do you not know?'

'Belatucadros does not concern himself with such trivial matters,' Umar told her. 'Kel would be the one to ask about this.'

An almighty splintering sound ripped through the air as the elm split down the grain. The men balancing on the side limbs leapt to the bank before they fell into the water. The split was clean, running from top to bottom, missing the remaining branches, and they were able to drag the top side of the tree onto the far bank. Taratus flung himself down on the grass and called the men to rest. It would take them all day, splitting slices away and hauling them from the moat.

Shael came up beside them, her hands full of mullein leaves, ready for stripping down into candle wicks. She looked down at her husband. 'It is good that he has something to work his anger off with.'

'He is angry again?' Faela frowned. Taratus was always a serious child, but he had never been one for a temper. Over the last year, though, his moods had become more and more unpredictable.

'He was supposed to set off for Stanwick at first light.'

'My brother has been spending a lot of time at Stanwick of late.'

Shael's shoulders drooped. 'If I am honest, his absences grow more tolerable. He has not been easy to be around these last moons and it is only getting worse.'

Faela nodded her head. 'I have never known him to be like this, and this ire at Kariss... I have been secretly hoping that she does not turn up here after all, much that I would dearly love to see her again.'

Surreptitiously, Umar took in every word. He had sensed some bad blood between the siblings, but he had not realised the man's behaviour was so out of character. Ideas were forming in his head. He needed to speak with his father. He made his excuses and left the women.

As he walked, he felt a small frisson run up his spine and into his hair. His senses were immediately alert to the warning and he quickened his step. Kel lived slightly apart from the rest of the houses in the fort. Where they were large and spacious, Kel's was small and compact, with a tidy herb garden growing outside. In his old age, the druid had begun to spend all of his time in the fort. He could no longer manage the walk into the woods to his retreat, but he refused to move into a more comfortable house. His solitude was too important to him, and his small flock respected it. Only when his door covering was open were they free to approach.

Smoke was still filtering through the thatch but as Umar neared, two crows flew out of the doorway and circled overhead. There was no mistaking whose birds they were. Inside, his worst fears were confirmed. Nantosuelta stood at the head of the bed. In her right hand she held her tall pole with its small birdhouse perched on top. Her left hand rested on Kel's forehead. The man himself was peaceful in his demise. Umar leaned forward and gently closed his eyelids. Never again would those eyes look at him with ill-concealed guilt.

'You never had anything to be regretful of,' he told him, his soft voice barely louder than a whisper. 'You could have left me to flounder, but you didn't. You took me to the one person you trusted to look after me.' He glared up at the goddess. 'It was the gods that drove the woman to suicide, the gods who needed to take me for their great Albion-saving plan.' His emotions bubbled up inside him as he spoke, filling him with the remorse he had tried so hard to bury over the years. 'Their selfish, selfish plan,' he said more forcefully, kicking the bed with every syllable.

Nantosuelta did not reply. Tears welled up in Umar's eyes as he watched his father failing to breathe. 'This place was supposed to be your reward, the honour of serving the mighty Kariss's home. Did you ever even know?' He glared at Nantosuelta again. She nodded her head but remained compassionately silent.

Umar looked back at his father, his anger gone as quickly as it had arrived. Dropping to his knees, he took hold of his hand. The skin rolled loosely over the bones within and his nails were grubby with earth. Umar glanced around and saw a basket by the door, in which meadowsweet and marigold cuttings lay wilting. 'I could have done that for you,' Umar told him, 'I should have done so much more for you.' The tears fell in earnest now. 'Why did you not let me know how sick you were?' He squeezed Kel's bony hand as if he could pump life back into him.

All his days he had been unable to cut through the barrier the gods had forged between them. Their relationship had been stiff with formalities and withheld emotions. Now that barrier had come crashing down and with it came everything he had held in reserve. It was a shock. Umar had always held himself so tightly, he had forgotten the feelings his younger self had locked away inside. Now those feelings poured out of him. His own guilt at the sacrifice his father had been forced to endure was something he had refused to recognise, even in private. He rocked back and forth on his knees, crying barely audible tears of grief. No one in Wendell approached the little dwelling place. The door was now covered, they had no way of knowing what was occurring inside.

Do it now.
I cannot.
You must.
It is too much for the man to bear.

It is necessary.
It is cruel.
It is necessary. It is for Albion.

Unhappily, Nantosuelta finally accepted what the other gods were saying to her. This part was down to her, she pushed her misgivings aside and stamped her foot. 'Stop this nonsense at once!'

Umar barely heard her.

'What is done is done.' She raised her voice until it filled the conical room, though not a trace of it could be heard from outside. 'Do not concern yourself with these silly intricacies. Your father would be ashamed of you, wailing on the floor like a child.' Her face was a mask of stone, so unlike the goddess her druids knew and loved.

The room had taken on an oppressive air. Umar sat on the floor, bewildered at her anger.

'He has known he was dying for many moons. Did he send word to you? Did he make any attempt to see you?' Umar was too stunned to answer her. Where was the compassionate goddess of a few minutes ago?

'You are here for other reasons, remember that.' Nantosuelta continued her scolding. 'Your father lived believing you did not care. Have the decency to let him rest now in the same knowledge. To do otherwise would cause his spirit great unrest. How cruel a man are you, Umar?'

For once in his life, the druid was lost for words. How could his love possibly cause his father unrest?

'I do not need to hear you speak to know your words, Umar. Your father loved you beyond measure. His greatest regret in life was that you did not return such feelings. What parent could live happily, knowing their child failed to care? To learn of your love now, when it is too late...' her words hung in the air, needing no further clarification. 'Your actions are your own doing. If you feel regret then it is of your own making. You will carry your penitence with you for all your days.' She looked down at Kel and gently stroked the side of his face before looking back at Umar, her eyes bright with tears. 'I hope it festers.'

Umar felt his face burn with shame as he looked down at his father's hand, still clasped in his own. Though he longed to kiss the papery skin, to hold it to his face and claim a closeness that had never existed in life, he slowly, and with great care, placed the hand onto the bed and got to his feet.

'You must leave this place now, Umar.'

'But what of his funeral? I must be allowed to conduct the ceremony, surely?' His voice wavered. Even a druid of such standing could not face the wrath of a god without quailing.

'Be gone from this place,' Nantosuelta was almost shouting now. 'Be gone and do not return. Your father will be interred by those who loved him. That was not you! Your time here is done.'

With a last lingering look at his father, Umar backed from the room. All attempts at decorum forgotten, he stumbled away. After so long in the dim room, the sunlight was almost blinding.

Nantosuelta watched him go, her heart heavy with remorse. *It is done,* she told the watching gods.

Umar could hear a voice calling him, and for a moment he thought the goddess had followed him.

The voice called again, and a hand touched his shoulder. He flinched, but it was only Faela.

She eyed him warily, she had not forgotten his strange behaviour when they first met, but his red eyes betrayed him.

'Whatever is the matter?'

Umar grabbed her arm. 'Quickly,' he hissed, pulling her along with him. Once inside his quarters he began hurriedly throwing his belongings into his bag. 'I must go,' he told her, his urgency leaving her in no doubt that something was strangely amiss.

She pulled a face. She had lost her annoyance at the druid over the last few days, but still, he had a habit of making the people around him feel uncomfortable.

'I cannot explain, but you must promise to meet me at Stanwick.'

Faela had not expected such a demand and she was about to refuse when he took hold of her shoulders and shook her. 'Promise me.' His voice was filled with a passion that alarmed her. 'You could be in danger, I do not know.' He flapped his arms over his head to indicate his confusion. 'For some reason you were marked out for me to find, but now I must leave before I have learnt why.' He grabbed her again. 'Promise me!'

'I, I, I... will,' she stammered. He was starting to frighten her. 'But why? I am nothing to Kariss now. What can I possibly have to do with all this?'

'This is bigger than all of us, the gods in their wisdom have used some of us in ways which we would rather they had not.' He hurled the last item in his bag and threw a glance at the few remaining lobsters he had left in the bucket by the door. 'You can eat those. I have no time to sort them now.'

Faela was still reeling from his admission. She had never heard a druid speak dispassionately about the gods before. 'What do you mean about the gods?'

Umar turned back to her and let out an exasperated breath. In his distressed state, he had said more than he should and now he was going to have to form some sort of explanation. 'What I tell you now goes no further.'

Faela nodded her head.

'I cannot tell you much.' He took a quick look outside to make sure they would not be overheard. On seeing no one, he continued. 'There is a reason your druid Kel was placed here. It is all to do with Kariss, as was my reason for coming here, but now Kel has passed away and Nantosuelta has bid me leave.'

Faela let out a cry of alarm.

'It was peaceful,' Umar reassured her. 'Nantosuelta was with him at the end, and is with him even now. I, however, need to leave...' He held a hand up to stop her as she made to speak. 'I can say no more than that; already I have said far more than I ought. But you must do everything you can to try and find out why the gods have an interest in you.'

A noise from outside made them jump and Umar wiped his hand across his face. He needed to be alone. Making for the door, he had one last parting comment. 'Speak to no one of this. Look for me at Stanwick, and watch your back. There is something we cannot see yet, we may not know what it is until the last moment.'

33

A blackbird flew scolding through the trees, frightened from its perch by the boy creeping through the woods. At the cave, they were immediately on the alert. Anniel and Garth stood forward of Kariss and drew their swords. Cloud crouched low, his hackles raised in warning. A low growl rumbled from him, not loud enough to hear from any distance but menacing all the same. All of a sudden the sound stopped and his tail thumped the floor. He rushed forward to greet Naraic as he emerged from the trees. Everyone relaxed.

'There is someone in that little cave down the river,' Naraic told them. 'A man. On his own, I think.'

'Did he see you?'

Naraic shook his head. 'I don't think so. I was careful. He was bathing in the river, splashing about. So I heard him before I saw him. I could not tell if he were a Brigante or a Roman. I waited and watched, but he walked back to the cave naked.'

'We must find out,' Garth said, sheathing his sword. 'If he is Roman, there will be more of them.' He looked at Anniel, 'If I am not back by midday, get yourselves away.'

The small cave cut into the base of the rock wall was only a few steps from the river and prone to flooding when the waters ran high. Garth had been inside it once before, there was not much room, barely enough for one person. A pair of nervous does had watched him as he made his way down the river, a sure sign that no one else was hiding nearby. Still, he would not relax his guard until he knew for certain who the stranger was. He waited, dagger in hand, the summer undergrowth giving him plenty of cover on the wooded bank. Whoever it was clearly felt no threat. He was making no attempt to be silent. Garth could hear a single voice echoing inside the stony vault. The words were too indistinct to make out, but their tone implied the speaker was agitated.

All of a sudden a naked man burst out of the cave, threw back his head, and let out a holler. Garth was so shocked, he lurched backwards into a patch of angry thistles. He winced as the spines sunk into his flesh. The man looked his way. Garth kept his head low and cursed his stupidity.

'Who is there?' the stranger called, his accent reminiscent of Torwain's.

Garth relaxed somewhat; not a Roman then, but he kept his grip firm on the dagger nonetheless. The man had the body of a warrior, he could still be trouble. Garth stayed hidden as the man took a few steps towards him then paused. Calmly, the stranger crouched down, keeping his eyes looking ahead. All of a sudden, he rushed forward, stout stick in hand, yelling like a madman. Garth leapt to his feet, ready to defend himself. There was no time to draw his sword now, the man was almost upon him.

Surprisingly, he stopped a few feet away. Holding the stick like a baton, he glared at Garth. 'Name yourself,' he demanded. 'Why are you spying on me?'

Garth was affronted. He pulled himself up to his

full height. 'Who are you?' he returned. 'Why are you hiding out here?' He looked the man up and down. 'Your voice tells me you are no Roman, but there plenty of reports saying that they are using Albion spies.'

The naked man dropped his arm. 'I am a druid. Just passing through. I thought you were a Roman.'

The two men glowered at one another. On the far river bank a pricket buck bent his head to drink, ignoring them. The men held their breath as it lifted its head, water dripping from its mouth, and let out a loud bark. Stepping into the water, the deer barked again. Then it was off, leaping in graceful bounds until it was out of sight.

The druid threw down the stick and held out a hand. 'My name is Umar,' he said. 'And you must be someone very important. The gods could not be any clearer about that.'

Garth tucked his dagger away and grasped the outstretched arm. 'I am Garth, guard to Anniel of the Vacumagi.' He grinned, 'I did not realise druid's bodies were so fine. I took you for a warrior.'

Umar looked down, as if only now realising he was unclothed. He laughed, 'Then I congratulate you my friend. You stood your ground well. I can only imagine how absurd I must have looked.'

Dressed, with his belongings in hand, Umar made his way through the woods with Garth. They arrived at the cave a short while before midday to find the others packed and ready to flee.

As soon as she heard his name, Kariss relaxed. 'Tell us all you know of what is happening. We have had no news since Torwain left; even before that, we knew very little.'

'I only wish I had more to tell. I have been at your birthplace, Wendell. Led there by Cailleach herself. It would appear that your cousin Faela is a key factor in the balance between you and Martaani.'

Kariss felt her heart drop. 'We had heard it was Taratus who was causing concern, not Faela.'

It seemed to her that there had been no good news for weeks now. Kariss longed to speak with Cailleach for some much-needed reassurance but it was too risky to call her. She had to hold faith that the goddess would come to her when the time was right. She looked round at the bedraggled group. If someone had told her back in London that she was to become the heir of the Brigante people, she would have expected castles and notoriety. Certainly not skulking around in caves, hiding from a ruthless rival. Her eyes flicked to Naraic's right hand. His wound was healing nicely now but every time Kariss saw it, a shiver of regret took hold of her. Naraic himself was much stronger now. He had matured immensely since they had first left Brigantia, all those moons ago. She did not want him to come to Stanwick. She wanted him to stay here where he could be safe. He had protected her when she needed it and now she wanted to do the same for him, but when she had brought up the subject he had been hurt and annoyed. The goddess would not have saved him if he could not be any further use, he had insisted. Besides, he had assured her, if she left him behind, he would only follow.

'I believe,' Umar reassured her, 'that she is very

much in support of you. I could find nothing to suspect otherwise. Her brother, however, is something of an enigma. He is a dutiful man, working hard for his people. Yet we have all heard the rumours; indeed, the man is displaying many unusual behaviours of late. He is very unhappy. I sensed a great deal of turmoil inside him on the brief occasions we met. Though it appeared he went to great lengths to avoid me.' He looked down at his brightly coloured robes and shrugged. 'Faela, on the other hand, was warm and friendly, once she got used to me. Despite questioning, she could think of no reason why the gods had singled her out. Can you?' He pointed at Kariss, his serious face pulling into a frown.

Kariss shook her head. 'She was the best friend I had in Albion before I was taken away. My memories were kept from me then and I only remembered about Wendell and my cousins after I returned.'

'Could she be a target for Martaani, if she found out about your closeness?' said Anniel. 'She is not to know there has been no contact between you.'

Umar clapped his hands together. 'That is my own conclusion.'

'But why?' Naraic asked. 'Martaani would have taken her by now, surely?'

Garth had been quietly listening to the conversation, but now he spoke up. 'She may be Martaani's last hope. If she has not managed to stop us before the Gathering, she will be getting desperate. We must find this woman first and keep her close.'

'Indeed,' Umar agreed.

34

The camp was deserted. The hot ashes in the fire pit and the half-eaten pigeon left slung on the floor suggested they had left in a hurry, and not that long ago.

'Span out, find them!' The Pontiff struggled to hold onto his decorum. He had set out from Dumpender Law four days earlier. His mission there had not been a success. King Inida's wife, Claudia, was dying. The healer had taken one look at her and known immediately. Her body was wasted, her pallor grey, and her breathing slow and laboured. Nothing he could do would save her. Inida had railed and cursed when he saw how much she had deteriorated since he had left her. In just those few days, his wife had become a shell of her former self.

Her eyes flickered open when she heard her husband's voice. She managed a brief smile but refused the food and drink he offered her. Her eyes closed again and she appeared to sleep for a while. The Pontiff moved around the bright room, blowing out most of the candles. He added fragrant herbs to the fire and the floor rushes to cover the smell of incontinence, which hung in the air and clung to the skin.

He rested a hand on Inida's shoulder and said quietly, 'Libitina will come for her shortly.'

'How soon?'

'It is not for me to say. A few days, perhaps, not much more.'

Inida nodded, words were useless to him.

'Try to encourage her to wet her lips at least, but do not force sustenance on her. She has no need of it where she is going.'

Claudia opened her eyes then. They focused on something the two men could not see. 'Mother,' she said, smiling. 'Can I come home now?' She must have received an answer which pleased her for she closed her eyes contentedly. A few moments later, her breathing lightened, and she slept.

The Pontiff had left the following day with a couple of guards to guide him. Inida had no need of him now, though he left the healer there for reassurance. The previous night had been spent at one of the contuberniums in the woods. The Pontiff had no option but to take to one of the leather tents and hope for a good night's sleep. It was not to be, however. The night was dogged with mysterious calls, rogue fires in the near distance, and even one of the tents being cut down onto the sleeping legionaries inside. First light revealed a stake, thrust into the ground at the entrance to the Pontiff's tent. From it hung a dead black raven, the glazed eye staring at the Pontiff as he emerged. His fury was immense. He railed and cursed at the Decanus for keeping such an unruly bunch of men. No legionary worth his salt should have let someone into the heart of their encampment or place such a warning in the ground.

The deserted camp had not been hard to find, being only a few paces from the roadway. The Pontiff stepped carefully, searching the ground. From the indentations on the grass he could see that three people had slept here. With at least one man constantly on watch, that meant a minimum of four. His curiosity was roused; could it be?

High up in a nearby oak, Torwain watched. He was taking a risk, getting so close to the dreaded Pontiff, but from the moment he had realised who the person visiting the camp was he had been intrigued. The raven had been Cailleach's idea. At least, Torwain presumed it had been. The bird, so indicative of that great goddess, had flapped down beside him as he rolled around on the ground to form the imprints of three sleepers. Its eyes were dull, with a film of death over them. Torwain had wasted no time ending its misery. He grinned as he imagined the Pontiff's face when he found it. It was hardly subtle but then these Romans were past the need for such tiptoeing measures.

Beneath him, the Pontiff had seen enough. He barked orders in his native tongue and strode off, his two guards hurrying to catch up. As soon as they were clear, the druid moved lower down the tree to where two stout branches grew out from the trunk. Here he curled himself up and went to sleep. It would be a long time before it was safe to leave his hiding place, and he had been up all night.

The journey back to Stanwick did nothing to improve the Pontiff's temper. He had now spent the best part of eight days in the saddle and his body was protesting. Never one to sit comfortably on a horse, he winced at every pace-change and stumble. The chariot was his preferred mode of transport but here in Albion even a horse was preferable to the bone-jolting ride such rough roads caused. His lip curled at the vulgarity of the place. He had heard it was a beautiful isle but beauty was in the eye of the beholder and he beheld nothing exceptional here. The land was obscurely diverse, making it tricky to navigate, especially amid the plethora of trees. He longed for the sight of marble columns and intricate mosaic flooring. Order and efficiency instead of this chaotic scattering of the population. Brigantia's capital had also come as a huge disappointment. There was no order to the layout. Buildings sprouted up as if grown from seeds scattered on an ill wind. In many places there was not even room for a horse to pass. Yet still the people felt it worthy of a protective barricade complete with guards on the gateways.

The sentry today had been ill-bred and bad-mannered. The Pontiff had noted his face; he would pay for his insolence when they took this nation. The paltry accommodation given to them was on the far side of Stanwick, giving him the chance to stretch his aching body as he walked. He pretended not to notice the wary looks from the people, especially when they saw what he carried. Let them stare, he thought, I neither need nor require their acceptance. Wreathed in superior disdain, he strode forward, looking neither right nor left.

He found Martaani deep in conversation with Proculus and the Augur. Wasting no time on courtesies, he threw the dead raven onto the table. 'See what you can read into that.'

The Augur took a long, measured drink from his goblet, making no attempt to move. His self-righteous counterpart had no business ordering him like a common slave. A glint of amusement flickered in his eyes as he watched the Pontiff striding around the room, unable to control his boiling emotions. Arrogance may have got the man far but combined with his lack of self-control it would be his downfall. Martaani glared at the Augur and flicked her eyes towards the bird. He took another sip of wine and rose. In truth, he was intrigued by the offering and would have rushed to inspect it had he been alone. He pulled it towards him and ran his hands above the feathers, taking care not to disturb how they lay. There was meaning in everything.

The shock he felt was instantaneous. A little like the feeling of hitting his elbow in the wrong place. It seared at his palms and sent shockwaves up his arms. He pulled his hands back and gave a sharp look to the Pontiff. 'Where did you get this?'

'It was strung on a stick outside my tent this morning.'

'Were there no sentries?' Martaani snapped.

The Pontiff flourished a hand in the air. 'Apparently they saw nothing.' His voice was laced with sarcasm. 'They had a number of incidents throughout that night and the one previous. Though they failed to inform me of their problems when I arrived.' He poured himself a glass of wine from the decanter on the table. 'We searched the area and found a camp.' He looked pointedly at Martaani, 'It would appear there are at least four people in the group.'

Her eyes became slits, she looked at Proculus. A whole conversation seemed to pass in that glance.

'How did you come by that number?' the praefectus asked.

The Pontiff bristled. 'Three indentations on the ground would say there were three sleepers. Presuming they had at least one person guarding them...' he let his voice trail off.

Martaani was grinning. 'I think we have them.'

All eyes turned to the Augur. He rubbed his hands down his sides, steeled himself, and tried again. This time he was ready for the sensation. He noted the position of the feathers, some broken, many laying contrary to how they would have when the bird lived. It spoke to him of confusion. Wasting no time, he took out his blade, lay the carcass on its left side and sliced the bird open from crop to vent. The innards remained fast inside and unreadable. The Augur tutted internally, this seemed to happen far too often in this cursed land. Externally, he showed nothing but calm. Laying a hand on the bird, he could feel the firmness of the breast beneath the skin. He pressed lightly. Still nothing emerged. The briefest of frowns appeared on his face. He pressed harder, but still nothing. He pushed his fingers inside the slit and felt a cavity. Unable to believe what he had felt, he flipped the bird onto its back and pulled open the belly to peer inside. It was indeed empty. He checked the body over carefully, looking for another way the innards could have been removed. He found none. He looked up at the others. 'This is a strong message.'

'Is it him?'

'There is a strong sense of the druid here, yes, but it is not his message. Whatever god this bird represents is telling us that we will find nothing but confusion.'

The two priests exchanged looks. For an inferior Albion god to directly challenge a priest of the mighty Roman gods was unthinkable.

'How do you know it is a god's message?' Martaani snapped, her grin long-gone now.

The Augur lifted the raven's head. 'Its neck has been broken, you can see where some of the feathers were damaged as someone wrung its neck.' He dropped it back onto the table and ran his thumb along his fingers as if to wipe away any contamination. 'For that the bird must have lived. Its size and the scars on the legs and face tell me it was a good age. Yet it has no innards. Tell me, who else could have done this?'

Martaani swept the carcass onto the floor and spun around to Proculus. 'Find them,' she hissed, 'I will not be frightened by an empty bird.'

At once he turned to leave.

'You will find nothing,' the Augur called after him.

Proculus raised his eyebrows at Martaani, pulled the door covering aside and left.

35

Rain had been falling for the last two days. Under the trees there was some relief, but only where the canopy was really dense. Even then there was the constant *drip, drip, drip* from the leaves above. The plants, of course, loved it. There had been next to no rain for weeks and the ground was parched. The land was full of rich, vivid colours again and small rivulets re-appeared where they had ceased to run.

Umar had been right about the neglected building they had found when they stopped the previous evening. In the morning it had guests; travellers who had arrived during the night. Leaving the others in their makeshift shelter some way off, Garth crept closer. Whoever they were, they were not wary. They had set no watch, and made no attempt at keeping quiet. Brigante voices could be heard complaining inside. Evidently they were not so fond of the rain. Garth smiled to himself; Umar had been right about that, too. The roads were much busier than normal: The Midsummer Gathering was always a well-attended event, this year it would be even more so. The Brigante nation would be out in force to throw their weight behind Kariss.

Lord Hightern had ruled for many years; few people remembered his succession to the throne. Those that did remembered an easy transition. This time, with no heir apparent, those with a right to the throne would appear before the nation. They would present their individual cases, then the people would vote and the result would be binding. No one but Brigantes were eligible to vote but the sheer numbers of support would hopefully be enough to stave off any Roman thoughts of trying to take the nation by force. Martaani would see the north standing firm. She would not just be taking on a nation, she would be taking on a large part of Albion.

All these people now travelling to the capital needed to be avoided at all costs. Luckily, the rain made their journeys miserable; they kept their heads down and ploughed onwards, seeing nothing but the path ahead. Umar had thrown his arms wide and spun with joy when the heavens opened, calling out his thanks to Bodach for his aid. Taking advantage of the weather, Kariss's group had set out for Stanwick a day earlier than intended. They had kept to the smaller paths, often nothing more than deer tracks, but still they had to divert regularly to avoid travellers.

Garth got no information from listening to the people in the abandoned building; he headed back to the others. They were camped beneath the branches of a fallen tree. Not much protection from the rain but better than sleeping out in the open. They were cold, but not hungry. Food was plentiful at this time of year. Wild strawberries and elderflowers were abundant, as were hawthorn leaves, mushrooms and plantain. They were in no rush to set off but the need to warm up drove them on.

By nightfall they found themselves in the little house where Kariss had first met Naraic. They had come full-circle. Kariss sat fingering the little hare amulet he had given her before they set out.

'We have come a long way, you and I,' she told him.

'And been through much,' he added, looking at his hand.

Kariss pointed to his other arm, 'But look what your bravery got you.'

He ran his remaining fingers round the silver cuff Galan had given him. It would be a few years yet before it fit him properly, but he would not remove it.

'And look what your bravery got you,' Anniel kissed his wife on the forehead and sat down beside her.

'Lord Alpin's blessing.' She took his hand. 'I wonder if everyone who goes chasing blessings is as lucky as I was.'

The hut was much the same as they had left it. There was even a pair of coneys left on a rock outside. A sure sign the goddess approved of their stay. Assuming, therefore, that it must be safe to light a fire, Garth set about preparing the meat whilst Umar brought the dry kindling from underneath the overhanging roof. For a short while, the rain eased, and they were able to get somewhat dry.

'Will you go and visit your parents?' Kariss asked Naraic when they finished the meal.

He shook his head. 'I cannot.' He rubbed Cloud on the head, looking troubled. 'I am still a murderer.'

Garth opened his mouth to argue but thought

better of it; this was not the time to fight that charge. There would be time enough later.

Talk turned to the Gathering and their best approach to Stanwick. Surrounded by the earnest faces of her friends, and knowing there were many more people relying on her, Kariss once again began to question herself. No matter how hard she had fought it, how often she had pushed the feelings to the back of her mind where she could refuse to acknowledge them, she had known deep down that her resolve was beginning to fail.

'Do you know what you are going to say?'

Kariss realised Umar was speaking to her. She looked at him, confused.

'Your speech. You do know what you are going to say?'

The ground moved beneath her, she felt herself sway and Anniel taking hold of her. The speech. She had forgotten all about it. How could she possibly get up in front of all Brigantia and explain why they should trust her to lead them, when she herself didn't even believe she could? Her insides churned, the rabbit she had enjoyed not long before was boiling in her stomach. She had to get away.

'I... I'm sorry.' She stumbled from the fire. By the side of an elder she dropped to her knees and retched. She was barely aware of Anniel arriving at her side. When she had emptied her stomach, she leaned into him.

'Come on.' He helped her to her feet and moved a short distance away, sitting her down next to a tree. He brushed her hair away from her face and looked at her. 'Tell me.'

He looked so worried, it reinforced just how disappointed everyone was going to be in her if she failed. Her hand went to her hare amulet. How she wished she could call on Cailleach. Or that Brigantia or Verbia would just appear as they had last time she had been in these woods. It was just too dangerous now. She needed to keep her faith, but it was failing, and she was at a loss to know how to get it back. She made to get up; she needed to get away, to run from everything, if only for a little while. They didn't know, couldn't possibly understand, and she did not know how to tell them. Anniel grabbed her hand and pulled her back down.

'You need to talk to me,' he insisted. 'You cannot run; you know it is not safe. There is nowhere you can run to get away from all this.' He stroked her face. 'And besides, my feet are too tired. It would be cruel to make me run after you.'

'How?'

'How do I know?' he said. 'Because I love you. Because I can see it in your eyes. You are carrying so much weight on your shoulders, you were bound to crack sooner or later.' He leaned forwards and placed a long kiss on her forehead.

She felt his love, it tore down the last of her reserves, and she buckled beneath his kiss. Tears welled up, finding release at last, and with them came every doubt, every worry, all the negatives that she had been refusing to accept. With great heaving sobs, she let it all out. Clinging to her husband as if she would fall and never stop falling if she let go. Anniel held her tight, crying with her. The gods were putting her through so much, and for a moment he resented them for it.

Then he remembered why they were there. The very lives of the gods were at stake, and with them the welfare of every true-blooded native of Albion. Kariss was the only one to save them. If the gods had not stepped in, she would be dead by now. Killed by the Romans the minute they realised she could block their return. Without the gods, she would never have made it to him; they would never have fallen in love, and he would be reduced to a life without his soul-mate. He closed his eyes and willed the gods to hear his apology for doubting them.

At last Kariss's sobs eased. She felt empty, but still full of fear. It was as if her very breath had become tainted with it. There was no escape, she was trapped. The tears kept streaming down her face but her body was too tired to cry with them and she lay curled on Anniel's lap, too exhausted to move.

'I don't know what to do anymore.' Her voice wavered. 'I cannot do it, Anniel, I don't know how to go on. I need Cailleach, but I cannot call her.' A few straggling sobs escaped her. 'How did I ever manage to come this far?'

Anniel knew it was time.

He lifted her gently and leaned her back against the trunk of the tree. She was like a puppet in his arms. With his thumbs, he wiped the tears from her face, his heart aching at the sight of her red, blotchy skin and swollen eyes.

'Cailleach warned me this would happen,' he said, his own voice croaking with emotion. 'She did not know when, or where we would be, but she knew that at some time it would all become too much.'

Fresh tears streamed from Kariss's eyes. Her goddess was still caring for her, even when she couldn't come to her. Kariss could see Cailleach's wizened face, those piercing green eyes that she loved so much. Her hand reached again for the hare amulet. It was Brigante's amulet, but who was Brigante but a daughter of Cailleach? Kariss loved them all, though she would always hold Cailleach the dearest.

Anniel wanted to stall his next words, but he had to do this. He took a deep breath. 'She told me that when this happened, no matter what, or where we were, I was to place you by an apple tree… and leave you alone. So that is what I am doing.' He squeezed her hand. 'I will not be far, you only need to shout and I will be back.' He kissed her again. 'Lean back,' he whispered.

Then he stood and slowly walked away, hating every step that took him from her. Despite what he had said, he had no idea what was to happen now. Secretly he feared she would be taken away again. Even though he knew Cailleach would only act in her best interests; he did not know how he would cope with losing her, even for a short while. He walked back to the fire. The embers were almost out. He added more dry sticks and soon the fire flared once more. The rain was falling steadily again and he realised how sodden he was. Kariss too must be soaking wet. He jumped as Umar held out a dry cloak. Slipping out of his wet clothes, he wrapped the cloak around him.

'There is a fire inside the house,' Umar said. 'I

will get these dried for you.' He did not ask where Kariss was, nor did he comment about Anniel's appearance.

The tree felt hard beneath her back. Kariss tried to clear her mind but all the turmoil inside her refused to dissipate. Focusing on her breathing only served to let in more thoughts of inadequacy. Her mind could hear nothing from the tree. She didn't notice the first bug land on her arm; only after several more hand landed on her did she realise something strange was happening. The bugs, green and shield-shaped, kept on coming, one after another. She was mesmerised. Everything else seemed to fade as she watched them.

Hello Kariss. She jumped as the tree spoke in her mind. *I am Quert.*

Remembering this was what she was supposed to be doing, Kariss greeted the tree in return. The bugs became still.

You have become tainted with the negativity you are fighting, Quert told her. *You do not have the luxury of time to heal yourself, but have no doubt. Positivity is the only antidote you need.*

Kariss was about to point out how incapable she was of this, but was distracted by the bugs flexing their wings.

You are not in this alone, Quert said before she could speak. *Albion is with you. We are all here to help you succeed. No one could ever expect you to do this alone. You are but a part of the whole. If we all give in to doubt, Brigantia will fall, and Albion will not be far behind.*

Open your heart. Your strength has not gone far. Breathe in the scent of healing in the air, your spirit will not fail you.

Close your mind to the uncertainty you feel, drive out the rot of anguish. You must learn to armour yourself from any doubt. For only then can you succeed.

Kariss inhaled deeply; the air was tinged with the smell of apples, though no ripe fruit graced the tree's branches. It filled her with a sense of calm, and much to her delight she could once again sense Cailleach nearby. She closed her eyes and saw her. The crone was nodding to her, that enigmatic smile she knew so well fixed firmly on her face. Next to her stood Brigantia, just as she had before when Kariss had nearly died on the way north. She put her hands to her mouth and blew a reviving kiss towards her. Beside her stood a god she did not recognise. He was immense, muscular, with a pair of ram's horns protruding from his head. He looked fierce, and he did not smile, though he bowed in respect. At once she was reminded of Umar. The thought had no sooner entered her mind than the god nodded and raised his mighty fist against his chest in a sign of power. Kariss continued to breathe deeply, the gods faded. She sensed all her misgivings shattering into pieces and falling away and in their place a wall of resolve rose up. She carried on her meditative healing for a long time until the scent of apples faded.

Go back now, Kariss, Quert told her. *Anniel awaits you.*

She opened her eyes and gave herself a shake. The shield bugs took to the air, their job done.

When she reached the edge of the camp, she paused to look at her friends, still gathered around the fire despite the rain. No one had seen her yet so she took a moment to reflect. Anniel was pale, she could tell how worried he was by the way he hunched his shoulders and worried at the cuff of his tunic. Garth and Umar were deep in conversation; probably planning tactics, she thought with a smile. For someone who had come to Albion knowing no one, she had managed to gather a wonderful group of people around her. Not just the few she was with now, but everyone else who had helped her on her journey and even now were amassing to help her if all went badly at the Gathering.

Naraic and Cloud were nowhere to be seen and she wondered if he had gone to the village after all. She doubted he would let anyone know he was there if he had. He would be lying at the top of the rise just outside the houses, as they had both done all those months ago when she had first come to Albion. They had been through so much together in that time, had done the unthinkable and not only survived, but come back stronger than ever. He was like the brother she had never had. She sighed. When this was all over, she must find a way of reuniting him with his family. They must be beside themselves with worry about him.

She must find a way of reuniting her own as well. There was still no word of her parents coming back to her, but once the ceremony was over there would be no more need for them to stay away, surely? Her spirits lifted even further. They would like Anniel, she was sure of it. He was kind and caring and dedicated; everything anyone could want in a man.

She wondered again about the ceremony and

how it would play out. It was going to be such a monumental day for her. She would meet Lord Hightern for the first time, and his two druids, not to mention the other key figures around him. The people of Brigantia must be eager to see her. What would they think of her? Would they like her immediately, or would she have to win them over? It was no longer such a daunting thought. The shield bugs had done their job well; she felt a flutter of nerves but no more.

She thought of Martaani. At the Gathering she would come face-to-face with her rival; the woman who had terrified and maimed Naraic, killed Dei, Lord Alpin, Inan and Anyetta. The thought gave her a frisson of fear, but again the shield bugs' charm protected her. What would protect Anniel? Her eyes sought him out again. Just the sight of him made her chest fill with love. She would love him no matter what happened and she knew he would love her, too. She saw him look up to the trees again, this time noticing her there. He rose to his feet looking anxious and Kariss went to him.

A slit of light spilled down onto the floor of the small cell-like room. Outside, the sounds of sawing and hammering had been going on for most of the morning. He wondered what they were making. There was no point trying to reach the tiny window, he already knew it was too high. The first few weeks after he had been taken, he had tried everything he could to escape. Each futile attempt had led to a beating. Now it was all he could do to keep his mind from slipping into the pit of despair that had become his constant companion.

A curse filled the air and he smiled at the knowledge that one of his captors had hurt themselves. He could not understand what most of them said, they spoke a different language; and when they did speak his, they spoke in such a guttural, almost musical, accent that he struggled to understand what they were saying.

He knew midsummer could not be too far away now. Darkness only filled his cell for a few short hours every night. He shivered. Would he have the strength to deny her again?

He had known she was keeping him here for something. That much had been obvious for a long time, he would not still be alive otherwise. Early on, they had forced him to watch as she questioned others then killed them without blinking an eye. Yet he had refused to give her any of the answers she had demanded from her endless questions but his injuries had never been too severe. Painful, debilitating and incapacitating, yes, but never life-threatening. Then, the last time she had arrived, she had him dragged out in front of her. He remembered how she had laughed at his anxious face. Once again he found himself plunged back into that last meeting.

'You think that your silence will protect her? You think that you can keep her safe by denying me what I need?' She stepped towards him and ran the tip of her fingernail down his face, trailing it down his throat, over his chest, and finally stopping over his heart. She stabbed the nail hard into his skin. 'I do not need you to speak, your heart has already sealed her fate. You fell in love with the wrong woman and it will lead to the downfall of

Brigantia as you know it.' She laughed again at the disbelief on his face.

He could feel himself trembling. This was a new Martaani, one he had not seen before. She was too confident, too sure of herself. Before, she had always been searching for ways she could defeat Kariss. Now it was as if she had no doubts that she had found what she needed... and that he was the key. 'Kariss will succeed Lord Hightern, she will rule Albion and defeat you.'

Martaani's face hardened. 'Love is a weakness; it always has been. Already it has cost you so much.' Her eyes raked over the filthy, dishevelled man in front of her. 'You can argue with me all you like, there is nothing you can do to change what will happen. If the vote goes against me, you will be all the leverage I need.'

His heart hammered in his chest. 'She will never give in to you. Albion means more to her than I ever did.'

The light flickered as a bird flew across the window and he was brought back to the present and the sound of hammering. He was the only prisoner left here now. Not that he knew where 'here' actually was; somewhere in the Votadini lands, he presumed. Where else could there be so many Romans for so long?

There was a sound outside. His door was being unlocked. A man came in, grabbed hold of him and dragged him from the cell. Once outside, he was forced onto the back of a covered wagon and into a coffin-shaped box that lay there. It smelled of fresh shavings. 'Not long to go now, traitor.' The legionary laughed as he slammed the lid down, blocking out the light. One word echoed in his mind. *Traitor, traitor.*

He shook his head refusing to let them get to him. His captors had been calling him Traitor ever since his last meeting with Martaani. It unnerved him, even though he knew they were wrong. He would never betray Brigantia. He felt the wagon start to move and pushed on the box lid, it did not budge.

Martaani's words came back to him again as he lay there. *Love is a weakness. It always has been.* Love was not a weakness, it was a strength. Without it, he would never have survived all these months as a captive. It gave him hope, strength to keep going. He hoped the woman he loved felt the same. That what he had told Martaani was true, that she loved Albion more than she loved him. He hoped his words were right… but deep down he knew they were not.

The End of Book 2

The Albion Chronicles story continues…

The Battle for Brigantia

Now also:

Queen of Betrayal

(short story prequel)

**for news on these and other titles
by Nelly Harper visit:**

www.nellyharper.co.uk

www.goblinhouse.co.uk

Also by Nelly Harper

The Jet Necklace
A POWERFUL SPELL, ONCE UNLEASHED WILL NOT STOP UNTIL ITS WORK IS DONE.
~ However long it takes ~

Centuries have passed since the jet necklace was made and imbued with a magical calming spell capable of stopping even the strongest hate and hostility.

Oonagh is forced to flee the invading Vikings, hiding the necklace from them as she runs. With everyone she knows dead, she builds a new life far away from the troubles.

When an act of ultimate betrayal brings the past crashing back, her daughter Bethoc, must return to her mother's homeland and try to retrieve the necklace before it is too late.

www.nellyharper.co.uk

www.ingramcontent.com/pod-product-compliance
Lightning Source LLC
Chambersburg PA
CBHW031018120726
47905CB00007B/1968